Mallory and Derek Attend Secret Parties
Ruan Willow

I0599569

Table of Contents

R.U. Ann is a pen name for Ruan Willow for Romantasy, paranormal/magical/dark/horror tropes.
Edited by All the Proof Editing
Cover by theredfoxcreative.com
Certified Human Authored by The Author's Guild 2546131

Dedication

This book is dedicated to lovers who play in and out of the bedroom, those who never stop playing, and those who desire to please their partners and get off on getting their partner off, plus celebrate who they truly are because that's how it should be. Mutual pleasure is mutual bliss. Aftercare matters. Before care matters. During care matters.

This book is an erotic romance, specifically erotic polyamory romance, please read and enjoy it knowing this is the genre it is in. Marinate in your sexuality daily.

FYI the triggers are on the next page so you can either read them, or skip them, as you desire.

Get book 2, Power Plays, coming 2026
https://books.ruanwillowauthor.com/powerplays

Triggers: language, explicit sex scenes, swinger lifestyle theme/ alternative lifestyle, multiple partners, LGTBQ themes, sexual health, empowerment of women, sexual exploration, polyamory, love triangle, BDSM, ultra high spice open door, exhibitionism, voyeurism, dark desires.

Chapter 1

"You're my powerful vixen," Derek says as Mallory emerges nude from the bathroom, her flesh dewy and shiny.

She blushes with a giggle. She presses her arms together and her breasts mash as she shrugs. "Well, I feel incredible, anyway. Thank you for the bath bomb. The name fulfilled its promise. I feel like a goddess after that."

"You are a goddess," he says slyly. "Only you don't know it."

She shrugs. "I'm super nervous. Are you?"

"Yeah. I am, too," he admits as he swings his legs off the edge of the bed. "But I'm so happy we're doing this together." He clasps his hands. "This is our dream, Mal, what we've talked about for so long."

Mallory stifles a shiver, but the reaction prevails, and her skin erupts into goosebumps. "I think we should go, it's just that I'm scared to death."

"Me too," he says, rising. "But if we're together, nothing can stop us." He embraces her, and she drops her head.

"It's not just a party."

"Nope." He grips her chin and raises it up, so their eyes meet. "It's not just a party."

"What if we see someone we know?" That worrisome reality has been nagging her.

He laughs. "If they're there, then they are the same as us and there will be no worries." He clears his throat and cocks his head.

"True. Horny and curious?" She adores him, and how he's suddenly confident is a surprise, but she likes it.

"Yes," he cradles her closer and rocks them together. "You're my everything."

"And you're mine," she parrots back softly.

"I'm more nervous than you are," he states with a serious look.

She scoffs. "What? Oh, I don't think so."

"It's true."

She caresses his cheek. "I guess that makes sense." Her mind spins on the possibilities ahead of them. Some seem scarier than others, but her biggest fear is that she won't like the party. That would crash all her dreams and hopes. "You're ready."

He presses his lips together. "I think I am. Yeah." He releases a big sigh. "Screw all the negativity. We don't have to buy into their BS."

"Nope. And it's total BS." She pauses as she holds his gaze. "Oh, I'm so excited. It's going to be epic. I'm so ready to just try it out, you know? It's like a fantasy coming true." Anticipation grips her, and butterflies spring through her. "We're doing this. We're really doing this. We're going to live out our fantasy in real life." She bites her lower lip. "No one gets to do this."

"All the party-goers do," he says with a tilt of his head and a heckle after.

"True. But all our friends, everyone we know, no one matches up." She leans back as he supports her. She sucks on her lower lip. "We're the lucky ones."

"We are the lucky ones. And I'm with you, I have high hopes, despite being terrified."

"Our life, our rules."

Derek nods. "Our life, our rules."

"It's normal, right? To be terrified of something like this?" Her nerves keep switching her mood from confident to worried. She makes a fist before she says, "We do this. And we do it kick butt, full on."

"Kick butt," he says with a nod. "I'd say we should do a quickie, looking at you looking all luscious and sexy, but we should save it, I'm thinking."

"Agreed. I want to go into this as ripe and wanton as possible. We can't break our setup. We've gone this long without it."

"Yes. Exactly." He steps away from her. "Then I need to stop being so close to you." He heads over to the closet. "And I need to stop looking at you." He scoffs. "I can't control myself. You're way too sexy."

"I love your libido," she coos.

"I love yours more," he copies, then disappears into the closet. "I have no clue what to wear to something like this," he shouts.

"Wear what you're comfortable in. Your orange and gray flannel?"

"Oh, come on. I can't wear that to this kind of party."

"And why not?" She enters the closet. "There was no dress code listed."

He quickly flicks through his shirts, and the hangers scrape across the bar.

"You're not helping me abstain from fondling you by coming near me," he protests. "You weren't supposed to follow me," he jokes.

"I have to get dressed too, silly. Just pretend I'm not here." She gives him a flirty glance.

"Fat chance of that." He points to his groin. "Plus, that bath bomb made you smell like heaven."

She watches him peruse his shirts, sliding them across slowly, one by one.

"How about I pick for you?" She prances in front of him and bumps him backward with her bum.

"Well, that's definitely not helping," he says sarcastically.

She cackles and then chooses the flannel shirt she suggested. "You look hot in this one, and it's super comfy. Ruggedly manly. It's perfect."

"It's so casual, though. Too casual?"

She shakes her head. "No, it's the one. You'll feel good in it, and that's exactly what you need." She tips her head to the side. "Think comfort clothes. All the things to help you relax."

He pulls the flannel off the hanger and slides his arm in. "I guess you do know me."

"I do." She moves to her side of the closet and chooses a dress she feel sexy in. She slips it over her head, her confidence returning to normal with the dress in place. "I'm so ready. And you're going to be amazing. I just know it."

"You're better equipped for this," he sighs as he pulls his jeans on. "If I disappear, know that I'm hiding in the bathroom." He releases a big scoff. "Ugh. Why is this so hard? We both want this."

"It's new, but soon it won't be," she says, then blows him a kiss. "Let's go. We're going to be late. We'd better hurry." Of course, this is harder for him; he has all that awful backstory of being shamed constantly running as a script in his head. She strokes his arm.

He stares at her with a lewd, wanton gaze. "You're so hot. You're going to kill it, and I look like a frumpy dude who just crawled off his couch."

"You look burly and masculine, and I love you in that shirt." She hooks her arm in his and tugs him out of the closet. "Let's get ourselves there before we change our minds."

The drive drags, and Mallory reaches for her phone to try and dissipate some of her nervous energy. She scrolls through social media and stops on an image of a sexy woman she recently started following, who is a content creator and is now launching into adult films. The woman is a phenomenon. She's impressive and empowered. Mallory's legit got a woman's crush on her. She's harnessed her power and is charging headlong into her vision of sexuality and femininity, and she's owning it. The woman is an absolute legend. Mallory's admiration for her grows as she peruses her profile page.

"Wow. Incredible," she says, shaking her head. "You know that woman I was talking about last night, now she's doing films." She glances at Derek to see if he remembers the conversation.

"Yeah, I remember. The one with big titties and long straight hair in two tones of blond?"

"Yeah, that one. In the interview I watched, she said she's making more per day than she used to make in a whole week in her old job. That's truly an accomplishment."

"It is, and what a nice way to make money." He scoffs. "I'd live that way."

"I know, right? Make a living off her sexiness. And dang, she's killing it." Mallory scrolls the woman's content way down the feed on her page. Her interest in how she's doing it grows, fueled by both curiosity and a hint of jealousy. "Using her own self to make this much money, what a power move. What a woman!" She's proud of her and the keepers of the patriarchy must be groaning in pain. She snorts. "And more power to her. I should subscribe just to support her cause." She taps subscribe.

"Indeed. Good idea." He stops at a stoplight. "I think it's the next turn. Will you check?" He pulls the car over to the side of the road once they pass through the green light.

"Yeah," she says, leaving the app to check the map on her phone. "Yup, it's the next one." Her nerves bloom into a bigger ball of frenzy, not unlike what she'd imagine a panic attack feels like. "I think I might explode, I'm so excited and so nervous. I want to jump out of my seat one second and cower the next."

"Yeah, me too. Part of me wants to turn the car around and just go out to eat." He looks sheepish. He laughs.

She swats his arm. "No, we can't do that. Not after all we've gone through to join." She lets her phone fall into silent mode. "Plus, think of this, after today we won't have to go through the first time again. We won't be the newbies anymore. Plus, we want this." She pauses and stares intently at him. Worry fills her. The last thing she wants to do is make her lover uncomfortable. Consent is everything. "Don't we? I mean, we've talked to ad nauseam. But Derek. Honestly, if you want to pull the plug, we can. Just say the word, and we can go home. We can think about it some more. Talk some more." She reaches over and places her hand on his. "Are you having second thoughts? I'm okay to not go in."

He pauses, staring at his hand on the steering wheel. "No. I'm in. And that's a good point. After today, we won't be the newbies. That helps." He looks more nervous than she feels, but she expects that, coming from the painful life he's endured. "Let's do this, and never have to do it green again. If we don't like it, we just never go back. Right?"

She squeezes his hand and gives him a reassuring look. "Right. Yes, now let's pop this party's cherry and get it on." She throws her head backward and gives him flirty eyes. "Whew! I'm ready to scream my head off from the pleasure overload."

"Same," he says with an equally excited look. "Let's go!"

They drive down the street. Mallory's heart pounds as she gazes at the houses. Her mind imagines the party house, beautiful, majestic, and luxurious. Inside its walls will be a whole new world of experimentation for them, a mini-universe of the potential of their needs being met, and new connections to enjoy, not to mention so many climaxes they might never want to leave. Though others might help launch her arousal, her heart belongs to Derek, and it always will.

She touches her heart and reaches over to place her hand over his. "Heart to heart. I'm yours, and you're mine. Nothing will change that." She holds direct eye contact with him as he quickly glances her way.

"Nothing," he says as he slows the car. He looks at her more intently, agrees with a generous nod, and clarity in his eyes. He brings the car to a complete stop in front of a random house.

"We do this together."

"Together."

He plucks her hand off his chest and kisses the top of it.

She's convinced he's ready. His nerves make him seem not ready, but then her nerves are screaming in freak-out mode to her, too. But this sexual adventure is what they've wanted from the start of their relationship, and that hasn't changed. It's time to enact what they've dreamt about, and no last-minute jitters should stop them. Derek is right. If they don't like it, they can just stop. No harm done.

"Honesty is our superpower," Derek states while holding Mallory in a direct eye lock.

"Honesty is our superpower," she agrees. "And pleasure awaits."

Will it all be easy? No. Will it all be comfortable? Hell, no. There will be a learning curve, but if they stick to their boundaries, communicate incessantly without holding back, and are true to themselves, she's positive they will succeed in this adventure.

Together.

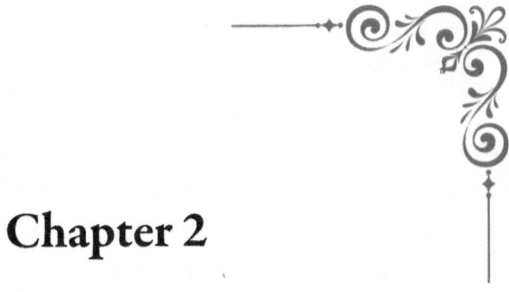

Chapter 2

Derek drives again. Even though their anxious glances flicker between excitement and nervousness, they proceed onward. Holding her hand helps him.

His heart beats out of control as they pull into the neighborhood area where the house is located. He can't stop the jittery feelings from consuming him, but he's resolved. He's doing this with her. No turning back. "Ready to get your brains fucked out?" He parks and gives her an affirming glance. "Let's do this."

"Let's."

They walk to the front door holding hands. Mallory knocks. She squeezes Derek's hand and gives him a reassuring look.

An older couple opens the door.

"Hello," the woman says. "Come in." She raises her arms open and wide, as if ready to hug. She wiggles her fingers, and Mallory goes in for an embrace. "Yeah, that's it," the older woman coos.

Huh. Derek is taken aback. They start right in with being open and almost overly friendly. He's ready to just immerse himself in their sensual culture, though. No turning back.

The man of the house comes up to Derek and says, "Welcome. I'm Sam. What are your names? And did you read and agree to the disclaimer we sent you for this party?"

Derek nods. "Yep. We did. We're Derek and Mallory, and we sent the signed form back as a response to the email address that sent it to us."

The woman smiles and nods. "Good. Glad to hear that. My name is Maria." She checks the tablet in her hands and scrolls. "Yes, I see your response here. Fantastic. We are always so happy to welcome newcomers. We hope you both feel comfortable here and will want to return. We are like a little family of fuckers." She grins big with a salacious look in her eyes as she chuckles.

"Oh, we are excited to try this out, but I have to admit, I'm scared to death. Well, he is more than me." Mallory points to Derek, who wholeheartedly agrees with an aggressive nod.

"That's...that's...that's the truth," Derek stutters out.

Sam pulls Derek into a hug but stops midway. "May I?"

Derek nods.

Sam, who has a bod to die for, even hidden under his clothes, lays Derek back slightly like he's going to dip him back, as if they're dancing.

Derek nods happily again with a giant grin.

Sam leans him fully and kisses him in a deep French kiss, then stands him up straight. "More?" he asks.

Derek looks shocked, yet extremely overjoyed. He nods with a deeper grin, making himself look starstruck, or like a brainless bobblehead, with all the nodding. "Yes."

Sam touches his thighs and snakes his arm around his side to his back, giving him a little spank.

Derek is a little taken aback by the spank, but he smiles, nonetheless. He's getting himself set to go all-in to do this party.

Mallory stands there, watching, dumbfounded. But this might just be what Derek needs, to be thrust into this by such a man.

Sam winks at her. "I like to start right away with physical contact, so it isn't such a shock when you enter the main room, given that you've both already given full consent via email and just now. We are big, huge, astronomical on consent here. It just sets the right tone."

Mallory takes a deep breath, but before she can say anything, Maria makes eye contact with her.

"May I kiss you?" Maria asks with a lusty twinkle in her eyes.

Apparently, she is of the same thought process as Sam, but she's definitely not complaining about a sexy as fuck woman asking to kiss her. Mallory nods with a grin. She's hesitant, but she thinks Maria is nothing short of a goddess and, hell, yes, she'd very much love a kiss from her.

The woman of the house grabs Mallory and gives her a kiss, a deep kiss that sends butterflies all throughout Mallory's body. Maria runs her hands down her breasts and then pulls away. She grabs Mallory's hand and tugs her toward the hall.

She keeps direct eye contact with Mallory. "Ready?"

Mallory can't quite speak after that kiss, so she lamely nods again. She's the bobblehead now.

"This might be a shock to you both. I'm sure you've both seen orgies on porn, but seeing one live can be a bit jarring, let alone the overwhelming feeling you will get once joining in. If either of you would like to step away for a break, for any reason at all, off to the left of the main room is a break room. It's filled with snacks, drinks, and comfortable chairs. There's a TV in there as well if you need some distraction. Feel free to go there whenever either of you needs to. There are also robes and blankets for comfort, and a bed if you need a nap." She winks. "Fucking this many people will wear you out in no time, especially when you aren't used to it."

Mallory is shocked that such a house exists for this type of thing. Do Sam and Maria live here? Or is this someone else's house? Are the homeowners a part of the orgy? Are there video cameras? Had she read that there were? No. So why was her brain going there? All these questions swirl in her head, but she can't seem to form words to ask them.

It's even more of a shocker that she and Derek are actually here. They found the party ad on a swinging website they had made an account on recently. They had no idea how many swinging groups were in their area, nor that they'd have so many choices to pick from, that the decision of which party to try had been a difficult one. There were so many, they'd likely be able to try things out for more than a year, each one a new and exciting experience. So many offerings out there, it blew their minds. They had no idea all of this existed. All this had been going on right under their noses, and they never knew such groupings happened. They were elated, both being sexually adventurous.

"That's amazing," Mallory whispers, realizing sheepishly that her response is rather delayed. She's practically panting; the anticipatory intrigue is almost too much to tolerate.

Maria chuckles. "We've been at this for over twenty years, Sam and I, hosting sex parties, that is, so we've figured out a thing or two to make it a smooth transition for people."

Mallory follows as Maria pulls her along. She glances back at Derek, who is likewise being guided by Sam. The hallway is way longer than Mallory had expected.

Sam's face is filled with joy, whereas Derek's face keeps flitting between uneasiness and joyful awe. Mallory thinks it's a beautiful thing to see him like this, and is so ready to see him take all the cock he wants.

He's had a hard time admitting his bisexuality, after having brought it up to Mallory after they watched porn once at the beginning of their relationship. She had immediately put him at ease by telling him she's bi too and has slept with several women. It had sort of helped, but Derek had a few hang-ups to work through, namely his dad's disgust for gay men, and the teaching he received from his church growing up that being gay is a sin.

Mallory had not grown up with such restrictions. In fact, her aunt had married a woman back when Mallory was eight, so being queer had been normal to her at a young age. She had been blessed with an upbringing not being ashamed of being human, rather differences were celebrated, which was drastically the opposite of Derek's life. He had been constantly shamed at every turn.

She nodded at Derek and did a chin-up motion as she smiled as if to say, 'you got this, baby.'

He responded with a smile that betrayed his nerves, but it was a smile nonetheless despite the doubts on his face. She'd take it in a heartbeat over sheer terror. He had suffered a nightmare a few nights ago about this party, where his dad had walked it as he was being fucked in the ass by a man. It was so strong he almost backed out of agreeing to come to the party. Mallory is proud of him for getting past that shame. Fake as it was, it was laced with reality.

The sounds of sex hit her ears before she sees them. The moans are loud, as are the grunts. And then the skin smacks become audible. Her heart pounds as they walk into the big living room with a high ceiling and see a bunch of naked people already fucking.

Malory gasps. Are we late to the party? It being in full gear already shocks her. She'd thought there would be a happy hour, a chance to get to know each other. But then she realizes all these people already likely knew each other, so that's silly. But, still, she kind of wishes she could make some connections first.

"We won't throw you into the dog pile yet." Maria points to the long tables on the other side of the room, where a few naked people are talking and sipping drinks.

Mallory lets out a sigh of relief. "Oh, thank goodness," she says in a very low voice.

Maria looks pleased. "Another thing is you need to have some connections to people, so we pulled out a few of our veterans for you and Derek to chat with and get acquainted. There's no rushing this. Just so you know. And if you both prefer just to watch this time, please, feel free to do that. You'll be invited back as long as you want, as long as..." she pauses, "well, we don't need to get into that unless we encounter it. You read the disclaimer, so you know."

Mallory imagines what she means, and it makes sense, but she feels uneasy about it all. What if she fucks up and they hate her?

As if Maria can read her mind, she says, "There are no rules other than consent which is required for all acts, as is respect. Don't violate those rules, and all will go well for you with our group."

Mallory nods as Maria leads her to the table. Mallory glances back and reaches for Derek's hand. They stroll along as a string of four bodies holding hands as they pass the massive pile of fucking and moaning people. Their facial expressions and sounds are like they are in utter bliss. Someone always seems to be coming or near orgasm. The orations they make alone are totally delicious to Mallory, and it drives up her lust.

Derek squeezes Mallory's hand three times. That's been their signal in bars for 'I'm okay' and it's worked out so well they've kept the practice alive. She squeezes his hand back three times. They hold each other's gaze for about ten seconds before their eyes wander.

As the four of them approach the people mingling, they all turn and smile. It seems almost orchestrated, but their friendly faces erase any creepiness Mallory had suffered from coming over here at first.

"Alexa, Matt, Josie, Malakai, this is Mallory and Derek. The newcomers I told you all about."

They all nod with pleasant expressions and wish Mallory and Derek a warm welcome.

Mallory keeps glancing at the giant mass of people fucking. It's like watching a train wreck, but hot. She's jarred by the energy the orgy emanates throughout the room. It's almost palpable, and it charges up her own sexual energy hugely, more and more by the second. Part of her just wants to tear across the room running, give a war battle cry, and leap into the pile of people having sex. She wants to assimilate herself. But the other part is hesitant, and this part of her also wants her to take it slow for Derek's sake, too. The apprehension in his eyes is still quite thick.

Derek is still holding both Mallory's hand and Sam's as he stares at the orgy scene. It's far more chaotic than he imagined. There's so much to look at and watch that his brain is telling his eyes to look here, look there, look everywhere all at once. He's overcome with trepidation, not unlike how he felt at fourteen years old, having to walk into a new school, only here everyone is naked and either putting parts into someone or accepting someone's parts into them. All he wants to do is run away, but there is also this draw that pulls him forward. It's not unlike a magnet, but way stronger. It's also the promise of a fresh start, and, of course, all the possibilities the opportunity could potentially deliver to both himself and Mallory. The freshness of the situation is intoxicating, and he gazes upon the scene as if in a trance. Inside, he smiles. Nothing is a memory yet, nothing is a mistake yet either.

Derek peeks at Mallory. She's just devastatingly gorgeous, and her eyes are lit with excitement. This look that she often displays to the world is exactly what drew Derek to her in the first place. It had been like her eyes shared all the beauty of her soul at first glimpse. Everything about her was upfront and energetically joyful. There were no games. He never expected he'd find a woman who would be more open to trying new sexual things than he is. But he's learning from Mallory, and this party isn't the first foray he has followed his sexy girlfriend into in the past few months. He'd had sex in way more places than ever before in his life, and he had way more sex than he'd ever had in any relationship prior to this one. That part made him very happy. Mallory had been good for him in so many ways, and he just hopes he can be as good back for her as she is for him. He seriously doubts he is.

Maria hands both Mallory and Derek a champagne glass. She raises her flute. "Toast to your first live sex party, that won't be your last." She looks proud and has a sexy air of confidence about her that both Mallory and Derek find very alluring. Sam is the same way, only even more so. Derek suspects he's a Dom. Maria could be one too, or at least a switch. There's an unspoken connection between them that is totally obvious.

The men and women in the middle of the room are all enjoying each other's bodies. A massive mix of clearly all bisexual men and women. With men and women with men, women on women, and mixed groups of gender for threesomes, foursomes, and even a fivesome tangle. And the people keep shifting around to new partners. It's fluid, like a moving, living creature, this orgy pile, and screaming of life and lust with gasps, groans, moans, sputters, choking sounds, giggling, yells, screams, skin slaps, and 'omigod' utterances. Both Mallory and Derek feel it's a beautiful phenomenon of chaos that has an order to it because it's all sex, and seems primal, instinctual, and oh so right, even though watching it now feels even more chaotic than expected.

One of the women hands Mallory and Derek each a chocolate-covered strawberry. "To get you in the mood. An appetizer of pleasure for your mouths." Her green eyes are gorgeous, and her body is kickass, curvy hot.

Mallory grins as she takes the strawberry.

Derek smiles meekly and takes his berry.

They hold each other's gazes as they bite into the lush, rich, chocolate-bathed piece of fruit.

"Mmmm. This is divine," Mallory says with a mouthful, while nodding and smiling.

"Totally. I could eat ten," Derek chuckles.

The woman, who's basically wearing a tied sheet like a toga, waves her arm across the table. "Well, help yourselves, there's more of those, and plenty of other things to whet your appetite for pleasure. That's what this party is all about. Experiencing and enjoying pleasure." Her pleasant facial expression puts both Mallory and Derek even more at ease.

"So, tell me more about your situation, your relationship. I read your answers on the intake form, but I'd love some elaboration," Maria says.

Neither Mallory nor Derek speaks up.

Sam's expression turns to one of total compassion. "Please, don't ever feel pressed or forced for anything. You don't owe anyone any explanations either. Do what feels comfortable to you, and if you suddenly need time away to reflect, or you changed your mind about something, there's no judgment." Sam's demeanor is that of a loving, caring leader, and his calm directness puts Derek at ease.

"Well," Derek says with hesitation. "I'm kind of new to being open sexually. Mallory is more open than I am, or more than I have been, but she's been supportive and helping me explore my own sexuality. But I admit, I'm a bit nervous about taking cock."

Sam's smile is genuine and kind, understanding and knowing. "There's no need to be nervous. I assure you, everyone here has been fully screened for their backgrounds, and anyone who has any nasty personality traits, narcissism, or greediness is asked to leave immediately. We are very selective in who we choose to let in here."

"Hence the extensive form," Mallory says with a nod.

"Precisely." Sam raises both hands. "And we do prefer couples. We do have one divorced woman in the group who is now single, but she's joining another couple in the group. They are polyamorous, and the couple is taking her in as their partner."

Derek's eyes widen. He had read about such things and seen posts about it on social media. The idea of a polygamous way of life definitely intrigues him.

"Do either of you have any questions?" Maria asks them with kind eyes.

Mallory finds her voice and speaks up. "I know the information said everyone gets tested for STDs, and women are on some sort of birth control or speak up about the need for condoms, but how often do people test? And I ask this because of the polyamory comment, cause if these people are having sex with people outside the group, that poses a risk."

Maria nods her head. "Yes. So, we talk about this one if a couple decides to join our sex club officially, and so before their second party. If a member of the club has sex with others outside this club, they must retest to prove they are clean. It's on the honor system, and we haven't had a problem with this in all the years we've been doing it. And that's in part due to how selective we are for who we let join us."

Mallory nods. "Fair enough." Watching the faces of the people blossom into orgasm after orgasm is driving her desire to join to fire alarm status. She needs to get in there. "What do you think, Derek? Is this still a go for you?"

Derek meets her gaze, and his eyes melt. He gives a single nod. "I'm nervous, but I want to do it."

Sam takes a step forward and turns to face them. "This is exactly what I like to see. You two checking in with each other. Communication is key. A dedication to each other's comfort and pleasure is also key. I think you two will fit right in. And be a great addition to our group." Sam draws in a long breath and releases it, as if savoring something. "One more thing, I'll remind you that you don't owe anyone explanations, nor are you obligated to finish any act you start. You should feel comfortable just leaving a person or group whenever you don't like something or aren't comfortable. This is a safe place. We want you to feel completely safe here, so please feel free to move on, leave the room, or even the party, if you ever feel the need to. And the hand signal for you is done with what you are doing, and moving on is your arm raised up like you are asking a question with your index finger pointed at the ceiling. We all know that a signal means you are moving on. No need to give a reason. Okay?"

They both nod at Sam.

"Good," says Sam.

The validation from Sam is like a hug to Mallory. Being called a "good girl" usually tweaks her clit and thickens her satisfaction. It's not that she's an approval seeker or needs that kind of validation to be okay; it's just delicious to hear.

"Do you need more time, or shall we enter this pile of sex?" Mallory squeezes Derek's forearm before she turns to face him fully. "I'm ready to do this if you are, but I'm also ready to walk out if you are. But if we do that, we are fucking the second that car door closes," she says with a chuckle laced throughout her last words.

He grins. "Oh, I get it. And I'm in too, Mallory." Derek's shoulders relax and his face clears of unease, well, mostly. "Let's go fuck and get fucked."

Sam grabs Derek's hand, and Maria grabs Mallory's. Derek reaches for Mallory's hand and the four stride together as a human chain toward the orgy. The people in the orgy are on a large, round piece of beige furniture, which is like an island. It looks like an ottoman, only supersized, like someone gave it steroids. Mallory has never seen such a large ottoman before and is amazed at how perfect it is for an orgy. It's like a large circular padded stage in the middle of the large living room.

Sam and Maria start to strip. Mallory and Derek follow suit, smiles on their faces. They are so ready for this sex party. It's just a big old pile of naked people, and an orgy of no end. There's so much moaning and groaning, lip smacks and skin smacks all around, it's like being immersed in a dream.

Maria faces them, but both Mallory's and Derek's eyes drift down her body. She smiles. "Okay. To orient you, there are bottles of lube strewn about and sex toys of all different sizes, shapes, and colors. All will be thoroughly cleaned before every party, as the welcome email stated. Use what you need and want. This is your sexual playground." Maria points to a colorful pile of dildos and sex toys on the edge of the ottoman nearest them.

Mallory dives right for them without hesitation and stands at the edge of the ottoman. Derek watches in amazement because she's instantly a part of the scene. A man grabs her and kisses her. He fondles her breasts.

Derek watches in awe at how she just assimilates in so easily, so naturally. He's proud of her.

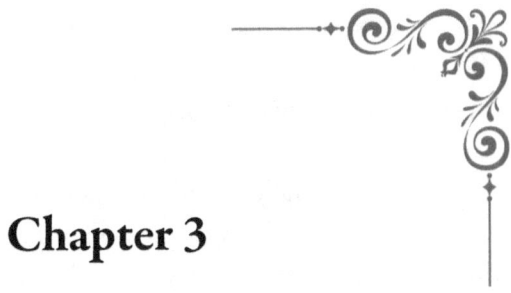

Chapter 3

S am puts his arm around Derek, who is shorter than he is by more than a head. "Take your time, Derek. This is on your timeline and only your timeline."

Derek desperately wants to be with Sam sexually. He glances down at Sam's massive erection but feels too shy to ask him to join him in a sexual act.

Mallory continues to deeply kiss the man who pulled her into the horde. She looks so happy and excited, Derek loves to see her like this. No matter how it happens, he loves to see Mallory have pleasure. He knows they are committed to each other, and he's just never felt threatened by other people because he and Mallory are so strong together.

Derek watches as the man's hands are traveling down her body onto her curvy hips, where he then walks his fingers to the back of her and grips both of her butt cheeks. He gives her flesh a hearty squeeze, lifting her slightly off the floor. She squeals and runs her hands along his biceps, meanders her hands over his nipples, and down his tummy. And then she gropes her way back up to his hair to play with it. They kiss more, maxing out the foreplay. Derek loves doing all those same things to her, so he smiles, loving that she's getting the touches she desires.

Mallory glances back, and Derek is just watching with a happy smirk on his face. She is very pleased and happy to have found such a wonderful man in Derek.

Derek makes eye contact with Sam, with what feels like way too much trepidation, cause honestly, he's ready to try this. "Do I just ask someone, or do I just lay myself in the group and let someone take me?"

Maria joins Mallory and the man, and Mallory's eyes beam with bliss. Mallory's smile blossoms with happy, salacious lust at the addition of Maria to their tryst.

Derek is dying to ask Sam to be that same someone for him that Maria and the man are being for Mallory, but he's so scared to ask.

Sam smiles deeply, as if he knows. "Would you like to have a partner as you join the horde? If so, I'm definitely the man to gently usher you into the ecstasy you're watching." His grin is lascivious and hungry, but confident.

He reminds Derek of a wolf, an alpha, a bull—which likely, he is.

Derek simply nods with an awestruck look on his face.

Sam drapes his arm around Derek's shoulder. Derek's eyes fall once again to Sam's very large erect cock, which is out and stiff in all its magnificent glory. He really has a stunning cock. Derek hasn't been able to keep his eyes off Sam's raging boner, ever since Sam undressed. The man is a living Greek statue.

Sam gently guides Derek to an open spot that just appeared on the ottoman. He pushes Derek to sit, which brings Sam's hard shaft right in front of Derek.

It bobs seductively in front of Derek as Sam moves slightly. He's hypnotized by the beauty of it, so near to his eyes. He cautiously reaches for Sam's cock, then glances up to make eye contact with him.

Sam nods his approval. "Keep your eyes on mine, Derek." It's a command, but Derek willingly complies because this is exactly what Derek wants. Mallory's statement from earlier today flits across his brain. 'If you see a cock you want, suck it.'

He opens his mouth and leans toward Sam's hard dick and takes it into his mouth. The feel of his cockhead filling his mouth is exactly what he's been longing for. But the sigh Sam gives as he begins to suck him and take his member deeper into his mouth is to die for. Derek's so turned on, his own dick couldn't get any harder than it already is. The sounds he's bringing Sam to make with his blow job alone are almost making him come. He doesn't touch his own dick as he sucks Sam's because he doesn't want to come yet. There's way too much to do before that should happen.

After a few minutes of enjoying blowing Sam, which Derek could keep doing for about an hour or so, Sam tugs on his arms, signaling he should rise.

Sam pulls him close and whispers, "That was very delicious and very hot. You give a very excellent blow job. But now I'd like to fuck your ass."

Derek's cock twitches, then he nods. He's realizing he's under the spell of Sam's sexy, dominant demeanor. And it's exactly what he's been desiring for years.

Sam kisses him, and the kiss sets off fireworks. He's always thought that analogy was stupid and unrealistic, but Sam is disproving that because Derek feels explosions firing off inside him. The tip of Derek's cock is pressed against Sam's, and they rub together as they move. It's so fucking delicious that Derek fears he's going to come too fast, and the fun will be over. He thinks of unpleasant things to stave off the climax, like cleaning a toilet and picking up dog poop to get his brain off this sexy, irresistible man.

Sam pulls out of the kiss, grabs Derek's shoulders to turn him around. Sam presses his body against him and caresses with his hands all down his torso before stroking Derek's cock.

Derek lets out a groan that sounds louder to him than the whole mass of fucking bodies. He's watching all of this going on in front of him, but it's like he and Sam are in their own microcosm.

Sam bends Derek over, and that act alone charges up Derek's lust to peak heights. Sam reaches to the side of Derek for lube and pastes a dollop at Derek's anus. Derek tips his ass upward for Sam, presenting it to him. He and Mallory had been practicing anal stuff with toys, so he's ready for this. He even let her peg him for the first time the other day to get him ready for the party, plus, he had wanted his first anal sex to be with Mallory.

His heart is pounding so hard, his panting is so rampant, he feels as if he will explode. As Sam presses a finger into Derek's ass, Derek gasps. His body, mind, and soul are ready to accept the best cock he will likely ever have in his entire life.

Sam pulls his finger out of Derek's asshole and leans in. He rubs his cock all over Derek's ass cheeks and spanks his ass with his hard shaft.

Derek whimpers. "Oh please," he says in a soft, pleading voice. "Please, Sam. Do it."

Sam grins deeply and presses his cockhead gently into Derek's anus.

Both men groan. The satisfaction is unmistakable in their sounds. This is heaven to them both.

Sam begins to increase his thrusting and proceeds to fuck Derek as if he's never been fucked before in his entire life, at least by cock. Derek loves how aggressively Sam slams into him from behind. The skin smack sounds alone turn Derek on even more. He bounces forward from the thrusts, grunting with each one. But in keeping his hands on the furniture to stabilize himself, he's not able to stroke his own cock. His cock swings with each pounding of his ass that Sam delivers.

Derek's orgasm peak is looming fast. He's helpless, as he can't stop the rise, not even slow it down. Derek spews his cum, despite his dismay to do so this early on in the orgy. He feels shame at coming already. Plus, he's sure it's landed on the ottoman. He worries about that slightly. But then he almost chuckles, this is likely not the first time cum has landed on this monstrosity covered in upholstery. He's being ridiculous.

His panting is out of control, and his heart is beating ferociously. He doesn't remember ever coming that hard in his entire life. The spasms keep going, and so does Sam. Sam's not done with his ass. As Derek recovers a bit from his massive orgasm, his cock thickens as he watches Mallory getting fucked from behind by a black man while her tits are being sucked from beneath her body by Maria. It's a lovely and delicious sight he won't likely ever forget.

As Sam continues to slam into his ass like a machine, Derek's body is gyrating in the air as a woman slides beneath him from the side. She's a very cute and petite redhead, who looks about his and Mallory's age. She smiles at Derek and reaches up to caress his cheek.

He smiles and nuzzles his face into her touch. She presents her pert little nipple to his mouth.

"Suck," she says in a commanding tone, but which also implies a bit of a question.

He immediately obeys and takes her nipple into his mouth. Suckling her proves tough because of the pounding Sam is giving him, but she moves with the rocking to assist. He suckles her nipple sloppily, and she drops her head back with a moan.

After a few minutes, she sneaks down lower to fondle Derek's balls. His dick is so hard again, and he's ready to blow once more. He laments his weakness that he can't control his climaxing but, then again, he's in the middle of an orgy. That's to be expected.

Derek gets brave and tries to balance on one arm as he's being fucked and starts grabbing at breasts all around him, reaching for and touching hair, grabbing butt cheeks, all parts of the people around him. The whole scenario is overwhelming and in constant motion; it's as if the mass of people is one animal and as alive as any single one of them.

Derek listens as the sex sounds in the room seem to be reaching a crescendo, or maybe he's just slipped out of the post-orgasm fog. Oh, the moaning is driving everybody wilder. All the people are gyrating. It's a big pile of skin. A big pile of sex.

He can hear Mallory's moans, so he searches for her.

He spots her quickly. A man is spinning her around for doggy. He pushes her against the woman who's lying in front of her. She smiles and begins to kiss the woman, fondling her breast as the man fully penetrates her from behind.

"Ooh. Oh yeah," Mallory mutters in great appreciation of his cock inside her, her face blooming into pure ecstasy as she leans back from the kiss.

She returns to trying to kiss the woman, but their mouths keep slipping off each other because they are both getting pounded by men. She moans in between the kisses. She almost giggles at how difficult it is to kiss another while being fucked by someone else. This was not something she had considered before actually being in this situation. The woman she's lying on is now being double penetrated by two men, so it becomes nearly impossible for the two women to kiss. Since she barely fits in there anymore, she slides away as they start to go at it, heavy and hard. She's happy to leave them to their threesome.

Mallory focuses instead on the man who is fucking her. She's in the way of the threesome and wants to enjoy this man's cock now anyway. Mallory moans happily as she takes his hard rams on repeat, her generous tits swinging below her like mad.

Sam finishes his pounding and pulls his dick out of Derek. Hot cum spews across Derek's ass cheeks. Such warmness had never felt so satisfying on Derek's skin before.

"Oh, oh, mmm, oh fuck," Sam groans out. Sam gives Derek's right butt cheek a light slap.

Someone licks Sam's cum right off Derek's ass. The warm, wet tongue is so nice on Derek's skin that he releases a sigh. Derek glances back and it's a woman he saw being fucked on the other side of the ottoman not more than a minute ago. How yummy that she ran over to do this. Derek gives her a big grin.

Sam taps Derek on the back, so he stands up and spins around to face Sam.

Sam's face is so full of satisfaction that Derek is deeply pleased that he brought Sam this pleasure.

"Good boy," Sam says, and kisses his forehead, strokes his hair, then pulls him into a hug. He whispers into Derek's ear, "That was perfect and delicious. You are a very good fuck." He steps out of the hug and tips his head to the left as a questioning expression of concern flits across his face. "Now. Are you good? Or do you need any more aftercare from me?"

Derek would love more of Sam's aftercare, but he doesn't want to hamper either of them from enjoying others, so he nods and says, "I'm good. But, seriously, that was epic." He releases a big sigh. "Thank you for being with me." Derek can only hope he gets to hear this from this amazing, impeccable Dom again as his eyes threaten to fill with tears. He's not going to allow himself to cry, though. He nods sheepishly, feeling a bit foolish, or at least inexperienced, but his little smile tells Sam he loved every second.

Sam leans in close to Derek and whispers in his ear, "Oh, it was most definitely my pleasure. Now that you are warmed up, get in there and get after it. Take whatever pussy or cock you want, and just remember, we're all here for the same thing. So be bold, my new friend." He pats Derek firmly on the back.

Derek nods as this realization fully floods his consciousness. It makes most of his trepidation vanish. He's ready for more.

His eyes again float to Mallory. She's moaning and groaning, groping all the bodies within her reach. Every piece of flesh near her she can find, she consumes in some way with her own body. She finds a cock and starts to suck it, while caressing the shaft, meandering her fingers down to fondle his balls. He moans and rubs his hands into her hair. Mallory falls off his cock as she starts to come from the man pounding her from behind. He leans down and grabs her and rams as he just goes to town, railing her, thrusting into her so hard in the jackhammer motion Mallory so often enjoys.

Mallory climaxes hard and intensely. Her body is shaking from the strong contractions her clit is sending throughout her pelvis and spreading throughout her whole body. The entire orgasm lasts longer than she imagined it could have as she steadily continues to pant.

As Mallory floats down from this huge orgasm, another one is ramping up as the man does not stop fucking her. She glances back and feels the rush of his wet cum splatting inside her as she rages into another orgasm herself. Consumed by feelings of vulnerability and pleasure, Mallory enjoys the sensation that she's drenched as all the orgasm hormones flood her brain and body. She feels sleepy, satisfied, and still turned on as fuck.

Her pussy feels rather sloshy, and it has for quite a while now. Each time she stands or gets fucked, it leaks out. Her thighs have been soaked from cum streams many times over in such a short time that it's blowing all her expectations through the roof.

As she glances behind herself, she sees a man mount the man who is on her. They start a threesome fuck: the man who has been fucking Mallory from behind, the other new man on the scene, and Mallory. This is so overstimulating but excitement flares within her. This will likely be the most epic experience she could ever dream of. This is something she's seen in porn and has always wanted to try it. Her being fucked from behind and him being fucked by the man behind him. The thrusting increases as they go in unison, their three bodies rocking back and forth. They lurch forward at the same time with the thrusting motions. As they find the rhythm that works, the skin slaps drive Mallory wild. As she gropes for his ass, people are under her writhing. They rotate but they're all squirming and moaning and like a big pile of skin just fucking. She is drunk on all the eroticism, the pleasure, the moaning, the joy created by a whole mess of people pleasing each other, and themselves.

It's a dream come true. She's being fucked by a man who is being fucked.

She hears the pleasure sounds emanating from the man, kneeling on the ottoman in the middle. He is clearly coming. The one immediately behind her is orgasming as well, and he grunts and growls. His body jerks against her, and the moans drive her wild. She hears another man nearby enjoying the pleasure. And she can't tell if it's the one behind him or if it's someone else, but it's hot.

But it's just the way of the party. People are almost constantly coming, moaning, groaning, and enjoying each other to the absolute max. She feels euphoric like she's floating in a fantasy that's also a dream, but still real. The whole thing is a level of unreal to her.

The men have each come and step from Mallory. Someone comes down to eat her, to eat the cream pie that the previous man has just deposited. She's moaning and thrashing against his sucking. He crawls up her body and gives her a cream pie kiss.

"Mmmm," she expresses happily. She tastes the salty cum and knows it's a mixture of hers and a previous man's, likely with traces of many someones' spunk. What sexual bliss this is.

They begin to kiss harder and deeper. As a man gropes her from the side someone else pulls the man slightly back on top of her. She opens her eyes, and she sees a woman with a strap-on behind him. She's yanking on the man's hips as she fucks his ass. Mallory gasps. That was fast, but every new encounter at this party tends to happen quickly.

It's all so dizzying and changing by the second. Someone is kissing her hips, tugging on her nipples, another is readying to press his cock into her, but she's in a mass of people and emotions that it's hard for her even to see him. He pumps into her as she moans in delight, as she focuses on the feelings, rather than the who.

Mallory's head falls to the side. She watches the woman in the strap-on as she rubs the dildo against his ass before inserting it again. The man moans and continues to reach for and kiss Mallory. He groans out and grips Mallory hard. She's hard-fucking him from behind like an animal, and it's delicious to watch both her face and the face of the man being fucked. They appear to be enjoying each other immensely.

The man fucking Mallory has cum and he leaves, and immediately someone takes his place between her thighs. It's like she's constantly serviced to pleasure without ever having to move. She feels like a queen, and she feels used, and both satisfy some of her strongest fantasies. The man with his mouth at her pussy has blond spiky hair. She watches the top of his head as it bobs as he begins to eat her out. Her view of his head gets blocked as another man is still lying on her. He's the one being fucked from behind with the strap-on. To Mallory, this is just pure ecstasy, and an all-out feeding frenzy of limitless lust. She's both in each moment and lost in the chaos, but it's all bliss on overload.

Mallory comes again from being eaten out. As her body jerks from another orgasm, of which she's had way too many to even try to count by this point accurately, but likely it's nearing thirty, she turns her head and sees her man nearby. Derek is fucking a woman lying next to her. The woman is so overwhelmed with her own orgasm that she appears to be in a daze. Her eyes are either rolling back, closed and fluttering, or dashing around wildly. She's clearly enjoying a string of multiple orgasms. It floors Mallory that she had been so into her own ecstatic moment that she didn't even notice it was Derek next to her with this woman at first.

She grins while making eye contact with Derek, who smiles back. She then turns her attention and kisses the woman with Derek. She knows that the woman must taste the cum in her mouth because Mallory can still taste it too. She passionately kisses the woman that is being fucked aggressively by Derek. She makes a move. She stands up and brings her womanhood to hover over the woman's face.

The woman Derek is fucking begins to eat her out. Mallory rides her beautiful face, slipping and sliding around, mashing her lower lips into the woman's mouth. The woman's lips are moving, her tongue is licking, then her mouth is sucking Mallory's pussy and clit alternating between the two actions. The woman is so skilled that Mallory is ready to come already. The woman grips Mallory's thighs and pulls her closer. And she moans as Mallory aggressively rides her face again, loving every second of riding the face of a woman her man is fucking. Mallory looks into Derek's eyes, and they both smile and grin. Both of their eyes are so full of satisfaction and insatiable lust. So many of their fantasies are being fulfilled at this one party today that it's mind-blowing. They are intensely fucking a woman together, each in their own way. Actually doing it is a million times better than what they'd fantasized about together all those times.

The woman below her is moaning. She's gonna come again any second, Mallory suspects from her sounds. She falls off Mallory's pussy because she is indeed coming and loses her ability to suckle momentarily because her orgasm overtakes her.

Mallory repositions and is grabbed by someone. He gently tugs her arm and makes eye contact with her as he asks. She smiles her approval as he then pulls her across the pile of people. It's a whirl of action and bodies, and way too fast for Mallory to even count how many. Someone wants to fuck her, the look in his eyes is unmistakable. And she is so ready. She aligns her body with his as he pulls her close and they kiss. He has long brown hair and a mustache. He is kissing Mallory hard and strong, mauling her curves, grabbing her, his hands admiring her on repeat with savoring caresses. She meets his desire by grabbing his torso.

He lays her back. Now that she is still, she can count. There are four heads in the middle of the ottoman. But that changes again. There are five heads in the middle, now six, like spokes of a wheel. All the people with their heads together are getting fucked or in the process of starting to get fucked. Some of them are facing up. Some of them are facing down being fucked from behind, some with asses in the air, but all their heads are in the middle, all being fucked around this fuckwheel.

The man with the long hair presses his erection into Mallory's pussy and both she and the man groan out. It feels just as good as every first penetration she's ever had. It's beyond satisfying to be a part of the sex wheel. It's like they are all a part of the same sex act yet are being fucked separately and it's wild to be a part of it all. She wishes someone were above them videotaping it for later. Mallory is positive she will never top this sexual experience ever in her life.

Mallory is in luxurious ecstasy, moaning and groaning out her enjoyment as she's writhing, grabbing the people beside her, kissing them all as much as she can. A dick appears and she sucks it. The actions become a whirlwind of sexual activity. Someone creampies her, another man spurts cum on her face from above, then a woman appears and licks it. A man leans down and licks the cum off that just landed on her tits. He then gives her a long, thorough kiss. Mallory floats above herself, but she's in herself at the same time, being pounded by a man with a big dick that fills her to the point of near pain. She grabs him as much as she can, but all the action on her and around her has her feeling a bit unreal, like this is not possible, but very real all at once. All along his skin, she's gripping, squeezing, and pinching his nipples. Her head is thrashing back and forth as she's about to orgasm again.

And Mallory climaxes, it's a massive orgasm, her biggest at the party yet. Her body shudders, and she flat-out screams as her body convulses like she's seizing. Her vagina squeezes the man's cock voraciously. Her orgasm launches her vagina into an onslaught of strong pulsations. The contractions are too much for him and his cum blasts inside of her. She imagines her pussy must be draining him, but he pulls out and finishes coming on her tummy in grand streaks of creamy white ejaculate.

"Fucking wow holy fuck me," the man gasps out as he lies beside Mallory in an exhausted heap. "I couldn't hold off once your pussy started squeezing. I just lost it."

Mallory smiles and says dreamily, "That's the power of pussy."

He chuckles. "No doubt. And a power I'd like to experience again at the next party, that is, if you come to one again."

"Oh, I'm definitely planning on coming to one again." She's not fucking missing out on this massive amount of pleasure.

"Good. Maybe we can hook up and satisfy each other again, then." He smiles a genuine smile.

"Oh, for sure," Mallory says, returning his happy look.

An older man, maybe sixty appears and licks the man's cum off Mallory. And he climbs up to give her a kiss afterward. She moans as the man travels his mouth in constant kisses down her neck and goes to visit her nipples. He begins to suck and the man who was just fucking her, who just came, leans down to suck her other one, both men's heads are bobbing on her chest. Her moans rise as she thrashes. They follow her movements, her orations blooming from their incessant suction. She arches her back expressing her thorough gratification, humming from her enjoyment. She smirks, wondering how sore and tired her body will be after all this heightened pleasure.

"Mmmm, you have such tasty and attractive nipples," the older man says when he momentarily lets her breast slip from his mouth.

"Thank you," she murmurs.

It's an exquisite time. She hears the man next to her hitting his apex. And then a woman on her left is coming, as well. The skin smacks, the delicious sounds of sex are still all around her. As she writhes in the big pile of naked people, she savors every little sound, every movement, every slap. It's all ingrained in her brain for life.

But then, suddenly, everyone is leaving the ottoman like it's over, so she shifts her gaze around, trying to figure out what's going on. She's immediately sad about this change. But she's curious about how everyone is suddenly acting as if it's done. She watches the whole group moving in one direction together. She is confused but follows their lead anyway.

Derek watches Mallory follow the group. Everyone lines up against the wall. Well, on second look, he realizes it's all the men with their backs to the wall. All the women randomly pick a man and kneel in front of him. He watches as Mallory situates herself in front of Sam, and by the look on his face, he's thrilled she chose him.

Mallory looks ready and happy to please him.

Chapter 4

Maria has her hands raised in the air like she's ready to announce something. Her beautiful tits with erect peaks are delicious looking to Derek. He regrets that he never sought her out to suck on them during the orgy. Next time, he will make a point to.

"Yep, many of you heard the bell. Don't berate yourself if you were in the throes of passion and didn't hear it. But it's group contest time, which most of you know signals us moving on to the next phase of the party. And today we are doing the cocksucking wall contest."

The group cheers, and many people laugh with delight.

"My favorite," a man says, which elicits more laughter.

"Ladies, and any men desiring, you've got ten seconds to get ready to suck. Ten, nine, eight, seven, six, five, four, three, two, and one. Go!" Maria shouts.

The women all start to suck the cock in front of them. There are a few men on men who organize themselves in the lineup as well, including Derek. He kneels in front of a man he hadn't gotten the chance to play with during the orgy session but wanted to. The man smiles big, looking down at Derek with big blue eyes as he caresses Derek's cheek with rough fingers. To Derek, this man looks like a lumberjack, even without wearing a plaid shirt. Derek's lust rages, anticipating getting this man off with his mouth.

Maria continues, "For the newcomers, this is a contest to see who can make their man come fastest. The winner gets a prize."

All the kneeling women and men are sucking, the slurping sounds seem extraordinarily loud to Mallory. She imagines this must be quite the sight for Maria to watch. There's a woman with blond hair next to her. And she is obviously very good at giving head. She's deep-throating all the way down to the man's balls, which is something Mallory cannot do. What Mallory lacks in experience, she makes up for in enthusiasm, however.

Mallory giggles with her mouth full of Sam's cock and he groans deeply. Oh, he likes that, so Mallory hums. Sam groans out more and plays with her hair. Mallory keeps working on Sam's cock as she hums to send the vibrations of her vocal cord across his member. She's trying her hardest as she's grabbing at his thighs as she's sucking. She knows that even with her hardest efforts, she and Sam will not win.

Sounds of a man in the throes of near climaxing spill into the air. The man next to her with the blond cocksucking goddess must be about to come.

Mallory glances at him as she sucks Sam, watching him bursting into peak climax is driving her closer to coming herself. His body starts to curl forward toward the blond at his cock, and he howls. Mallory smirks a grin, her lips trying to smile around Sam's hard shaft. Sam chuckles and tousles her hair.

Yep, the blond wins as he comes down her throat and she swallows his load. She's clearly had enough and comes off the cock, more cum sprays across her face.

Watching the act causes many other people to come, and many moans and groans fill the air. Many other men, and a few women, come as well, as evidenced by their sounds.

Mallory sighs, loving having been a part of such a grand sexual group act.

"And we have some winners! Max and Alexa win!" Maria announces loudly.

The crowd cheers and erupts in clapping.

Mallory sucks as hard as she can and grunts as she squeezes Sam's balls lightly. He responds by pulling out and guiding his cum to splatter across Mallory's tits. The blond woman who won leans over and grins before she licks Sam's cum off her flesh.

Mallory gazes around, looking for Derek.

The contest comes to an end with only two couples still engaged in a blow job.

Mallory has loved this party and is sad to see it end. It's been epic beyond her wildest dreams. She knows she and Derek can come back to another party, but she still feels ready to do more. She still can't locate Derek, but she can't wait to hear how this contest went for him.

Sam tousles Mallory's hair softly. "Thanks for the kickass sucking babe, now it's time for us to eat."

Mallory nods.

"You're a good girl, Mallory, the best."

Mallory beams from his declaration. She longs to tell him how amazing that makes her feel. She opens her mouth to say it, but gets interrupted.

Maria claps her hands together loudly. "Okay, great job, everyone! It's now time for intermission, and it's time to eat some food. Dinner is served." She sweeps her arm toward the table, which is full of steaming metal pans containing food of various colors, baskets of bread and rolls, piles of meat and fish, platters of fruit and cheese, and tons of glasses of wine at the end.

Mallory's eyes widen in amazement.

"Intermission?" she asks meekly, rather a bit in shock.

"Yep, that was round one," Sam says as he squeezes her shoulders, then assists her to stand. He gives her a hug. "I'm loving that you and Derek have joined our group. You are both a great addition. I so enjoy both of you very much. I hope you both decide to come back again and again."

Mallory blushes at the compliment, which is rare for her. "Oh, I plan to for sure. I've been enjoying this very, very much. And thank you." It seems weak, but it's all she can manage to say at the moment.

"That's my good girl. Now let's go nourish our bellies," Sam says as he grabs her hand and tugs her toward the food.

Mallory warms inside again at him calling her that once more.

Naked, all the people line up at the food tables. They are all talking and giggling, belly laughing and touching each other, all smiling because everyone is on board with doing what they're doing. Mallory recalls how she had thought this was how the party would start, but instead, it's the intermission. But then, all these people already know each other from past parties, so this makes sense to her now. And it has been a life-altering, luscious party. No doubt.

Mallory finds Derek, and they join hands. He squeezes her fingers.

Sam makes eye contact with both of them. Smiles. And walks off to leave them alone.

"How are you?" Derek asks Mallory, his voice full of happiness.

"I'm amazing. But I'm a bit stunned. That was just mind-blowingly wow! Wasn't it? What did you think?"

"Yes, geez, fuck, my mind is reeling. My dick is throbbing, my balls are zinging. I think I came like four times, which is a lot for me in a small amount of time." He chuckles and pulls Mallory close, giving her a kiss on the top of her head.

"I lost count of how many orgasms I had, but honestly, it feels like I must have reached forty. I don't know but my pussy is still throbbing like mad."

"Nice, I love that. I love it when you get pleasure." He raises his eyebrows as he bites his lower lip. He asks, "Are you thinking you want to do this again?" He's so hoping her answer matches his.

"Oh, most definitely, absolutely, hell-fucking-yes. Try to stop me!"

He laughs. "Same, babe, same for me."

"So did you suck or get sucked just now?" Mallory asks with a sly grin.

"Oh, I sucked. And it was epic. I scored time with the lumberjack looking man. Oh, Mallory it was so damn good." He points to the man, who is chatting with the woman with long red hair and a daisy tattoo on her right breast. Derek had loved slipping his cock into her anus. She had squealed so loud he almost came from her sounds alone.

They both smile.

"Good for you. I'm so proud of you, Derek." Her smile deepens. "Yeah, he fucked me. He's quite the yummy specimen, isn't he?"

"Oh, for sure. Lots of those here." His eyes scan the room for Sam.

Derek pulls her along with him, and they line up to get their food too.

Mallory finds it quite interesting to see the faces of these people who she just fucked in a different light as they converse and smile. It's not that they look that different, but it's just new to see them this way, yet it's also helping her to know them a little better, to watch them. She feels as if she belongs to them and they to her. She's a bit taken aback that this feeling is settling in her when she just met these people, but it's the whole experience together that has already bonded them. She can't wait for what being a part of the group will bring to her life in the future.

"Let's eat," Derek says. "I'm positively famished."

"Me too," Mallory says with a joy-filled expression.

Everyone is cheery and seems to enjoy the ambiance, the company, and the food because they all know once they're done eating, and after they've relaxed for a little bit, had some cocktails, there's going to be a round two to restart as the party continues.

Both Mallory and Derek know they are ripe and ready to go again.

Chapter 5

Mallory squeezes Derek's hand. They gaze into each other's eyes for a split second before Derek rings the doorbell. The LED lights make Mallory's skin glow, making her look even more ravishing. She turns her head and tries to peer into the partially covered front window.

She shivers and it triggers his thoughts of how hard she had come during the morning's fuck session they had indulged in. New Year's Eve day is perfect for satisfying sex in the morning, and a wild sex party in the evening. He grins deeply, so ready for what will come. The unknown elements are particularly enticing.

"I'm a lucky man," he says in a soft voice, his breath coming out like a little white cloud when he speaks.

When she glances back at him, her facial expression is pleasant, full of happiness and excitement. "I think I'm the lucky one here," she says, giving his hand a shake. "I'm so fucking excited I can't stand it." She shifts back and forth on her feet with a little grimace. She rolls her eyes with a smile.

He laughs. "Thong shifting?" He knows exactly what she's doing. She's trying to maneuver the panties in her crack without using her fingers, and he loves it. The image of her bottom with the strip of fabric threaded between her buns floods his brain and strengthens his lust further. "I could help, you know."

She smirks at him. "Yup, but it's all good, a nice little scrumptious extra pressure."

Derek knows this time at the club party will be different. The first sex party had been daunting, though satisfying. But even just coming to the house, no longer a newbie, feels not only more relaxing and arousing, but also offers a nice aura of the familiar.

The door opens, and it's Sam. He has on a tuxedo and looks so debonair and sexy that just looking at the man makes Derek's cock fill completely.

Sam gives them a huge grin. His gray hair and eye crinkles at the corners make him so distinguished and dashing, his smooth, masculine aura packs a punch. It doesn't hurt that the man really is an amazing bull.

Derek blushes as he remembers how Sam had shoved his cock up his ass last time and made him cum without even touching his dick. The man and his moves were that powerfully sexy, and Derek hopes he will get the same experience with Sam at this party.

The glint in Sam's eyes tells Derek he remembers their intense encounter, too. That recognition in the man's eyes arouses Derek even more; it's pure golden lust, and his heart pounds in anticipation.

"Ah, come in, my new friends. Derek, Mallory, how are you? And Happy New Year's." His commanding stare is not only friendly, but he has an air about him that suggests he owns everyone he looks upon. It ensnares Derek's sub kinks in a flash. It's as if his gaze coats Derek with a net. And yet, it's deeply gratifying. He wants Sam to own him and on repeat, not that he expects any kind of ongoing claiming by him.

"Oh, I'm so very excited about this party. We haven't been able to stop talking about it since we got the invite." Mallory rolls her shoulders as she releases Derek's hand and falls into Sam's open arms.

Rather than be offended, Derek is thrilled. He realizes not all men are of his caliber on such things, but it's something that endears Mallory to him.

"Ah, baby, it's so good to see you. To touch you. Let me warm you up. It's frigid out there." Sam gives her a squeeze with his arms, then reaches his hands toward Derek. "Come on in here, my yummy young man."

Mallory shakes slightly as another shudder overtakes her body. "Brrrrrr."

Derek grins and shuts the front door. He quickly nestles his body along Mallory's and lets Sam's hands consume him in their three-way hug. Sam jostles them both, and Mallory squeals happily.

"Yes, more of that, and while naked, please," Mallory says in a seductive voice.

"Did you bring your paraphernalia?" Sam asks with obvious excitement. "I love this idea of everyone bringing their favorite sex toys because we will get such a wide variety, plus, we will get to learn something about everyone's sexuality. Last year we did a rope theme on New Year's, which was fun, but I love this idea where it's more open."

Derek takes a step back from Mallory, but immediately misses her ass pressed to his erection. His dick won't be lonely for long though. His girlfriend has changed his sex life in ways he had never imagined possible, and her suggestion of joining this lifestyle club has been the most significant fodder for his personal sexual growth. He can only imagine what kinds of kinky stuff he'll get exposed to at this party alone, and he's so ready.

"We brought a few things." He reaches back and pats his backpack.

"Paddles? Handcuffs? A strap-on? I'm dying to know," Sam says with a lecherous look and a deep chuckle as he releases Mallory.

Mallory gasps with delight. "Oh! We brought more than one item apiece. I hope that's okay? I know we're breaking the rules, but I kind of wanted to, just to see if you'd punish me." Mallory slips her coat off, revealing her deep cleavage. In this dress, her breasts look like perfectly round cannonballs wrapped in glitter.

The fire in her eyes thickens Derek's cock even more. He adores it when she's lit with excitement like this. He wants to punish Mallory too, and he wants Sam to corral them both and flog them into the submissives the man deserves. Well, he hopes he'll react that way anyway. The truth is, he has no clue how he will react to being flogged by Sam. He's so ready to find out, though.

Sam laughs heartily. "Oh, my, well fuck, I have no doubt that can be arranged." He whistles. "Whew, baby. Mallory, that dress is fucking killer on you."

Derek swells with pride. Mallory is indeed a gorgeous goddess, and he loves showing her off. She had debated buying it in the store last week when they shopped after receiving the party invitation. He had laughed at her like she was insane. He'd never seen her look more beautiful than she did in the sparkly silver low-cut, high-thigh cocktail party dress. It cost more than they could afford, but he hadn't cared. She needed to be seen in this outfit. It would have been a crime not to.

Sam cocks his head and then leads them into the familiar hallway.

Mallory and Derek join hands as they follow. Mallory gives Derek a hand squeeze, just as she had the last time they graced this hallway. Only this time, it's more of a gesture of anticipation than reassurance to Derek.

In the main room, no one is fucking yet on the giant ottoman, but instead, they are mingling with drinks and plates of food in their hands. The ottoman is set up and ready, though, with enticing toys of domination, pleasure, and titillation strewn across it. Derek smiles as he scans the multicolored dildos, paddles, floggers, blindfolds, clit stimulators and slappers, handcuffs, crops, and even a large wooden spoon.

The room is positively glowing with all the bright white strings of lights strung from the high windowsills to the fireplace mantle, to the sliding door that leads out to the hot tub on the deck and the pool on the patio beyond. The area surrounding it is fully aglow with lights, too, and steam billows out of the hot tub and the pool.

"Wow," mutters Mallory. "It's so beautiful in here. Like a true winter wonderland."

Derek beams. She fits right in the décor with her dress, and her face positively glows. "Yeah, and that pool looks magical."

There are all kinds of sex toys laid out beside the large ottoman, too. In all, it's a sexual cornucopia that's literally blowing Derek's mind. If only he'd get to try them all tonight. There are strapons, monster creature dildos that look like they came from a Dungeons and Dragons game, a pair of leather handcuffs, a spreader, and various other sex toys in the colors of pink, purple, and black. Flashbacks invade Derek's brain of the last time they were in the house. Bodies had been tangled and gyrating as they had walked in. The whole 'pile of sex,' as he had thereafter referred to it, had jarred his brain and his cock into the most lecherous delights he'd only seen on porn. The whole experience had left a glorious stain on his sexual self that he cherished immensely. Tonight is already promising to provide the same treasured phenomenon, and it makes Derek's heart race. "It's like sexual heaven in here."

Mallory points to a large wooden structure in the corner. It's one of those stocks like from Medieval times where there were three holes, one for a person's head, and two for hands. That device could lead to all kinds of wicked debauchery.

Derek knows that look that flashes across Mallory's face, her clit has just lurched. She'd shared with Derek about how she'd always wanted to be forced into one and used like a whore.

She claps her hands and meets Derek's eyes.

He nods. She'll get her wish list item checked off tonight, and he can't wait to watch, participate, and enjoy her body jerking against the wooden restraint as she comes like a shrieking banshee for all in the room to see. "That has you written all over it."

She nods enthusiastically. Derek loves her exhibitionism kink. He has it too, but she's so much more willing to actually do it than he is, which is why the last time they were at the party house, she dove into the massive pile of fucking people like a seasoned champ while he stared in awe. He totally respected her lack of inhibition, but being completely dumbfounded and frozen, he had needed Sam to gently usher him into the orgy horde. Not this time, he won't, though. He's proud of his progression and newly earned sense of accomplishment. However, having Sam lead him again is more than appealing.

"Oh, what a treat to be able to try that, Mallory. I can't wait," Derek says with a salacious grin. His lust is growing by the second to unmanageable levels, and it enrages him further as he scans around the room, noticing erections pressing out the trousers of most of the men. "Fuck, Mallory, this is going to be an epic night."

She nods as she grabs his hand and pulls him toward the refreshments table. She briefly greets those they pass by, and Derek returns their smiles as she tugs him along. Once they reach the table, she snatches two glasses of champagne and hands one to Derek.

"Cheers to the best New Year's Eve of our lives." Her eyes twinkle with delight.

They clink their glasses and take sips while gazing into each other's eyes. Derek mirrors her lusty look as he takes another drag.

Their eyes are drawn to the smacking sounds coming from across the room.

Someone is starting the games. A tall regal-looking man is striking a paddle across the thick ass cheeks of a bent-over, half-naked woman. Her hands struggle to hold her upright each time he slaps the large wooden paddle against her flesh. She cries out with each one, her body jerking forward. With the next hit, her breasts spill out of her dress as if someone is squeezing her. Her facial expressions alternate between shock and euphoria.

"Fuck," she says loudly as she twitches, expecting another spank. She moans as the man instead of hitting her again rubs the wooden paddle in circles around the flesh of her generous ass. "Again," she pleads.

Her face flashes from ecstatic to a grimace as the man repeatedly spanks her ass in hard wallops. His thick long cock moves in the air ceremoniously with each swing of his arms as he delivers the smacks. Derek is overcome with the urge to sneak under him and suck his cock while he spanks her.

"Should I join?" Derek whispers in Mallory's ear as his heart races. His own willingness to leap right into the scene surprises even him.

She nods vehemently. "You'd better or I'll spank you with that paddle next for not acting on your desires." She swats his ass playfully with an encouraging look. "Go," she says in a loud whisper.

He grins with a flirty pucker of his lips and then downs the rest of his champagne for some extra liquid courage. He hands her the glass with a raise of his left eyebrow. Next, he strips off his suit and leaves it in a pile next to Mallory. His expression grows positive as he struts confidently toward the spanker. Wow. He's so proud. He looks around to see if Sam is watching, but he is nowhere in sight. Derek stuffs his disappointment and keeps walking.

The man is taller than Derek with dark skin. The contrast of his dark skin against the white skin of the woman he's punishing is both stark and beautiful. This will be Derek's first black man's dick he has experienced, not that it matters, but it's new to him so therefore hot. His heart pounds as he slides beneath him.

The man's eyes are appreciative as Derek grabs for his erect cock.

"Good boy," the older black gentleman says. "You ever taste a black man's cock?"

Derek gulps and shakes his head. His confidence deflates a little, and his smile falls. "No, sir. I haven't."

The man stops mid-swing and grabs Derek's chin. "Don't you do that. You will be amazing. And I'm already so turned on by you." He gives Derek a libidinous grin. "If you make me come too fast, this paddle is riding your ass next." He grins even deeper, and Derek loves seeing his intensely white teeth glisten between his dark lips.

Derek wants to kiss his lips, but this gorgeous statuesque man's cock is commanding his attention first. His cock is long and thick, damn near ten inches. Derek knows he won't get much of it in his mouth, but he desires to try. He wraps his lips around the head, and his eyes grow wide. His cockhead seems even bigger as Derek consumes it in his hot mouth. Derek grips the man's penis shaft and begins to pump it with his tight grip as he sucks.

The man jerks slightly from Derek's sucking as he continues to spank the woman. Derek dares not look back but he imagines her ass must be pretty red by now.

This opening act spurs on others as Derek watches three naked people approach the ottoman. Derek keeps on with the blow job as the man groans delightfully. Derek's cock can't get much harder, it actually almost hurts. He resists touching it as his mouth rides the man's dick.

The man's hands meander into Derek's hair. He massages Derek's scalp as he works his cock. Derek loves this move and often does it to Mallory when she sucks him off. To him, it's affectionate and meant to reassure her, and now, being on the flip side of that, it's confirmed for him. His nerves melt away and he focuses on the sensual feelings he's getting from running his tongue and lips on this man's dick. It's empowering to indulge.

The man begins to thrust his hips, pumping his cock deep into Derek's throat forcing him to gag. His eyes water from the strain. He feels helpless, but he keeps his mouth and lips firm as he struggles to steady his body. After about thirty seconds of the man thrusting his hard-on down Derek's orifice, he abruptly steps back, stealing his cock from Derek's mouth.

Derek remains still, bewildered and blinking.

He almost asks the man what happened, but the African American man swings the paddle in the air and nods his head upward.

"You almost made me come. You deserve a spanking," he growls. His anger spills out of his eyes in dominant passion.

Derek acknowledges this is a dominant's game and gives him a nod. He grins inside but is too overwhelmed by this power play to let it surface on his face.

Derek scrambles to stand as quickly as he can. The man grunts; he's impatient and demanding, which honestly turns Derek on even more. He spins Derek around and bends him over so fast that he barely has the time to draw in a deep breath. Derek presses his fingertips into the soft cushion of the ottoman, bracing for the first impact of the paddle. As his heart races, he feels a little light-headed.

He doesn't have to wait long. The first smackdown of the paddle is so loud that Derek isn't sure if the sound or the impact jars him more. The spanks come in rapid fire as Derek's penis drizzles precum. He's only ever been spanked by Mallory, and the hits are so much harder that it literally takes his breath away. This man makes Mallory seem like a weakling.

It's agonizingly more painful than he thought it would be. Derek gasps and sputters as his ass is whacked. He's perplexed; the pain is both erotic and disturbing at once.

During a short lull in the spanking, Derek watches the couple across the ottoman fucking doggystyle. It's so sexy, it's bringing him to the brink of an orgasm. The man behind him wielding the paddle clears his throat before he smacks Derek's ass again. It stings so harshly that Derek cringes as he cries out.

As Derek catches sight of the people having sex around him, he begins to realize the only thing that is preventing him from coming is the pain of each smack. He's feeling oddly grateful for this because he doesn't want to come yet. The hits are succeeding at edging him. This tactic has never occurred to him before, but it's clearly a useful tool to get his erection to last longer. He can't wait to talk about this with Mallory after the party.

He gazes around the ottoman at all the people engaged in various sexual entanglements. There is a foursome fucking to his right that garners his attention. A thin-framed woman is laid out on the big piece of furniture and a fat man is shoving his cock into her pussy while the man behind him is fucking his ass.

Finally, he spots Sam. He's behind that man shoving his cock up the guy's ass. The image of the four of them gyrating together and groaning out is too much; he feels himself rage over the peak of his orgasm. He can't stop it. He comes hard, spewing his cum all over the upholstery beneath him, even despite the spank he just endured.

"Damn it," he whispers. He's so pissed at himself for coming so soon. He smirks, it's kind of funny though, he literally had the cum spanked out of him. His face feels flushed, but more from anger at himself than embarrassment.

But the man behind him delivering his punishment does not falter, even though Derek has climaxed; in fact, he hits Derek harder. It's so gratifying to be punished as his cock is jerking out the last spits of his cum. He deserves this for coming so early.

The spanks stop. He's so turned on his dick stays hard as the man next massages his stinging flesh.

"Good boy for taking your punishment like a man. Now I'm gonna fuck your red-spanked ass." He's so commanding, and Derek wants desperately to comply.

Derek nods. He wants this man's cock up his ass. The man rubs his massive dick head along Derek's anus. Derek is honestly nervous. Though his cock being about the same size as Sam's gives him the confidence he can take that dick, only this man's is a touch thicker than Sam's. He draws in a deep breath and assumes he might be able to take it, with enough lube.

Derek's eyes drift to the left as some people join the ottoman. It's Mallory, the woman of the house, Maria, who has on a red leather strap harness across her breasts, torso, and hips, and a man, Derek, doesn't know. They're all kissing each other and caressing, their passionate grabs getting more aggressive by the second. Derek rides the edge of excitement, giddy for what he is about to watch them engage in. And he's super excited for Mallory, since she's so turned on by Maria, and she really loves female-female-male encounters.

Mallory glances at Derek and smiles her little smile that tells him all is right with her world.

The man at his backside speaks, "I'm Eddie. What's your name, son?"

The use of 'son' makes Derek's cock twitch. He does have a Daddy kink that he has never really ever had the chance to explore, other than the leadership he enjoyed from Sam. Likely, it stems from his dad's disapproval of all things male-male, but he's decided recently that his history is what it is, and he has to accept it. However, he has every right to claim it in his own way and use it to get maximum arousal from something that had hurt him deeply in the past. It's like his way of making it okay in his head. As if he is now owning the cruelty and making it his own, making it allowed in a way that works for him, for his benefit. Only then, and Mallory had agreed, might he get some healing from the way his dad treated him.

Derek shakes his head, trying to get out of it. He needs to be present in the moment. "Derek," he says meekly, barely audible over the sounds around him of moans, skin smacks, groans, growls, and music that spills from the flat speakers on the walls. "I'm Derek."

"You are a very good boy, Derek. I'm going to claim your butthole now. This is the first time we've interacted, and I'm sure you know our club's universal sign for stop, but I can't get off if I don't confirm it with you. Do you know the signal?"

Derek smiles sweetly, even though Eddie can't see his face. He almost lets an 'aww' spill out of his mouth, but he mans up and nods instead. "Yes, sir, I know."

"Please say it for me. It's part of my kink for you to fully acknowledge and accept what I'm posing to do to you." His tone is sincere and no-nonsense.

Derek understands and respects this. He feels this need, too, when he dominates Mallory. "I point to the ceiling." He pauses. "Or I could yell stop."

"Yes, good boy. Now I can fuck your tight ass." He presses his cock at Derek's anus, pulls back, and reaches for the lube next to Derek. He squirts a large dollop on Derek's skin and spreads it all across his pucker. "This isn't your first ass fucking, son, is it?"

Derek breathes a sigh of relief at Eddie's generous spread of lube across his butthole, and he especially likes the concern in his voice. "No, sir, it's not."

"Good to know."

Derek savors his view as Eddie readies to enter him. Mallory is kissing Maria as Maria is getting pussy fucked by the dark-haired man with a goatee. His face is set in utter delight as he rocks himself into her womanhood. Maria is caressing Mallory's hair with one hand and pinching her big, erect nipple with the other.

A Christmas song blares as Eddie gently presses his large dick into Derek's asshole. Derek gasps deeply, his body tensing upon the penetration, and he worries again he won't to be able to handle Eddie's enormous cock.

Eddie pets his back and whispers, "Relax baby, you can take this cock. You just need to let go of that tension. You are in control, and I'll stop whenever you want me to, so you can relax and be confident in that."

His soft, reassuring tone helps Derek loosen up. He takes another deep cleansing breath and relaxes his body and his anal sphincter even further.

Eddie gently proceeds to insert himself into Derek slowly. He groans deeply with the insertion, which hardens Derek's cock further. Derek gazes upon his pile of cum which has spread into a wet spot beneath him on the ottoman. He maneuvers to try and lick it up.

Eddie chuckles. "Go ahead, baby, you can have it." He stops pumping into Derek so he can swipe his tongue and clean up his jizz off the fabric. "That tastes good, baby?"

Derek nods as he savors his own taste. His favorite way to taste himself, though, is always off Mallory's tongue, but catching her in an eye lock as he rises back into his bent-over position for Eddie is a close second.

She grins at him with a nod as a man grips her hips from behind and bends her over the ottoman's edge. She glances back at the man, then returns her gaze to meet Derek's.

He loves that they will both be fucked doggy at the same time while maintaining an eye lock. The thought of that alone is driving him right to the peak of climax again.

The new man about to fuck Mallory is older, and chubby with a belly overhang. Derek knows Mallory must be excited, she's always wanted to feel a man's pudgy stomach bounce off her ass cheeks. It's been on her sexual bucket list forever to be fucked by a larger older man.

Chapter 6

Mallory wiggles her butt at the squishy-bodied man, who honestly reminds her of a teddy bear. He digs his fingers into her flesh.

"Pussy or ass, sweetheart?" he asks with genuine interest.

"Pussy please," she answers in a seductive voice. His mention of ass doesn't sit well though. The mere question of it from him makes her think he wants it, and her experience is already sullied. She wants to stand up and declare heatedly 'no anal' but reigns in her anger. She needn't kink shame him. She scolds herself. She knows she can't get mad at him for wanting to fuck her ass. It's just not her thing, but he hadn't known that. She draws in a deep breath to simmer herself down. It works, sort of. Her temper needs its own tempering, or someone to tame it. Would this man be the one to do it?

"You got it. You're so sexy, honey, I saw you at the last party, but I never made it to you before we had the dick sucking contest. And then I had to leave, so I missed my chance. I was excited to see you walk into the room tonight." His voice is soft and kind.

Tingles travel all around Mallory's body. He was looking for her; however, she hadn't even noticed him. No matter. To be desired deeply is also her kink, which is why she thinks she loves exhibitionism so much. To be wanted by many people turns her on immensely; it's admittedly a top desire of hers.

"Awww, that's so sweet. Well, I'm so excited to be here for you."
Her lust swells at his appreciative grin. She wants to make this man
cum hard.

He presses his erection to her buttocks and sways her gently back
and forth. It comforts and arouses her at once. He moans and leans
over her back. "You feel amazing already. Just looking at you gets me
hard." There's no mistaking the extreme lust in his tone.

Her eyes widen. That sentence ticks up her need for him inside
her even higher. "Mmm, I love to hear that." She glances at Derek,
and his little smile tells her he heard the man's comment to her, too.
He looks excited for her.

Derek's smile flits away into an expression of ecstasy as he is
pounded hard by the man fucking his ass. The dark-skinned man
rocks his body, pelting his backside aggressively with pelvic slams.
Derek's eyes fall open and close several times as the man behind
Mallory penetrates her, too. There's something so hot about them
both being fucked from behind at the same time.

"Oh, fuck," she whispers as yummy sensations travel her body.

The man groans, verbally expressing his deep pleasure. "Fuck,
you feel amazing." He grunts and slowly pumps his hard dick into
her. "I'm Max, by the way," he utters between pants.

"I'm Mallory," she says while glancing quickly backward between
her own heavy breaths.

"I know," he says with satisfaction.

Warm fuzzies envelope Mallory; she loves that he knew her
name. He's hitting her needs to feel special really well, which is
hugely satisfying.

"Mallory, can I blindfold you?" he asks with hope.

"Oh, yes, you can definitely do that to me." She loves being
blindfolded. The loss of control, of submitting to another human is
always extraordinarily delicious to her. Plus, there's something about
not being able to see, that heightens the sexual tingles for her. It's like

she can really focus on them rather than being distracted by what she sees. Maybe that's her ADHD rearing its multiheaded self. With her vision taken away, though, she can really be present in her own bodily sensations and feelings. The blinded experience becomes all about her and what she's feeling moment to moment. She seriously can't wait for him to slip it over her eyes.

Joining this group has been one of the best ideas of recent decades. Fucking strangers is hot, but then being in this sex club is also proving to be scrumptious. It helps her feel more comfortable because in the group, others have already been vetted and proven themselves to be safe, courteous, and careful with each other's hearts. She feels safe even though she's never been with this man. The fact that Maria and Sam allows him to be here serves as a glaring green light. These thoughts help her relax her body even more.

She can't restrain herself any longer. She reaches for the black blindfold.

"Please, let me. I get off on taking care of you." He caresses her back softly. "I appreciate you helping, babe, but I love to do it all for you. I'm going to make you come hard, big, and often."

What is this? This is a totally new feeling. Mallory's spirit rolls around in the comfort and excitement of his words as they blossom in her. She already wants this man to push her boundaries and get her to come like a geyser on repeat. His confidence that he would is particularly yummy to her. The fact that he desires to please her warms her heart and stokes her libido.

He reaches past her, his soft, pudgy stomach brushing her right side.

She smiles. She just wants him to wrap his body around her. He is such an intriguing person, and she is so excited to have him fuck her into multiple climaxes.

She releases a tiny squeal. "I'm so excited."

He chuckles. "Oh, well, you have no idea how excited it makes me to hear you say that."

Her breathing increases as he carefully lays the blindfold across her eyes. She promptly closes her eyelids as he pulls the fabric flush to her eye sockets. Her pussy lips flare in response as he secures the blindfold tightly behind her head. He's taking charge, and she's wholeheartedly submitting.

"Now, which toys are okay with you? Flogger? Paddle? Sex toys? Anal beads?"

She's never done anal beads. The thought scares her a bit. She's a bit irritated he doesn't catch on to her choice of pussy earlier. Did she have to scream it? Anal is not her thing! She's startled and vows to calm down. He isn't forcing her to do anything. Her anger is not cooperating with simmering down.

He takes a step back from her and gently caresses the tops of her ass cheeks. "You've gone still and quiet. Please be honest, sweetie. I don't want you to feel any pressure at all. This is about mutual pleasure only."

She breathes a sigh of relief, and her muscles relax.

"That's it, relax now. You can tell me. I won't be mad."

She takes another deep breath, then slowly releases while counting to three. She's cleansed and calmer. "Okay. Thank you. Nothing in my butt," she says confidently with a bit of indignation, which really, he doesn't deserve.

"Of course," he says quickly, his tone apologetic.

"I'm sorry, it's just..."

"No apologies for what you like and don't like. Just tell me your wants and desires you wish to share with me." He rubs her flesh. "I am just happy for any time with you, honey."

How is he so kind and understanding? He reminds her of a caring dad or grandpa, except that he wants to shove his cock inside her and make her cum. She snickers. Age gap is her thing, but not so much in the familial way. But if he's someone else's dad or grandpa, then she can really get into that.

"Ah, I like to hear that little laugh." He pets her back again.

"Okay. I'm okay with your cock, and any sex toys in my pussy or on my clit and the flogger right now." Her voice sounds meeker than she feels, and it confuses her somewhat. She's a lion, and usually so much more confident. Must be it's just the newness of this man, or perhaps the mention of anal that has thrown her. She shudders slightly to try and throw the nasty feelings off. She can't wait to accept him inside her body, within her boundaries she stands firm.

He nestles himself against her backside once more and presses his cock gently, but solidly, into her pussy.

The penetration is quick, luscious, wet, easy, and she moans out.

"Mmmm. Perfection," he says, then chuckles as he slow-fucks her from behind. "Right now, I just want to fuck you, but I'm very happy to know what you're okay with in case the mood strikes me." He lets out a big sigh. "I'm more of a lover than a punisher." He slows his thrusting. "Pausing to savor you." Then he restarts entering her, slowly increasing his pumping.

She nods as a grin spreads across her face. She's getting a sense of such goodness from him, and she likes it. He's even potentially pushing her closer to thoughts of exploring, and honestly, of spreading her boundaries by those statements alone. His deep understanding and expression of the fullness of consent and enjoying pleasure are intoxicating. She ponders what experiences she'd let this man deliver them both into together in the future, something taboo is one idea. It must be his age, she surmises. This understanding and his smooth, natural way of putting her at ease. Dare she say she's feeling extra comfortable with a man she's just met?

He lays his groundwork well and she settles into the lush world of visionless submission as he continues to sensually slow fuck her from behind. She is more than ready to be pounded into though;

she's getting so turned on and is beginning to crave the rough body smacks of urgent fucking.

Again, Mallory's thoughts flit to Derek. She marvels at how wonderful her relationship is with him. Not being able to see him getting fucked anymore is a bummer, but it's now time to focus on her own experience. She can ask him later. They are in this life together, but they still have their own too. Derek understands that and agrees, unlike men she's dated in the past. The fact that they both acknowledge makes Mallory believe she and Derek might stay together for the long haul, which is a scary, but mysteriously wonderful thought.

Max's cock feels amazing. Having an older man is fucking delectable. The age difference is filling her kink bucket up to full charge, which will be fabulous masturbation fodder for later. He keeps blissfully rocking his erection back and forth against her G-spot. He reaches around and jostles her clit. She moans extra when he does because she wants him to know she loves being attended to for her pleasure, too. He reaches forward, laying his body on hers as he fondles her breasts and nipples, pulling them smartly away from her body.

"Oh!" she exclaims, jerking and shrieking the harder he tugs. The cock ride never stops and she is on the rise to her peak real quick. If he starts to ram into her or accosts her clit hard, she'll come.

"Fuck, Max, that feels amazing. I'm getting close," she murmurs while squirming from the increased sensitivity. She likes being able to use his name. It feels like they've known each other longer than just an orgy allows. She adores the whole fucking a stranger thing, that being a newbie in this club offers, but this familiarity of knowing a bit about him is also nice. "So heavenly Max."

She sinks into her enjoyment as Max ramps up his fucking, pounding against her ass cheeks making them jump. She loves bouncing off a man's pelvic thrusts, loving the body-spanked feeling of a man behind her, and him getting aggressive, his want for her hitting an urgent plateau. The act of being rammed always spreads jolts through her entire pelvis and even though her clit isn't getting hit directly, it is incredible. Plus, she relishes that luscious feeling of being dominated, which drives her lust to peak heights. Her realization of being more of a sub is something she'd recently understood, though she could Domme Derek whenever he desired it. She had a well-used strap-on at home to prove it. But in truth, lately, she's been thinking it wouldn't work with anyone other than Derek.

She moans ever louder. The darkness of the blindfold forces her to focus on every blissful bit of sensitivity. The intensity grows quickly to a superb level. Each smack of his soft abdomen against her ass is like a body spank and each grunt he gives ticks her closer and closer to her climax. His cock constantly rubbing her vulva lips and internal walls has her about to scream. She's most certainly ready for her next orgasm.

"Please," she begs, "Max. Please, more. Make me come."

"My pleasure," Max says breathlessly. He thrusts into her so fast and hard, his plush tummy a squishy match for her round ass cheeks.

He mashes himself into her body, and with the combination of his grunts, the pleasure sounds of those around her, plus his aggressive grip on her hips, she tips over that edge of ecstasy and explodes into her orgasm.

The loss of control is fucking bliss, especially with so many others fucking around her. Her clit sends out pulses that cause her vagina to convulse repeatedly. After about the fourth contraction, Max groans and comes inside her pussy. The wet flesh-on-flesh sounds of him entering her on repeat increase as his balls are emptied.

She loves the smell of cum, more so than she loves the taste, and she yearns to reach down and dip her fingers in her pussy so she can smell his particular brand. She smiles, wondering what he'd think.

She bites her lip. She doesn't care. She wants what she wants, not gonna deny herself. So she reaches back and slides her finger along his shaft and wiggles her index finger inside her pussy.

He laughs lightly. "Fishing for buried treasure in there?" he asks.

"Kind of. I want to smell you." She presses her finger in deeper and caresses his cock with the pad of her finger. She pulls it out and brings her finger to her nose to sniff.

He takes every advantage, still pumping himself into her, though now very slowly.

"Mmm. Love the smell of cum on my fingers," she coos tasting his spunk. "Good sauce."

"Care if I join you? I'd love a taste of our combined cum, if you don't mind." He pulls his cock out and kneels behind her.

"Go for it," she says as she inhales the juices on her finger again to savor them, then she sticks it in her mouth. "Mmm. Me too. Love it."

He voraciously eats her out, his nose poking between her ass cheeks as he rides his tongue all over her vulva and inside her slit. His grunts as he works over her pussy are deeply satisfying to Mallory, she can't stop smiling, writhing, and moaning. She will certainly seek him out in the future. He's eating her out so fiercely, she approaches her peak point again. Max has definite pussy eating skills.

Her moans increase as does her panting, and she grips the ottoman hard, resting her head down on it. She's too weak to stay up. The next orgasm overtakes her. She tenses, then her body jerks and undulates in response to the climax. She freely releases her mewling of pleasure, adding to the sounds all around her.

As the orgasm slows, then stops, she quickly realizes he's not anywhere near done. He keeps relentlessly eating her out with ferocious fervor. She rages into another one immediately. He's sucking her clit so damn good. She comes again, and even harder this time. The sounds of the room dim as the orgasm flurry begins. She comes again, and then again as he keeps going. She gasps and flat-out screams as she comes so hard once more.

She slumps onto the ottoman, her body now flush fully resting upon it. She can't speak. It takes her about a minute of just lying there to recover, and the whole time he just lays atop of her, not moving, cradling her in her vulnerable post coming phase. Their bodies both heaving as one with heavy breathing, her heart pounds and her whole vulva and clit throb like mad. She senses others moving around her, which magnifies how still she is.

Finally, she's able to say, "Holy fucking fuck shit. That was so big, and so many."

He caresses her back. "Did you enjoy that, baby?"

She nods against the ottoman because words are hard once more as she falls back into the memory of it all.

"Good, I'm so thrilled. I'm going to let you rest for a moment before you move on. I think you need it. You seemed like you had many orgasms."

She nods, still mute.

He places a soft fleece blanket over her body and hugs her tight from above. Then he's gone. She soaks in her hormones, the exhilaration, and the overwhelm as a beautiful thing.

MALLORY WAKES WITH a warm, safe, satiated feeling despite still being blindfolded. She removes the fabric and opens her eyes. She's a little startled as the nap makes her temporarily forget where she is. In front of her are two men double penetrating a sexy woman with dark skin. Her silky hair gyrates against the ottoman as they fuck her. Her head thrashes from side to side as she grasps back at the men with one hand. She grabs at them wildly, then shakes, clearly climaxing.

Mallory smiles. What an amazing thing to wake up to. She's refreshed from the nap, from the endorphins she's been gifted from coming so many times. She stretches, flooded with feelings of amazement and satisfaction. She rolls to her back, then sits up. The blanket falls off her breasts, and Max appears before her as if by magic.

"I've been watching you sleep for fifteen minutes. You were so beautiful. It was an honor to fuck you to sleep." His eyes are so kind and soft. "That's a sign of triumph to a pleasure Dom." He's grinning hugely, she can't not grin back. "I wish I'd been close enough to be the one to remove your blindfold. Maybe next time you'll be willing to wait and allow me to do it."

She bobs her head quickly, yes, she wants that. The desire to please him overwhelms her. She yearns to hop up and hug him, and she's not quite sure why she doesn't do it.

She notices gray patches of hair above his ears for the first time. She's feeling so safe with him, plus, he has taken care of her sexual, emotional, and exhaustion needs. A true Daddy Dom, no doubt, but pleasure Dom was a new concept. She instantly adores him and wants to bask in his brand of afterglow in the future. She smiles even deeper at him with a sheepish shrug of her shoulders. The idea of a hug still seems awkward, which is crazy given the man just had his dick up her pussy.

"I didn't mean to fall asleep. You know that doesn't mean I wasn't aroused. I was extremely so, and I loved our interaction."

"Oh, I know, baby. I know. I could tell, sweetheart." He reaches for her and hugs her face to his hairy chest.

She melts in, grateful he's made the first move. She nestles against his soft, thick body.

"I really enjoyed watching you come so many times." He sounds like he means it. He caresses her head.

She squirms slightly in his arms. He smells like whiskey and BBQ sauce.

She tries to stop it by squeezing her belly muscles, but it's no use; her stomach still growls.

"You need a snack. Can I help you get some food?" He pats her hand and pulls her to stand.

She wobbles a bit but steadies quickly. All the moans, groans, and skin smacks have her wanting to fuck again, but she's also ravenously hungry. He pulls her along toward the table of food as she glances back at the orgy behind them, scanning the group of people for Derek.

As they reach the table, he points at the chicken wings. "These wings are to die for."

"I think I just smelled them on you," she says with a grin.

"Yeah, I ate them while I watched you sleep. It was quite enjoyable." The twinkle in his eyes blooms brighter yet. "My night is complete after being with you, though. I don't need anyone else. You were my goal, my desire, and my deep pleasure. I can only hope you allow me to pleasure you again in the future. It would be my honor."

"Wow," Mallory whispers. He's such a gentleman, the likes of a partner she's never experienced before. "Oh, yes. I'm definitely in for more. You were incredible." She relaxes her shoulders and releases a short, light laugh. "You blew my mind, to be honest."

He beams. "And that made my night even more."

She struggles with how to convey to him how he made her feel, that she truly loved it. It was so new to her, but unbelievably wonderful. She wants time with him again and again. She hadn't thought about developing actual lasting relationships with people in the club until now. Before this, she'd only thought about getting off in different ways with different people, like just sex acts, but this is something entirely different. It's jarring, yet still feels so good, so how could developing a connection with him going forward be bad?

She'd have to talk to Derek about this. It's not like she'd ever leave Derek, but this has the beginnings of something she likes.

Even though her head is heavy with such thoughts and utter confusion, she smiles as Max points at a salad.

"This salad was to die for. And this bread, whew! Watch it! I'm addicted."

He grabs her a glass of champagne and a bottle of water as she fills her plate. He leads her to a table that overlooks the lit backyard.

They sit, and he touches her hand. "I hope you are okay with me joining you. It's more fun to eat with company."

"I love it, Max. Thank you. I'd love more of your company." She returns his happy expression. This party is showing promise of being even more interesting and endearing than she thought.

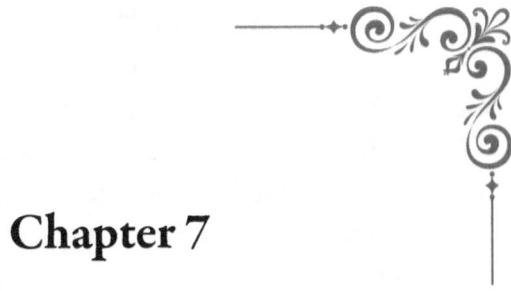

Chapter 7

"So, tell me about the old guy." Derek opens the door out to the back, pressing lightly on Mallory's back to usher her out first. He finds her new prospect very enticing, Daddy kinks and all.

"Oh, damn, this is so cold," she shrieks as she steps outside. "It's beautiful, but this sucks." She releases a light laugh as she tosses her hair. "A winter land is also a frigid land."

"Not for sex," Derek says with a snicker.

Derek scans the patio area. Several people are swimming, and two are in the hot tub. Both are lit up with slow-changing LED underwater lights, giving the water a glowing appearance.

"True," Mallory states as she watches the skinny dippers. "That looks lovely. I can't wait to get in."

"This way," Derek says, grabbing her hand. "I can't stand this cold for another second."

They walk swiftly toward the outdoor shower, holding hands.

Mallory giggles, pointing to the sign above the door. "Ha! 'Wash the swimmies off before you swim!' Oh, that's hilarious!"

"Yeah, and the giant sperm looks like Moby Dick!" Derek cajoles.

She shudders. "Whew! This is bad. That's about a whale, right? It looks like whale sperm, no doubt! And millions of babies behind him," she says, snickering. She grasps the door handle in a rush and yanks it open.

"You like that older guy?" Derek asks again, feeling only curiosity over his girlfriend's union with the man, well, and maybe some lust, if he's honest.

"Yes, I like him a lot," Mallory says as they enter the steamy outdoor shower. "Oh, this feels way better. Mmmmmm."

The heater is blasting down on them as Derek reaches in to turn the water on.

They both begin to strip to the side of the stream as they make eyes at each other. Derek tests the water with his hand and nods. "It's good."

They collide in an embrace beneath the hot, flowing water, their open mouths seeking each other and landing in an aggressive kiss, writhing together for several minutes before Derek pulls back.

"I don't want to make you be sore, so let's stop there." Derek holds her face between his hands. "You look so sexy, though, I just want to fuck you."

She blinks quickly as she smiles back. "Yeah, but you're right. We have sex multiple times a day, so one day with just one time won't kill us. The point of this party is to fuck others."

He nods. "Well, I can see us fucking again once we get home," Derek says slyly as he pumps a dollop of body wash in his hand and begins to massage it into Mallory's tits. "Your tits look extra dirty," he says in a joking voice.

"Uh, huh," she says in a good-natured tone, a sexy knowing grin on her face.

Derek eyes her up as she reaches for the soap. "My cock is extra dirty."

She chuckles as she smears the bubbles on his hard-on. "I think we will either still be turned on when we get home and want to fuck each other's brains out, or we'll crash from utter exhaustion."

"You're likely right. I'm having a blast though, you?"

"Yes. And Max, he's a Daddy Dom, or what he calls himself is actually a 'Pleasure Dom.'" She grins as if experiencing pure bliss.

"Oh, I want one of those," he says, laughing. "He into men?"

"Nope, he's hetero."

"Damn," Derek says as he rubs suds across Mallory's belly. He grips her hips and urges her to spin. As he's soaping up her ass, he groans. "It's really hard to not just fuck you right now."

"I know, I'm fighting that urge myself." She steps away from him. "How about we just wash ourselves, it will be less tempting to fuck then?"

He nods, but pouts. He's noticing a calm about her that she lacked earlier in the party; there's something different, but he's not quite sure if that's what it's about. "Max really put you at ease, didn't he?" He's happy for her. "Will you play with him at future parties?" He makes a mental note to watch them interact next time.

She nods heavily. "He was actually waiting for me to appear tonight."

"Oh?" If he were a jealous man, he'd be bristling, but the look of total happiness on her face satiates him instead. "I'm okay with you being with him. I trust you."

"Yeah, you're my nesting partner, forever, Derek. I hope you know that." She looks a bit shocked but quickly shifts her expression back to happy.

"I do. And I know you'll be honest with me if that ever changes, as I will be with you."

"We didn't really talk about this club turning us polyamorous," she says, making eye contact with him. "How do you feel about that?"

"I think we need to talk more about it, but I'm okay with you enjoying time with him."

She shivers despite the billows of heat streaming from the heaters above and the hot stream of water between them. "We knew we'd chart new waters with joining this club."

He nods and pulls her into an embrace. "Hey, I love you."

She meets him with a peck on the lips. "And I love you."

He turns off the water, and they snatch their clothes off the hooks on the wall and deposit them in the plastic bags from the bin next to the door.

Derek opens the door, and the blast of cold air sends goosebumps across both of their bodies and hardens their nipples.

"Oh! Shit that's cold," she says as she tears across the deck making a beeline for the hot tub.

She drops her bag next to the basket of white towels and slides right into the steaming hot tub. "Ah, that feels much better." She glances at the people in the tub before making eye contact with Derek again.

"I'm so ready for this," Derek says as he climbs in with a deep sigh. "This feels incredible." He nods to the couple sitting opposite him and Mallory in the hot tub. "Hi, I'm Derek."

"And I'm Mallory," she says cheerfully.

"Hi Derek and Mallory," the older gentleman says. "I'm Steven, and this is my wife, Faye."

"Nice to meet you both," Mallory says as she squeezes Derek's hand beneath the water.

"Likewise," says the woman next to the man.

The couple appears to be in their mid-sixties; he has white hair, and she is blond.

"What a gorgeous backyard," Mallory says in a cooing voice. "I can't imagine living in such a haven."

"Yeah, they have it pretty nice here," Faye says, smiling. "You two are new, right?"

"Yup, just joined recently. This is our second party," Derek says, his older woman's kink flaring his bone to thicken. He'd love to play with her, and her husband too. He can't resist finding out more. "Bi or straight?"

"Both bi," Steven says with a sly grin. "You two?"

"Same," Mallory quips in quickly.

They both smile and bob their heads. "Nice," says Faye, her eyes flaring brighter with excitement. "We love it when new young people join."

Derek's passion seethes. She's clearly got an age gap kink in her, too. Perfect.

"Very happy you've entered the hot tub," Steven says with a grin. "I believe we'd be interested in discussing some interactions with you, right, Faye?"

"Oh, definitely, I'd love to do that." She meets Derek's gaze intently.

Derek's arousal stacks up quickly, not that it ever went back to baseline after showering with Mallory.

"Would you like to come and sit next to me?" Faye asks with an inviting gaze directed at Derek.

"Oh, yes, ma'am, I would love to." His heart begins to race as he gives Mallory's hand a squeeze, followed by a quick connecting check in glance into her eyes. She looks excited, too. Yup. She's all on board. He scoots over to sit next to Faye.

After smiling back at Faye, Derek watches as Steven slides closer to Mallory. Her face lights up as he moves in, their bodies almost touching.

"I like how you're looking after her," Faye says with a twinkle in her eyes. "Shows good character."

The praise kink in him eats her words and demeanor up. "Yeah, she can take care of herself, of course, but I'm always on the watch."

"You, too, seem very well suited for each other. You look at each other with love in your eyes." She smooths her hands palms down across the bubbling water. "You two remind me of Steven and me when we were young, like you."

He releases a slow breath, trying to calm his thundering heart. "Yes, we're very much in love." He widens his grin. "And very like-minded."

"That's a recipe for success," she states confidently.

"Have you two belonged to this club long?" Derek asks as he watches Mallory giggle, as Steven is bouncing her breasts in his hands, making the water splash up. Her giggling increases the rougher he gets.

"Yes, twenty years."

"Whoa! Seriously? Wow! That's incredible." Now he feels like a true youngster, and too inexperienced for the likes of this goddess.

"Yup, and we've never regretted it once." She softens her face even further. "We've had some discussions. It hasn't always been smooth sailing, but we've worked out any ripples. You can't expect any issues." She raises an eyebrow as a look of authority graces her face.

Derek's cock thickens. He's getting so aroused by her that he's ready to explode. He nods at her as he takes a quick peek at Mallory and Steven again, and he's pinching her nipples as she giggles. He tugs them away from her body, and she moans louder, her eyes beginning to roll.

"Looks like they are having fun over there. How about you and I have some fun?" she asks causally, as if she's asking him to pass the jelly at brunch.

"I'm game for whatever you are into." Derek instantly wants to please her, whatever that might be.

"Are you interested in playing with me, in a sexual nature?" she asks with a wink.

His cock throbs. "Yes, ma'am. Very much so," he says as he drops his eyes to her erect nipples that tip her small tits.

"Wonderful. I'd really love that. May I touch your splendid looking cock, young man?" Her eyes burn with mischief. "I could go for some nice stiff young meat in my mouth and pussy."

Derek's panting. This woman is so hot, she's fire. "Yes. My cock is all yours. As much as you want." He wiggles his hips to make his dick sway in the water.

She scoots closer to him and her hand is on his manhood in a flash. She pumps her hand up and down his firm flesh in the water, and within seconds, he feels the urge to come.

He writhes, pressing his hands to the plastic beneath his ass as he tries to not come quickly. He looks around and sees Steven tit fucking Mallory, which makes his cock lurch. "Oh, fuck," he mutters as he quickly rises up out of the water. "I'm gonna..."

The frigid winter air freezes the water on his skin instantly, and his cock calms down. His arousal clams shut when his genitals hit the air.

Faye still has her hand on his cock and when he meets her gaze, she giggles. "I do love young men, and your ability to climax multiple times. You can relax and come if you want. There are tissue boxes all over the edge of the hot tub for a reason."

She continues to pump him, and despite being in the freezing air, he hardens to her touch. She maneuvers in front of him and presses him to sit on the edge of the hot tub. "This is the ultimate in sensation play, cold for your top, hot for your lower half."

Her face transforms from mischief to horny maiden as she opens her mouth ready to take him inside it.

Derek shudders in the cold and wonders if he can come with half his body frozen.

She mouth mounts his cock and closes her lips around his swollen member. She pumps her sealed orifice on his dick while she strokes his shaft.

He leans back on his stiff arms, throwing his head back as the throes of ecstasy consume him.

She deep throats his cock down the base as she fondles his balls. She mouth fucks herself on his cock much more aggressively than her petite frame suggested she could.

Derek lifts his head and watches Steven's ass as he's ramming himself into Mallory doggystyle. He grins because once again, he and Mallory are both getting action side by side.

Faye makes eye contact with him as she bobs up and down quickly. His arousal clicks and his cum spews into her mouth. She keeps sucking him as his cock pumps out cum.

He sighs as his body contracts from the orgasm.

She pops off his cock and wipes the corner of her lips. "Nice big load. Love that from you, young men." She reaches for a tissue and wipes her mouth with it, then tosses it into the little garbage can on the edge of the hot tub's rim. "They try to keep too much cum from entering the water, or we'll all be swimming in it." She snickers as she sits back. She leans her head as she side eyes his naked body.

"That was amazing," he mutters as he sinks back into the steaming water. "Ah, and that feels incredible." The hot water soothes his shivers away, and he grins deeply at Faye.

"Looks like Steven is going after it," she says with a saucy look.

Derek watches as Steven aggressively fucks Mallory from behind, his hairy thick body making it look more like Mallory's being fucked by a bear than a man.

Steven grunts as Mallory's moan peaks.

"She's coming," Derek says to Faye. "I know her sounds."

"Nice." She smiles as she watches her hubby give Mallory some final hard thrusts. "I like this club for him being able to get off on the rough doggy action. I just can't do that anymore." She sounds a bit wistful, but her grin shows she is happiness about it too.

"Yeah, that's one thing we are learning. We can be together but still get all our kinks met this way. Like Mallory doesn't like anal, but I do."

"That's exactly right. That's what this club is for. Plus, it's a community of like-minded people. But we found that out too, and we've been coming back ever since." She slides closer. "And when you're recovered, I'd love a ride." She peers into the water at his crotch. "You look pretty ready already." She looks interested as she glances at his face.

"Oh, I'm ready whenever you are. However you want it, my cock is still yours." He can't believe his body is still making cum. "Hop on, if that's what you want."

She pops up and straddles his lap, then slowly slides down. She bounces for a bit, her face full of joy. "I can't do the water for long, though. How about we slip inside for a quickie?"

He nods and rises out of the water, reaching for two towels.

"We'll come back for them. But for now, you're mine," she says in a richly seductive tone. She wraps the thick white towel around her body and releases shrieks as she steps out of the water. She slips her flip flops on and dashes for the door, calling behind her, "Hurry, Derek, before you freeze that cock off!"

Derek chuckles and follows behind quickly, his cock bobbing as he hustles.

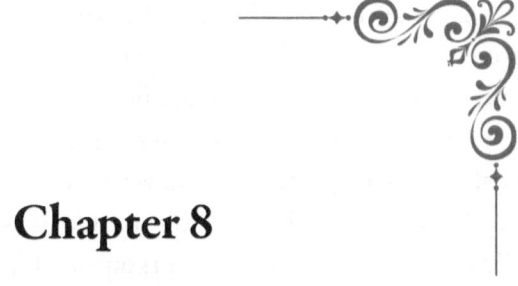

Chapter 8

Derek follows Faye to a bedroom. She scampers ahead of him, glancing back every so often. Her face is alive with excitement as she leads.

"This is my favorite bedroom here," she says as she enters the room.

"I didn't even know these rooms were available to use," Derek says as he looks around in astonishment. The room features a four-poster bed with a metal frame, topped by sheer white fabric draped around the black metal. The ornate design of the metal looks like vines with all their curls and irregular shapes. The bed looks lush, white, and fluffy as a cloud. The walls are a light pinkish beige, and the artwork is black-and-white images of people in various sexual positions. A fake candle flickers on each bedside table.

"Isn't it lovely?" Faye asks as she sits on the bed.

"Yeah, like a slice of heaven." Derek watches as Faye floats back and squirms. Her naked body nestles in the soft comforter as she moves. "You look beautiful in bed," he says sheepishly, as he caresses his chin. His erection is packed solid and he can't stop imagining fucking her down into that puffy comforter, her body writhing in pleasure and comfort.

"I need a bed these days, easier on my back," she states as she gives him a gaze full of electricity. "Eat me out, I'd love it."

Derek grins. He likes that she's directing him, just what he wants from a sexy GILF like her. "It would be my extreme pleasure to make you come." He settles between her legs and smiles up at her.

"That's a good boy," she says as she pats his hair. "Make my body shake and you can fuck me however you want."

Derek nods as his cock throbs. He likes this idea very much. His dick is certainly getting a workout at this party. He can't imagine how much longer he'll last, though. His mind wanders to what Mallory might be doing with Steven, and he wishes he could watch them, but Faye is quite a luscious woman. He's very happy to get to play with an older lady, another of his often-unmet kinks. Faye is right, this club serves a purpose in a controlled environment. He knows everything and yet knows their connection is valid, but Mallory is his home. It's no different from going out to eat with a friend, only they are bumping and grinding genitals instead of eating a meal.

He smiles at Faye as he nuzzles his lips against her right inner thigh, his hands caressing her flesh.

"Much warmer in here, too," she coos as her eyes fall partially closed. "I love your touch."

He brushes his cheeks along her inner thighs, and she moans, a light, airy ultra ultra-feminine sound, not unlike Mallory's when she's on the slow rise to arousal. He licks her flesh as he gently touches her vulva lips, then spreads them to reveal her flower. Her pussy is beautiful, pinkish hues with purplish flesh at the upper curve of her right lip. He swipes his tongue up her slit slowly.

She moans softly as her hands thread into his hair. She wiggles beneath his licking, and her torso curls upward when he tongue rides her bean. She presses his scalp more firmly when he applies stronger tongue pressure to her clit. "Oh, yes, just like that, Derek, that's perfect."

He continues his stimulation at the same force and pace as she ripples her body in response. He adds a finger and presses into her wet snatch and slowly pumps. He curls his finger up, stimulating the fleshy pad inside her, massaging the rises and valleys of her wet internal walls. He latches onto her clit with strong suction as he increases his finger ride inside her.

She flops and twists her head back and forth as her sounds crescendo.

He doesn't change a thing. She's close, and if he does, he fears he will ruin her orgasm, so he keeps up exactly what he's doing.

Within twenty seconds, she cries out, her torso curls, her fingertips push firmer against his scalp, and her body torques as she rides her climactic wave. Her whimpers are arousing him further, and he rubs his cock on the edge of the bed as he keeps eating. He won't move until she indicates they're done.

Her shudders subside, then her sounds elevate again as she jerks through a second peak.

"Oh, so good, Derek, so good," she says while panting. "That was so wonderful. You are so good at that."

"Nice double?" he asks, hoping she fully catches his happy tone.

"Yes, perfect."

"Good, I'm ready to fuck you into another one too. Prone doggy?" he asks, the idea of boning her making her body bounce off his thrusts on this puffy blanket loading his lust for her even more.

"Yes, I do like that position," she says, giving him a sly smile as she turns over.

Her cute little butt wiggles beneath him as she gets comfy.

He caresses her back and sides, massaging her muscles as he moves his hands across her back. Derek is loving the sensual vibes Faye exudes; he could stay there all night and pleasure her. He meanders his hands to her hips then cups her ass cheeks, giving them a nice firm squeeze.

She squeals when he spreads her ass cheeks apart, then giggles. "You like to look, don't you?" she asks in a demure voice.

"Oh, yes," Derek says. "I'm guessing you like pussy fucking, but I still do like to look." He looks longing at the puckered star of her anus.

"Yeah, just on the outside for me," she says confidently. "Never much got into anything anal other than that personally. Another reason I love this club because occasionally Steven likes to fuck an asshole, and I'm not too keen on ever obliging that request." She chuckles softly as she fondles the puffiness of the bed around her face. "A girl could suffocate in this." She turns her face to the side. "I'm not afraid of you pushing my face into it, though, I kinda like that."

Derek's urgency rages as he prepares to enter her. "Can't wait to ride you."

As he pokes the tip of his cock into her pussy, she groans.

"I adore how you're still hard, love that naturally hard cock," she says as she grips the bedding firmly in her fists. "Yes, oh, fuck yes."

Derek presses himself further into her and begins to pound rapidly.

Her sounds escalate as do his as he smacks into her bottom, burying his cock deep inside her pussy with each ram. He presses the back of her head into the comforter, the front of her face fully immersed in it. He rage fucks her as he pins her down, her silence telling him her face is fully crammed against the bed.

Her body shudders beneath him and her pussy clenches around his cock. She fights his hand pressing and turns her head to the side, gasping for air. He cowers, hoping he didn't push her too far.

His cum is ready to erupt. He pulls his dick out of her and splatters her right butt cheek with his jizz.

She's panting heavily, gasping and sputtering as her body twitches every now and then. "Oh, my, that was unbelievable."

"You're okay, then?"

"Oh, very much so, my boy. You've fucked me better than I've been in a long time," she says, chuckling as she rolls over. "I need young bucks like you. This old lady never has lost her libido; in fact, mine has only gotten stronger."

Derek loves that. "That's really hot."

"It is. Care to snuggle? We could even take a nap," she says with a wink.

He climbs on the bed. "I could definitely use both of those. I've been on my feet the entire party, almost, except for sitting in the hot tub."

"It's high time, then," she says with a knowing gaze.

They settle in an embrace, their heads upon the softest pillows Derek has ever had the pleasure to rest his head upon.

DEREK AND FAYE WAKE to a barrage of hoots and hollering. They meet each other's gaze and quickly scramble out of bed. Something big is afoot.

"Well, that sounds interesting," Derek says as he rises off the bed. He grabs Faye's hand and pulls her out into the hallway.

As they approach the main area, there's a crowd around the stocks. Derek spots Steven pushing Mallory into them among the cheers of the surrounding partiers. Mallory's face is one of pure delight as Steven brusquely shoves her into place. Steven spanks her bottom roughly, and her face erupts into one of strong pain. She whimpers as Steven does it again.

"Take that, you naughty whore," Steven shouts at her as he hits her again.

"Oh, goodness," Faye states. "He's in one of his moods." But Faye doesn't look worried, rather she looks amused. "It won't last long. He's fire, but he's got a short rope."

Derek cringes as Steven hits her butt again.

Mallory grimaces as her tits flop with each slap.

"Hey, that's enough," says a man on the far side. "Stop it."

Derek slides over to see who is talking. It's Max and he looks pissed as hell.

"You're going too far," Max says in gruff anger.

Steven looks at the man aghast, then his expression shifts to annoyance. "Hey, she asked for this," he retorts.

"She's in serious pain," Max protests. "I'm taking her out." He charges them.

Mallory looks too overwhelmed to speak.

"Hey," Derek speaks up, stepping forward. "She's my girlfriend, and she's always had a fantasy of trying this out. Don't ruin it for her."

Steven looks grateful, as does Mallory.

Max freezes in place. "It's not right. She looks too upset." His eyes soften with sadness and concern.

Mallory lifts her head and tries to look at Max, but she's unable to turn her head because she's pinned inside the device. "It's okay, Max, I asked for this."

Sam hurries over, and Derek swells with appreciation.

"Hey, all okay over here?" Sam asks, his face full of concern.

Derek finds his overseeing sexy, well, everything about the man is mega sexy, and so this doesn't disappoint.

"It's okay," Steven states. "He's out of line." He motions the paddle in his hand toward Max. "Mallory specifically requested I do this."

Mallory nods as best she can. "Yes, Sam, I did. It's all good."

Sam looks relieved. "Okay, carry on."

Derek jerks back and Max cringes when Steven slams the paddle hard onto Mallory's ass, making her tits flop. Her body jerks forward, but the restraint of the wood around her controls her. She gags and gasps as the spanks shove her throat against the wood. She looks miserable as fuck.

Steven grips her hips and roughly shoves his cock up her cunt. "Take this fat dick, you whore." Steven fucks Mallory with aggression as she gasps and whines.

Max shakes his head and hurries away. Derek doesn't like seeing Mallory in pain either, but he's not about to yuck her yum. He knows she may never do this again, but she's always wanted it.

Steven finishes and motions with his hands. "Anyone else want a piece of this fresh spanked ass?" He steps back, his cum dripping off the end of his sagging cock. "No anal," he instructs as the men line up.

Derek watches in amazement as every man in the crowd gets in line, and a few women sporting strapons do as well.

"Oh, she's ticking a lot off her sexual bucket list tonight!" Derek says as he waves at Faye. "I'm getting in on her fantasy."

Faye shakes her head. "Your cock is hard again! Your virility is certainly commendable." She reaches for him and gives his arm a caress. "And worthy of worship. Next time round, it's cock worship from me."

She waves and walks toward her husband.

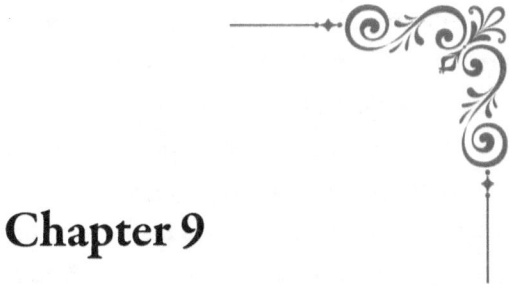

Chapter 9

Mallory sips her lemon water as she watches the people on the ottoman. Her body is in a state of utter bliss. She's climaxed so many times she feels floaty and woozy. She acknowledges her soreness but regrets nothing. She's had the most euphoric evening of her life, and she wouldn't trade it for a second.

She watches as Derek has sex with a pretty redhead. Her hair is like flowing silk as Derek pounds her, doggy style, her lovely, puckered mouth slightly parted. Mallory would get in on that action if she hadn't just been railed by the train of men who had lined up at the stocks. She smirks, then releases a slight laugh. That event was a solid sinking of her teeth in a long-held fantasy of hers, likely one she'll never top. She wonders with this club, though, she just might surpass it. The chances are that it's more than possible.

"Hi," says a male voice from behind her.

She turns, recognizing it's Max. "Oh, hi, Max."

"Are you still talking to me?" His eyes are cast down, and he appears sad.

It wrenches her heart, but he isn't the person she'd have sought out right now. She watches him as he motions to the chair next to her. "May I?"

She shrugs. "Yeah, sure." She swings her eyes back to watching her man.

"Mallory," he says, then pauses long enough to make it awkward. "I'm sorry."

She meets his gaze, and the forlorn, lost look in his eyes flips her switch. "Oh, Max," she says, feeling compassion, but nothing else makes it from her brain to her mouth.

"I was in the wrong. I was putting my own boundaries on you, and that's just not a fair thing to do. You're your own person, with your own kinks." He shakes his head as his face transforms to one of guilt. "I basically kink-shamed you. And I'm aghast at myself. That's not me. That's not who I am."

She reaches for his hand resting on his thigh and lightly brushes her fingers across it. "Oh, Max, I get it. Not everyone wants such extreme stuff." She shrugs her shoulders. "I really wanted to try it in real life. It's been something I've masturbated to, but you know, reality is so different. There's no pain, but then there is."

"I've been a member of this club for years, and I've never done such a thing before. Honestly, I'm embarrassed. It was truly an indiscretion on my part." He searches her face as he pauses. "I talked with Sam, and he urged me to come talk to you." He pats her hand with his other, sandwiching hers between his two. "I..."

"Max, it's okay. Thank you for the apology." She smiles sweetly at him, her heart loves his coddling, and likely, he wasn't even close to being done.

"Thank you. Very kind of you to forgive me." He continues to rub her hand. "I care about what happens to you, you know."

"Yes, I know. I get it."

"As I said before, I'm all about pleasure." He smirks. "And I can give a spank or two, but I can't go hardcore. It's just not in me to do it." He looks crushed.

"Oh, well, it's not something I'd want all the time. Am I glad I tried it? Yes. But I wouldn't do it frequently." She isn't entirely sure what she thinks, but for now, this is her stance. But she's also confident that her sexuality is extraordinarily fluid, more so now than ever before. "Don't forget, I very much enjoyed our time together."

A happy grin spreads from his eyes to his lips. "As did I." He looks so relieved. "They just put out some desserts and fruit. Can I get you any?"

She tips her head to the side as a warm feeling fills her. "Yeah, that sounds lovely. Some of both?"

"You got it," Max says and stands quickly. "Be back in a flash."

She watches him walk, noting he has launched into a semi in the last few minutes. His caretaking kink met her being cared for kink in a way she'd never tasted before. When she scans the ottoman again, she meets Derek's eyes. He's still going to town pleasuring the redhead. Likely, they won't have sex when they get home; they will be lucky to make it home without one or both of them falling asleep in the car, which could be disastrous. She instantly wishes she'd asked Max for a coffee. Derek's expression shifts to something unpleasant, and she wonders if he's hurt his cock or something.

"Here we are," Max says as he hands her a plate with two cookies, a small sliver of chocolate cake, strawberries, and mango slices.

"Oh, that looks amazing! Thank you so much!"

"Now for the drinks. Coffee, champagne, or water?"

"I'd love a coffee with cream and sugar."

He beams at her. "Be right back."

Mallory smiles as she watches all the people engaging in pleasure. She's tempted to throw caution to the wind and join them, but then, it's quite nice to sit with Max, too. She yawns as she stretches, and a shiver claims her as she shudders.

"I hate to say it, but I might need to get dressed. I'm feeling a chill." She glances down at her chest, nipples poking out.

"I have just the thing," he says, setting down her coffee. "Hot coffee, and I'll snag you a throw blanket." He rushes over to a basket and pulls out a fluffy white one. He wraps it around her shoulders and squeezes. "Shoulders or lap?"

The fabric is one of the softest she's ever felt. "Wow, what a luxurious little blanket!" She continues to finger the plush fabric as Max rubs it on her arms.

"We'll get you nice and warm and feeling good," he says as he moves over to his seat, then settles in beside her. "Now this is what I call a good time, and how I want to spend the rest of my evening."

The warmth of the blanket and his over-the-top taking care of her fills her with a sense of awe. Affection might be the right word, but she could get used to this.

She grabs a slice of mango and bites it. The sweet fruit is juicy and perfectly ripe. "Mmmm. Knew this would be so good. It's the perfect ripe color."

Max swipes his mango slice off his plate and bites into it, too. "Oh, yeah, it's at the perfect state."

She watches Max as she chews. She wonders if he has a woman at all, or if he only attends parties for such connections. Seems like he'd have so much to offer a woman on a daily basis that it seems a shame if he's all alone. But despite her curiosity, she wants to keep things light after the heaviness of earlier, so she keeps her questions to herself. She sips the coffee and the warmth, and the richness bathes her mouth. She closes her eyes as she savors it.

With the warm blanket, sweet comfort food, and the gentleness of Max, she settles into feelings of safety and appreciation. Not all lovers would be like him, as evidenced by her never having had one like Max until she did. She is beginning to feel the stirrings of attachment beyond his moment-to-moment caring for how she feels. Perhaps this comes from her past of neglect, but whatever it is, she's not analyzing it any further tonight. It isn't like Derek ever neglects her.

She watches as Derek approaches, his cock finally flaccid between his thighs. He looks wiped out. He sidles up beside Mallory and sits, nodding toward Max.

"Hi, I'm Derek, Mallory's boyfriend." He screws up his face into a mix of emotions. "We kinda met earlier."

"Hi Derek. I must apologize for my behavior earlier. I was out of line. I'm sorry." Max looks genuine, which Mallory knows will work on Derek's kind heart.

"It's okay. You seem to care about her, which means something to me." Derek slumps forward on his forearms at the table. "Whew, I'm pooped."

"It's taxing, I know." Max looks urgent. "I don't want to ruin a potentially good thing. This club is all about making personal connections, and I'm really pissed at myself for sabotaging it."

"Oh, Max, you worry too much," Mallory says with a wave of her hand. "It's all good. I mean, he was smacking the shit out of my ass, so it was a bit shocking, even for me. But I have to admit, I loved the domination and implied control of the whole thing. Especially that I was stuck in I place, then he offered me up." She snickers. "It was hot!"

"It was hot," Derek says with a grin. "And I enjoyed partaking in fucking your red-spanked ass with you in it." He chuckles with zero regrets. "I've fucked you so many ways, but that was a new one. And I liked it."

She met his lewd gaze. "As did I," she says, rubbing his hand. "Are you ready to go soon? You look as tired as I feel."

He nods. "Yeah, I'm game whenever."

Mallory watches as Derek looks at Max. "Hey man, don't worry about it. I may have done the same thing if I hadn't heard her fantasize about it so much."

"Thanks, I appreciate it. I'm relieved you both don't hate me."

Mallory coos a sigh, "Oh, Max. Don't go there. We're all good. I couldn't possibly hate you. You're a sweet teddy bear."

He laughs and pats his belly. "Well, I've got the body shape down!"

She giggles back and caresses his face. She hops up, the fluffy blanket falls to the floor as she straddles his lap, crushing herself to him in a flash.

"Oh, now what have I done to deserve this lovely lap sit?" His eyes shine with the gleam he shared with her earlier in the night.

"I just wanted to give you a hug and kiss properly before we go," she slurs as she takes his head into her hands.

"You're welcome on my lap anytime," he says with a sappy, blissful look.

She likes the idea of being in his lap as she squirms into an open-mouthed kiss. They kiss deeply as he caresses her back. His cock starts to grow between them.

"Look at what you do to this old man," he says with a twinkle in his eyes.

She desperately wants to ride him, though her pussy feels a bit beat up. She grinds herself against his cock as their kiss grows more heated. She leans back, pushing her tits in his face. He devours her breasts, giving a quick motorboat that makes her writhe and squeal.

She catches Derek's gaze. "One more quick ride, and then I'm ready."

Derek slumps. "Sure, baby, I want you to get it." He puts his head down on the table, his eyes glued to her and Max.

Mallory knows his wistful look. He wants to join in, but he knows Max isn't into that.

Max caresses her back and arms, riding his hands down to her tender bottom. She winces, and he pulls back abruptly.

"Forgive me, I forgot," he pleads.

"It's okay, I'm not going to die," she says jokingly.

"I'll keep my grabs north of your ass," he assures as he caresses her back and takes her right tit into his mouth. As he lets her nipple fall, he rubs his face all over her breasts. "Only you could do this to me."

"Well, I'm ready to ride that cock one more time, Daddy."

His eyes flare with passion and possession.

She wiggles her mound against his cock, then reaches down to stroke it. It's hardening quickly in her hand to full mast.

He reaches between her legs and presses her pussy lips.

She's tender there too, but she suppresses the wince this time.

His lust erupts on his face as he tickles his fingers along her clit. She moans, despite the slight discomfort, it feels amazing as fuck. She undulates her hips to his touches as he makes his way around her labia and slit, and back to her clit for a finger ride.

She glances around. "Any lube handy, Derek?"

He stands. "I'll find you some."

"Just a touch raw, but I'm so ready to fuck you," she says ardently.

He grabs her face, and they fall into a deep, devouring kiss, their tongues lashing inside each other's mouths. As he licks down her neck, she moans softly.

Derek returns with a tube of lube and squirts it on Max's dick.

"Such a helpful boyfriend," she says in a teasing tone.

He says, "Grabbing some water for the road. Want one?"

She nods as her panting ramps up. She rises and Max holds his cock for her. She slides down it as they both groan out. It's not pain-free, but she's aroused enough to feel pleasure. She bounces on his hard cock, her tits flopping in his face.

He sticks out his tongue, licking her flesh as she rides. He grunts as she takes his cock all the way to the hilt on repeat.

When he reaches to press her sensitive spot, she launches. She bounces harder the more voraciously he rubs her clit. She's rewarded as she's flung into yet another O to end the night.

Max's sounds explode as hers start to wane. As her walls encircle his cock in a multitude of contractions, he lifts her quickly off his lap and his cum bubbles out.

"Mmmm, that was so good," he murmurs as he pulls her into a peck.

"Yes, it was," she says, smiling with satisfaction. "A perfect way to end the night."

He hugs her body to his, burying his face in her flesh. "I thought you might be too sore for that."

"I'm good," she says through a grin. "Maybe we can text before the next party?" She's overtaken by sadness at the thought of no contact with him until the next event.

He nods against her, keeping his face snuggled to her chest. "I'd love that so much," he says, his voice slightly muffled by the tight hug.

She rises off him as Derek approaches.

"Done? Ready to go?" he asks.

"Yeah, I'm ready. Thank you, Max. I'll get my phone so we can exchange numbers."

Derek looks surprised but says nothing about it.

She hurries off to find their clothes and her phone. A twinge of worry worms its way into her heart, but she shoves it off. She's not going to let his look sway her. He might just be tired and ready to go.

When she returns, Derek is talking to Sam. They hug, and Derek walks back toward her.

"Okay, let's do this," she says as she points her phone at Max's.

"Got it," he says with a happy smile. "And thank you for asking. This has been a dream come true."

She hugs him and kisses him on the lips. "Goodnight."

"Bye," he says as he stands.

"Bye," Derek responds.

She meets Derek in an eye lock. "Are we good?" she asks him as they enter the hallway leading to the front door.

"We are, but we'll talk right? We have a lot to process."

She squeezes his hand. "That we do. And thank you. I loved it, and I especially loved when you joined the train when I was in the stocks."

"So you said," he retorts good-naturedly.

That's the Derek she's used to.

She smiles, and they put on their coats. "It's going to be so cold. I don't want to go out there."

He grimaces as he opens the door. The arctic blast rushes at them. "Yup, it's going to be brutal. Let's run!"

They rush out the door into the wintery night, the cold, brutal wind lashing at them as they dash into the dark.

Thankfully, Derek used the remote start, so once they are inside, the heater blasts the cold right out.

"Whew! That's horrible." She shudders as she rubs her hands together. "Thank goodness for remote starts."

He shudders too. "No doubt."

"Derek, are you sure you're okay?" She turns down the radio. "Did anything go too far for you?"

He puts the car in gear and backs up. He sighs. "No, not really."

"Okay. I just thought I saw something."

"I'm just tired, Mallory. I had a great time. I'd do it again."

"You would?" she asks, relief filling her. She isn't sure how she'd have reacted if he said he wouldn't.

"Yes, definitely. We both got to do some of our fantasies. That's what we wanted."

She purses her lips as her shivering stops. "Oh, this heat feels so good."

"Right?" he asks.

"Right, for sure." She didn't have a single bad feeling about anything she saw Derek do. "You'd tell me if you were bothered, right? That's always been our agreement." She can't help but worry, but then, she might just be too tired.

"I had the best time, I really did. I did things I didn't even expect I'd get to fuck someone like Faye."

"Oh yes, how was that? I can't wait to hear all the details."

"It was really good. Really good. She's an amazing woman. I made her come really hard. It was so good, Mal."

"Yeah, I bet. You are so good at making people come," she jokes.

"So are you," he says with a raised eyebrow. "We really did it, again."

"Yup, we did. When's the next one?" she asks with a laugh. "Can't come soon enough for me."

"I think it's January 19th. It's called Winter Ball."

"Oh, that sounds kind of like a formal. Did you read the description?"

"Yup. It is a formal."

She cringes. They likely can't afford formal outfits. "Maybe I can just wear this dress again. It's formal enough, right?"

"Yeah, I think it would work. And I have my suit I can wear."

"Good, we're all set." She pulls out her phone. "I'll RSVP right now."

She noticed a text notification had come, but she didn't feel her phone buzz. It's from Max. She enters the text and falls silent.

His text: Dearest Mallory, You're a delight, a breath of fresh air in this old man's life, and I'll forever be grateful that you allowed me to pleasure you and take care of you tonight. Please know that I would never harm you, and I apologize again. I'm sorry. It won't happen again. You do you, and I won't impose my boundaries on you, only play with you within yours. Bless you, and I can't wait to hear back from you. Yours truly, Max

She smiles. "Aww, such a sweet message from Max." She enters the app to RSVP to the party, her mind churning on what to respond to Max with. "Done, we are down as attending."

She returns to the text and reads it again, her body flooding with goodness. There's something extra sweet about a little love note like this from him. It's the cap to the perfect night.

Chapter 10

Derek keeps checking out the window, then glancing at his phone. Mallory has been gone for two and a half hours. Normally, he couldn't care less how long she's gone; he isn't a nosy control freak, but this time she'd gone off to meet Max. He likes their new foray into polyamory, and has met up with Faye several times over the past few weeks for dates and sex, and it has only served to make him uber happy. Mallory hadn't cared that he went, and all was good. They are both getting their needs met, are sexually satisfied, and their relationship is better than ever, which is why Derek's confused by this unease. Mallory loves him. He loves Mallory. Their sex has been off the charts hot, so much so that Derek hasn't even done his usual extra masturbation. The club has infused heat into their already hot sex life. It's been a magical potion.

He sighs and rubs his chin. Dang, he needs to shave. His stubble is going haywire. He moves toward the living room, aiming to turn on the TV. It's clear he needs a distraction. Watching for her to arrive is tanking his anxiety to an uncomfortable state. He doesn't want to be the jealous guy. He refuses to be that guy.

He scrolls the channels as time seems to crawl for the next hour. He rubs his eyes and grunts. Maybe he will start dinner unless she is eating out with Max. Ah! He has a reason to text her that doesn't seem like he's checking up on her. He pulls out his phone and readies to send the text, but then stops. Texting her this question basically is checking up on her.

He shoves his phone back in his pocket and stands up. He makes his way toward the laundry room to get his workout clothes. A good, hard run on the treadmill is exactly what his mind needs. Some nice adrenaline and a boost in his mood are always a guarantee with a workout. His mood is already lifted as he dons his workout shorts and tank top.

He looks up abruptly as he hears the front door slam, and he hustles out to the living room.

Mallory is in the doorway holding two full plastic bags, her face is beaming with a giant smile that lights up her beautiful eyes. "Oh, Derek! You'll never believe what Max did!" Her voice is high and full of excitement. She's absolutely glowing with joy.

Derek smiles back. "What?" he asks as he hurries over to embrace and kiss her. Her cheeks are cold against him.

"It was so amazing! You know, we were just going for a coffee, and the plan was sex in the car after, but then after that, we went shopping!" She holds up the bags. "Wait until you see! Max was so generous, it blew me away!"

Derek's heart sinks. "How was the sex?"

"Oh, it was amazing. I blew him and he ate me out, and then I rode him in the back of his SUV until we both came. It was really hot." She rushes to the couch and sets her bags down. She removes her winter jacket and drops it on the floor. "Look!" She pries open the first bag and pulls out a long garment cover encasing something thin at the top, but flaring out at the midpoint and on down. She hands the hanger hook at the top to Derek, then unzips it to the bottom. "This is so incredible!"

Derek watches as she pushes the plastic aside to reveal a shimmering, deep maroon metallic sheen strapless gown. His eyes go wide as she caresses the dress. "Wow!"

"Isn't it stunning! Max was asking me what I was going to wear to the ball tomorrow, and I said the same dress as last time. He wouldn't have it. He insisted on buying me a new one. And then he started going ballistic, bringing me different clothes to try on. Derek, it was a blast! I've never in my life been this spoiled on a shopping trip!"

Her excitement is contagious, but he frowns. He'd been hoping he'd make a big sale in the last few weeks so they could have afforded a new dress for the ball for her. He didn't mind wearing his old suit. But women, who shine and sparkle at such an event as a ball, especially when wearing new dresses, he wants that for her too.

"I can't wait to see it on you." He smiles at her despite the ache in his heart. "I love seeing you all dressed up. Will you put it on for me?" He watches her face as she stares at the dress with a look of lovestruck adoration.

"Yes, but first, look at all this other stuff he bought me. It was truly a shopping spree to beat all shopping sprees." She begins to pull out lingerie, bras, panties, slacks, jeans, long-sleeved tops, and even a bikini.

The next bag contains a winter jacket, gloves, a winter hat, and cozy, soft magenta pink pj's.

"He did go hog wild on you." Derek picks up a soft blouse that looks like it will be perfect for her to wear to work. "He was really generous."

"He insisted." She gives him a skeptical look. "You aren't mad, are you?"

"No, no. Not at all." He forces his smile. "Now to see you in this dress, unless you want it to be a surprise."

"No, I want to show you. It's the most amazing dress!" She shakes her fists in the air. "I never thought I'd ever get such a dress, other than maybe a wedding dress someday." She peers at Derek expectantly. "Guess how much it was?"

Derek shakes his head. He has no idea how much such a dress would cost.

"Just take one guess," she implores.

"Six hundred." His stomach churns.

"Nope! Twelve hundred!" She shrieks as she begins to strip. "I'm so excited! I'll feel like a true princess in this dress. I may not even want to take it off for sex at the party." She snickers. "Well, let's not go that far." She laughs heartily.

He feels sick to his stomach, but guilt seizes him. This is her thing.

She removes her bra and tosses it aside. "Help me get into it?"

The glow in her eyes softens his heart. His excitement begins to match hers as he removes the dress from the hanger. He unzips and holds it, widening the base of it between his spread hands. "Over your head?"

She nods, her eager eyes blossoming.

He helps get it over her head, then swivels her to zip up the back. The poofy skirt is multiple layers of sheer fabric, where the bodice is shiny and tight-fitting. He helps settle the dress into place. Her cleavage is mouthwatering, and the color makes her rosy cheeks even rosier. The darkness of her hair and the white creaminess of her skin against the fabric of the dress are exquisite. "Wow, you look incredible in this dress!"

She twirls, and the skirt part flares wide, the flowing fabric moving as if floating gracefully, like slow-falling snow. She squeals. "Isn't it so amazing?" She smooths down the skirt with her hands and scrunches her shoulders, which deepens her cleavage.

"You do look like a princess. You're going to steal the show tomorrow in that dress." Not that she needs a dress to steal the show, her beauty and bubbly personality do that alone.

"I've never been so pampered. I am just in shock at all of this. I kept fighting him and it just fueled him on to do more."

Derek scans the clothing. They'd never be able to buy this much in one shopping trip, let alone in a year. "I'm happy you had a good time and have this dress for tomorrow. You'll be the most beautiful woman at the ball for sure." He wraps his arms around her. "You are truly irresistible."

He opens his mouth to kiss her, and she meets his with her own.

They fall into a deep kiss within seconds. His cock thickens against her tummy. He kisses down her neck as he murmurs, "You look so sexy in this dress, I can't not taste you."

She drops her head back as soft moans escape her mouth. "Mmm, that feels amazing."

He nibbles her neck in the way that always fuels her, and she squirms in his arms.

"I need to be the first to fuck you in this dress," he says in a smooth tone. He unzips the back in a slow drag. He quickly unearths her right breast from the dress and devours her taut nipple.

Her head falls back as he moves to the other one and pops it out to slurp his tongue around her puckered skin. She caresses his head as he plays with her other nipple. "Fuck, I love your nipples."

She coos softly as her sounds of enjoyment begin to ramp up.

He chuckles. "It's going to be a challenge to find your clit among all this fabric."

She laughs too, and it's a light and sexy laugh that always makes him so happy.

He drops to his knees, a lusty gleam in his eyes. "I've always wanted to do this." He lifts up the hem of her dress and dives under it. He lets the fabric fall on his back as he caresses her smooth shins, slowly moving his hands up her silky thighs.

He can smell her arousal as he leans into her. He presses his fingers on her bald mound, admiring the fabulous shaving job he'd done on her during their bath last night. He moves his face closer to her pelvis and inhales her scent.

She presses his head buried beneath the dress, and though her sounds are muffled a little by the fabric, he can hear her usual sounds of her excitement ramping up.

He presses his tongue at the cleft and her lower lips, and she lurches away, but springs right back. He claims her thighs in a tight grip, securing her close. He wiggles his tongue between the divide in her flesh and presses it to her clit.

She cries out with a pleasure sound, and it eggs him on.

He presses his fingers along her slit as he tongues her, and he inserts his fingers into her wet hole and begins to pump them. Her little kernel is a hard nugget as he touches it at varying pressures, then he full-on clamps his mouth all around her fleshy bits.

Her body recoils, and she falters, but steadies herself quickly. He keeps sucking her clit, but puts both his hands on her thighs and gently presses her backward toward the couch.

She acquiesces and allows him to guide her to settle on the couch, all while still attached to her. Once there he backs off for a breather. She squirms as he pounces on her clit once more, and he begins finger fucking her at the pace he knows she will come from. The combo on her is killer, and he gets her to come fast every time with the technique.

She moans and writhes as he pleasures her to her peak. With a sharp, quick curl of her torso, she wraps herself around his head as she pulls his hair between her fingers. She hollers as her body twitches, and her pussy clamps down.

She's panting heavily as he rises out of the mound of fabric.

He smiles down at her. "You look so amazing topless in this dress, with that look of satisfaction on your face." He loves nothing more than making his woman climax.

She smiles a sweet, sexy smile. "That was incredible. And in this dress, it was so much fun." She touches the fabric of the dress as her smile grows.

"Now it's time for doggy," he says with a lewd happy grin, pulling his stiffy out. He may not have bought her the dress, but he sure as fuck was going to be the first to fuck her in it. "Get up and bend over," he says in his dominant voice.

She gives him a coy, sassy look. "Sure thing, Daddy." She obeys and stands up, her tits bounce as she shifts with exaggeration, then swivels to face the couch. She bends over and puts her hands on the cushions.

"Head down, ass up. Put that face into the crack."

She listens and presses her face into the spot where the top of the couch cushion meets the seat.

He digs through the fabric to bare her ass and flops it over her top half. The fabric of the dress completely covers her up and before him is just her naked ass and legs, and her holes bared.

He releases a man growl, and she shivers. He grips her hips firmly and rubs his cock along her slick flesh. He is putting out precum as he maneuvers to get his tip to glide along her slit.

She coos from beneath the fabric, "Fuck me, Daddy."

"I'm going to fuck you and make you scream in this dress." He presses his cock head at her hole, then pulls back. He dabs his cock at her slit several times, then spanks it against her clit. Her sounds flare his lust more as he teases her with his cockhead.

"Please," she begs in that whimpering voice he loves. "Please, put your cock in me. Please."

He loves how desperate she sounds. "You're mine." One thing he's found he loves after she goes with Max is the reclaiming of her when she gets home. He pushes his cock into her pussy hole, then takes it back out three more times to her heightening whimpering.

He smiles as he cock spanks her clit again.

Her whimpers peak and he plunges his cock into her roughly. It slides right in as easy as a slicked up dildo.

She groans as he fully enters her, matching his own deep one of satisfaction. He ramps up his thrusting quickly, making her ass cheeks bounce and the dress fabric flop rapidly.

"Take you as mine in this dress," he stammers as he aggressively pounds her body with his. The skin smacks fill the air as do both their vocalizations. "Get your clit," he commands.

She obeys and reaches up to rub her clit as he jackhammers his cock into her body. She shudders first, her body blasting into its usual orgasm curl.

As her pussy clenches on his cock, he launches. "Gonna," he says in a raspy whisper. He keeps pumping himself into her as his body tenses and readies to fly. He shudders as he ejaculates, coming hard as his cum spews inside her. He feels woozy from coming so hard, like his body is soaring in the air above him.

He slows his ramming as he empties his balls. He leans forward on her as he breathes heavily. "Wow, that was just...wow." He pants as he pauses. "I came really, really hard."

She giggles beneath her dress. "So did I."

"That was hot," he says as he stands up. His cock is still semi hard, but he turns and plops on the couch. "Didn't think I'd come that hard."

She stands up, and the fluffy skirt falls. She smooths it down and sits next to him. "Me neither. It was so damn good."

"I love this dress on you, especially with your tits out. That got me." He smiles. "Can't wait to see you tomorrow in it."

"Yeah, I have big plans. I think with this dress so princess-y, I'm going to curl my hair into big curls and go big on the makeup. Use glitter." She frowns. "Oh, shoot. I didn't think about shoes."

He caresses her face. "What about those heels you wore to my brother's wedding? Those would work, right?"

"Oh yeah, you're right. Those will be perfect."

He pulls her face to his and kisses her on the lips. "You know I love you more than life."

"As do I. Love you." She holds his face as she returns the peck. "Now, I'd better get this dress off before I wreck it." She chuckles. "Think the dry cleaners can get cum out of fabric like this?"

He smiles and says with humor, "I sure hope so!"

"Me too." She pulls the dress off and reaches for the hanger. "Not even going to bother bringing this upstairs." She puts it on the hanger and walks toward the entryway closet. She hangs it up and returns.

"Seeing you walk around naked makes me want to fuck you all over again."

"Same, but I need some food. That made me really hungry."

"Okay. Let's eat. I could go for something too."

"Any spaghetti left, or did you eat it for lunch?"

"Nope, I actually didn't eat lunch. That sounds perfect."

He watches her dress as he stands, slipping his cock back into his shorts.

"I love how you fuck me." She grabs his hand and pulls him toward the kitchen.

"Ditto," he says, his heart as happy as his cock.

Chapter 11

Mallory gazes upon herself in the full-length mirror in the corner of their bedroom, and joy courses through her. She looks and feels like a princess in the dress Max bought. Her hair is curled into cascading waves; her makeup is perfect so that she looks like a star. It fits so ideally that it's as if she had the dress tailor made for her body. She swivels and catches her image at all the angles. She's ready and she's especially grateful in a dress she'd never be able to afford, ready for experiences people like Max make possible for her.

The club is the best thing she's done in her life aside from dating Derek. Her stomach swirls with butterflies as she thinks about the upcoming pleasure of the ball. It's one thing to get to wear such a dress, but then to be gifted orgasms at the same time, the day is most certainly blessed.

She smooths her hands down her dress as her excitement surges. Derek approaches her from behind, all dressed and looking sexy in his suit.

He places his hands on her bare shoulders and softly caresses down her flesh. He smiles at her in the mirror. "You look stunning. So incredible, Mal, I'm in awe."

She smiles back at him. "Thank you." She is glowing.

He kisses her shoulder, then, hugging her from behind, he sways them together. "I want you to have such a good time today, so much pleasure it will blow your mind, that you think back to this moment in amazement at how unbelievably awesome the day has been."

"I feel that energy, too, Derek. And I want it for you, too." She knew they'd both be savoring sexual pleasure today, and it felt good to be about to do it alongside her man, who always wanted the topmost pleasure for her, whether it was from him or another. "We're really lucky, you know that?" she asks in a coo.

"Yes, we really are. And I wouldn't trade our way of life for another. You deserve all of it, even if I didn't join in with you, I'd want you to experience it all."

She turns to face him and they embrace. "You always prioritize me, and it's beyond incredible. You are an amazing man, Derek."

His face erupts into happiness, which is wonderful to see. He's looked a bit down all morning. "You are the amazing one, Mal. I'm just your sidekick, here for you in every way."

He does support her and uplift her like no other, other than Max. To be so triumphed by not one, but two men, she's on top of the world! And then, in this dress, she might explode with how stuffed she feels with goodness. There were a few days in her life so far that she had felt this extraordinary, and she intends to savor it.

Derek kisses her on the lips, then pulls back. "You ready to go, beautiful?" His grin is memorable, and it's exactly how she'd like to remember this moment.

"I'm ready, yes. And so excited I could burst!"

"I'm ready to go. Do you need more time?" he asks as he caresses her face.

"I'm ready too. Nothing else left to do but go and fuck our brains out." She bites her lip and raises her eyebrow. "You game?"

"One hundred percent."

He steps back and reaches for her hand. She offers it, and they walk out of the room hand in hand.

On the drive, her heart pounds. It being her third party, she shouldn't be nervous, but it's more of an excited nervousness, she supposes. She watches Derek, and he's still looking happy; gone is the evidence of worry from his face.

She checks her phone for any last-minute emails about the party, but sees no updates. As she scrolls social media, a text comes in. It's from Max.

Max: Hi babe, I'm excited to see you, and in that dress, I'm on pins and needles waiting. I'm here. When will you arrive?

She smiles as she reads and prepares to text back. She glances at their surroundings, then types: I'm excited to see you too. I love love love the dress! So much! Thank you again! We will be there in like ten minutes, I'm guessing. See you soon!

She looks up and catches Derek looking her way.

"Max?" he asks.

She nods. "Yup. He's asking when we'll be arriving." She has no desire to hide anything from Derek. He's never given her a reason to.

"Yup, I felt my phone buzz. I'm guessing it's from Faye."

The rest of the ride, Mallory's mind is full of ideas of what will happen, and she can't wait.

When they pull onto the street, cars fill the curbs, and Derek has to park a ways away.

"Geez, are we late? Or is everyone just eager?" Derek asks with a scoff.

"We're right on time. Yeah, this is crazy. We've never had to park this far away before." She zips up her jacket. "I guess everyone is really horny today."

"Well, I identify with that!" Derek says with a sexy sneer.

"Me too. Okay, you ready for the arctic blast?"

"No, but let's get it over with."

They both slide out of the vehicle and tear down the street, zooming as best they can across the ice and snow without falling down. They exclaim and holler as the brutal wind batters their bodies.

"Ugh," Mallory says as they reach the front door. "That wind probably wrecked my curls."

Derek peruses her and says, "Still looks beautiful." He presses the doorbell as he shivers.

Sam opens the door with a wide grin. "Ah, and here we meet again! I always seem to be near the door when you two arrive. It must be the pull of your auras approaching." He winks and motions for them to enter.

He takes Mallory's coat. "Wow, Mallory. You're gorgeous! So very sexy and beautiful."

Mallory loves the lusty leer in his gaze. "Thank you."

"Yeah, doesn't she look incredible?" Derek asks, looking proud.

"Very, whew. You look fit for a runway in that."

She shimmies her shoulders. "Max bought it for me on our date."

Sam draws his head back in realization. "Oh, very nice. And you two are getting closer, then."

"Yes, we are." Mallory looks down the hallway. "Looks like so many are here already."

"Yup, people wanted to get here before the snow starts, I guess. Hopefully it won't get too bad, or we will be having one big giant orgy sleepover." He laughs. "Wait, that sounds incredible, and might have to be our next party theme."

"Oh, I'd be in for that!" Mallory says in a soft, cooing voice. "Get some sexy pajamas or lingerie. Bring a sleeping bag. Middle of the night fucking!"

"I'm in too," Derek interjects.

"Come on, let's head in." Sam leads them down the hallway.

The great room is decorated with streams of flowing fabric, lights, and glittering balls hung from the ceiling. A photo booth is set up in the corner with a variety of props for pictures, and long tables filled with copious amounts of food and drinks line the walls, creating a large L shape that extends into the room. The place is aglow with festivities and chatter, lots of happy faces.

"I always love walking into this room; it's like walking into an enchanted land." Mallory scans the area and sees faces she now knows well, many of whom she's fucked and been fucked by. It's like walking into a fantasy playground where she feels safe to explore and be who she really is.

There is only one threesome on the ottoman, all three are still mostly dressed, but the woman's tits are out. The two men, one shorter and plumper than the other, are playing with and suckling her tits. She moans as she crashes backward to sit. They follow her like they are on strings tied to her body. They fondle her tits with fervor and Mallory's arousal takes flight. She watches them until she realizes she's stopped moving. Sam and Derek are a good half a room away from her.

"You're a vision of beauty," Max's voice comes to her from behind. "You look like a movie star, a queen. More incredible than I imagined." He smooths his hand across the small of her back as she turns. "There she is. I'm almost moved to tears," he confesses.

"Hi Max," she says in a soft voice. "You know how to make a woman feel incredible."

"I don't try. I'm just honest."

She relaxes her shoulders as he takes her in his arms. "I can't thank you enough for this dress. I feel like royalty." She shudders. "Not that I believe in that malarky."

His lips curl into a closed-mouth smile while his eyes dance with delight. "Oh, you're royalty alright. You're as majestic and epic as any queen ever was." He takes a curl in his fingers and playfully tosses it to and fro. "A queen who deserves as many orgasms as she desires, with as many dicks and pussies as she wants. And I'm your servant." He belly laughs before saying, "And wanna be my sex slave?" His expression shows he's being a bit facetious.

He legit knows how to make her melt. She laughs along with him as waves of elation course through her. "Yes, to all of that." She pauses, wishing to show her submission. "Daddy." She knows very well that leadership must be earned and bought into, and while previously, when she'd said it to Max, it hadn't reached the potential fullness of now, every step along the way had been delicious with him. She'd had a relationship where steps had gone forward with such things, but once the steps went backward, regaining traction was much too hard. That relationship had died long before she'd ended it. She likes to think she's smarter now than ever before, but it has taken Derek to help her really get it.

Max gazes at her. "I'm just in awe at how beautiful you are and that I'm actually holding you in my arms."

"I love your tux, Max. It's very sexy on you."

He guffaws. "I'm choking, so this trap won't last much longer." He motions toward the photo area. "Care to take photos before I free my neck?"

"Yes, let's do it. What a great idea they had to create a photo area when everyone is dressed up." Mallory follows his lead as he pulls her along.

"The photographer is there now, too. Let's get in line while it's short." Max seems urgent, so she hurries behind.

The couple getting their pictures taken appears to be in their forties. He has a tux on, and she has on a shimmering silver gown that reaches the floor. They are posing for photos like for a wedding shoot, that is until he pulls her dress down to expose her bare tits. She pretends to be surprised as the photographer keeps snapping away. The crowd laughs at her performance. The man sucks her nipples, then steps back, leaving her alone in front of the camera.

The cameraman looks in his zone as he instructs her on how to move her body, eventually urging her to fully remove her dress. He keeps on with the boudoir photo shoot as even more people gather to watch. She freezes in mid-pose, holds up her hand as an intense look overtakes her.

"Okay, I'm way too horny, I need to go fuck. I'm so turned on, I'm done." She waves at the cameramen, bends over to snatch up her dress, then skedaddles off after her man.

"Stay and fuck in front of us," calls a man with a long white beard, wearing a dark blue suit.

"Yeah," says a woman.

"Wow, I hadn't thought of this being a thing," Mallory watches with surprise and want splattered across her face.

The milling crowd expresses their disappointment, but that quickly shifts as the new couple enters the photo stage.

"Yeah, if you pay extra, you can get boudoir photos." Max raises his eyebrows quickly. "Then we can buy them."

"Buy?" Mallory asks, stunned, her jaw dropping open, and stays that way. She hadn't realized it would cost. None of the parties had been involved money.

"He'll do five minutes for free, and everyone gets to pick two poses digitally, but then you must buy if you want more. It's a business, and he needs to make money." Max holds up his hands. "With your permission, I'd like to buy the full package for you. I'll gladly share them with you and Derek, but I'd like the pictures to be mostly of you, if you're willing." He leans in to whisper. "I'm not supposed to share, but I will."

"Wow, I had no idea." She watches as the next group of three takes clothed pics, then begins to fuck as the photographer keeps snapping away.

"This is a very popular thing at the ball. I'm quite shocked the line is so short right now." Max looks energized.

"Oh, this is a tradition. What an incredible idea!" she exclaims, starting to get on board.

"Would you be interested in naked pictures? A few of us having sex?"

Her exhibitionistic bone thickens and falls into a full blaze as she scans the crowd watching the threesome fuck while the camera continues to flash. Watchers and pics? It's an exhibitionist's dream come true.

Her grin grows as her lust charges headlong into fire alarm status. "I'm so in. And really excited."

She watches as one of the threesome members comes in a blast of jizz that lands on the woman's erect nipples. She smooths it all across her skin as the other man enters her pussy. They fuck, both come, and quickly zip away.

Mallory glances around the room and locates Derek talking to Sam on the far side of the great hall. They both have plates of food and drinks in their hands, and neither is looking her way. She wants Derek to join, but she also can't wait to share the pics with him. They're up next.

She nods and clasps her hands together, shaking them up and down. "I'm in for this, Max. So in." She scans the onlookers, and her lust swells. "This is going to be so hot!"

Max grabs her hand with a smile and tugs her toward the photo staging area. The photographer's assistant approaches them.

She's wearing a low-cut, sparkly silver ball gown, and her green eyes shine with brilliance. "Hi, I'm Sierra. We offer three different packages. One is new." She hands them a laminated piece of paper. "One is the free route, you get two free digital images of your choosing. As an alternative, you can review the others and select the images you prefer. There are packages available at that level, which you can view on the website. They'll be available starting at 7:00 tomorrow morning. Then we have an exciting new option. Jasper has created a sort of temporary version similar to the Only the Steamy site, but it's short-lived. This means you can offer all your images for purchase to all club members, and they will be downloadable for one week. After that, they will be deleted and removed from the market. The awesome thing is, if you sign up for this, you can earn seventy percent of the profits of your sales to club members." She beams a huge smile. "And, if you pay a fee, you can also claim full rights to the photos to be uploaded to any sites you desire after the week is over. So, you could turn around and put these professional photos up for sale on Only the Steamy or such other sites if you desire."

Mallory blinks as she processes what she's saying. She could actually earn money for her and Derek, plus get her kinky needs for exhibitionism met on a larger scale.

Max grins. "It sounds appealing, doesn't it?"

She nods vehemently. "It really does. Do I need to decide now?"

"Yes, we prefer that, but you can stop by later and let us know if you want some time. We'll be here until midnight."

Max rubs her back. "You should do it, if you want to. You are so sexy, honey. You will get buyers."

She hadn't considered doing this until now, and she suddenly wonders why she hadn't thought of it before. She and Derek need money, and with both of them being so open, this is the ideal way. Her only concern is that she's heard of several people getting fired for participating in such sites. But if she were making enough money, that could be her job. It sounded too good to be true, but she's all about taking risks; she might as well be dead if she doesn't.

The desire to do it churns in her gut. She bites her lip and makes eye contact with Max. "Should I do it? We could use the money, and it would be super fun too."

The assistant smiles broadly. "You'd be paying a lot more to hire him to do a private photo shoot, to be honest. That's like in the thousands. If you have any desire to try it, this could be very economical, and get some kick ass sexy pics. I'd do it if you have any inkling at all." She motions toward the photographer, who is messing with his camera. "He's really good, and I'm not just saying that cause I fuck him." She snickers as her eyes dance with delight.

Mallory and Max laugh.

"Got it," Mallory says with a knowing glance her way. "Yeah. I'm in. Level three. Right, Max?"

His face spreads into the biggest grin. "Level three it is." He reaches for his wallet and pulls out a credit card. "Here you are, you delightful young lady."

She takes the card and heads over to the table.

"Wow, never in a million years did I expect this tonight. And in this dress? This is going to be incredible." She caresses his arm. "And all this is because of you, Max. So, thank you. You are so good to me, and you are giving me opportunities I wouldn't have otherwise gotten."

"Honey, it makes me so happy to spend money on you. I feel like the lucky one here, you even giving an old guy like me the time of day, let alone the chance to buy you clothes and make you orgasm, I'm the luckiest man on the planet." He takes hold of her arms. "And then I get the added bonus of putting my cock in you."

She grins back. "Oh, yes, Daddy, I want that." She's more than ready as she caresses his cheeks, tilts her head up, and opens her mouth.

They fall into a kiss, and the crowd hoots and hollers.

The assistant returns, and they break apart.

"I'll hold up these cards, and try to ensure you see them, so you know how much time you have left, so you can get in what you want in for the pics. Any questions?"

"Nope, I'm good." Mallory glances over at Derek and catches his eye. She waves.

He waves back, smiling.

"I'm good too," Max says. He looks at Mallory. "Okay, let's do this pineapple stand."

"Good choice of words," she says with a giggle.

She grabs Max's hand and pulls him to the circle on the floor.

The photographer approaches. "Welcome! It will be my extreme pleasure to work with you tonight. I understand we are doing some of the two of you together, and a good portion of you alone," he says, nodding at Mallory. "And you're Mallory and Max?"

"Yes," says Max. "And I'd like some nice clothed ones for SFW, then some of her as she is undressing and doing sexy unveiling poses, then some naked of, and then just a few with us fucking. Preferably with me behind her rather than to the side." He pats his belly. "I don't need picks of this," he says with a laugh.

The photographer joins in his laughter. "Understood. And you agree?"

The assistant hands Mallory a clipboard with paper on it. "Here's the release form. And there's one for the gentleman beneath."

Mallory signs her name without reading the contract, her hands shaking, her vision going slightly blurry. She hands the clipboard to Max.

"You'll both get a copy of this signed document emailed to the address you've listed. Good luck, and have fun!" She steps back and scurries to the sideline.

Mallory leans back into Max, pushing her tits out. He looks down at her lovingly as he places his hands on her belly. He caresses her as he gazes into her eyes.

She grins and raises an eyebrow because his erection is a log against her backside. "You have a nice friend. Are you going to share him soon?"

He laughs and says, "You bet I am."

The photographer keeps snapping photos.

She swivels to face Max, and they kiss.

"Okay, before you two get too hot, let's get some of those safe-for-work photos you wanted." He chuckles. "I can see the heat is pretty heavy between you two already." He smooths his hand down his chin. "I love shooting age gap couples."

Mallory startles at the word 'couple,' which she realizes she shouldn't be. She and Max had gone on several dates, and to the outside world, they appeared to be a couple. She just hadn't thought of them that way yet. She shoves the awkward thought from her brain and smiles for the camera.

"Beautiful," he says. "Keep that pose. Okay. Now, Mallory. You shift slightly to your right. Yeah. Like that. Max, move your hand down a bit." He gives a thumbs up. "Stellar."

They run through several innocent vanilla poses, and the photographer snaps his fingers. "Ok, sexy times start now."

Max and Mallory embrace and fall into a kiss. Mallory is hungry for Max, and she savors the urgency. They kiss until Max pushes Mallory slightly back, breaking their union. He gingerly grasps her dress and pulls it down to expose her breasts.

"Just a quick peek," he says, his eyes swimming with lust.

He spins Mallory to face the photographer and plays with her tits from behind.

She squirms, loving his touch and the attention from the camera and the cheers from the onlookers.

Max replaces her dress over her boobs, then steps away, bowing to showcase Mallory.

The cameraman guides her through a series of poses while she is dressed.

"Now, let's have you start undressing at a pace you desire."

If she felt like a princess earlier, now she's a star. A celebrity of significance as she twirls and poses for the camera. She leans forward to give deep cleavage and a puckered kiss of the air. She giggles and rights her body, then begins to seductively undress, unveiling her tits to the shouts of the exuberant crowd. She swivels, dips, twirls, cups, squeezes, pinches, and dances her way through all his suggestions.

She's never felt more alive as he suggests she bare more of her flesh to his lens.

The crowd blurs as she focuses on Jasper alone. His guidance is a seductive dance that is getting her so ready to be fucked that she can barely calm her breathing. She slides her dress down over her hips and presses it to the floor. His clicking of the button doesn't cease as she does the stripping, suggestively gyrating and exposing her body, including all her cracks and wet holes. Occasionally, she slips out of her reverie when a fan shouts extra loud, but she's in the zone and just follows Jasper's guidance.

Max enters the scene at Jasper's request. He gropes Mallory and humps her butt from behind.

She stops him and pulls her dress up to her waist. "I want some with my dress flipped over my back and my tits hanging as he fucks me, please."

Jasper grins with glee. "Fabulous idea."

Max complies and flips her puffy skirt up and onto her back. He fondles her ass, hips, and thighs, then reaches between her legs. He accosts her clit and rubs just how she likes.

With her tits hanging and Max playing with her pussy, her eyes flutter open and closed, she floats in her arousal, moaning and savoring all Max's touches, and all the eyes focused on her. When she opens her lids, she catches sight of Derek in the crowd. He looks turned on and happy, so she grins at him, making direct eye contact.

Max does his perfect manipulations on her clit, her tits flop and she holds her head up as a sigh escapes. Then she soars into her climactic peak, moaning and writhing, her head falling as her torso arches as she travels the orgasm.

"Head up, Mallory," Jasper instructs. "We all want to see your lovely O face."

Cheers from the group agreeing with Jasper launch her into a second orgasm, her body bounces off Max's in search of some support. She feels floppy and weak as the orgasm takes control over her.

As she calms, Max helps her rise to stand and he plays and sucks her tits for more shots.

"Fuck her," someone shouts.

Max nods in agreement, and Mallory seethes with arousal. He pushes her dress back off her body and carefully lays it to the side as she continues to pose for the crowd, now that she's fully nude.

She kicks off her shoes for better stability and allows Max to bend her over, her face closest to the camera.

He tickles his fingers along her slit, and drags them across her clit.

She grins as he lines up his cock. She adores that he's staying dressed and only his cock out, and she's naked, ready to be fucked at his disposal.

He penetrates her with a deep, primal grunt and begins to pound. Before too long, he pauses, "Get more skin to skin," he murmurs, then resumes his fucking of her, with more of his flesh hitting hers.

Mallory loves the plush cushion of his belly as he rams himself against her backside.

He reaches for a titty grab, and Malory struggles to keep her head up as he tugs on her nipples.

Her body twitches, she's gonna lose control to her satiation again and come.

"Oh, fuck. I'm gonna..." she says panting. The rhythmic sounds of their bodies smacking together add to the turn-on, and she launches into another peak. Her tits are rocked, and she hears people's comments on how hot she is. This lights her up even more.

He releases her nipples and grips her hips hard, and proceeds to fuck her from behind, rapidly slamming himself against her body, driving his cock deep inside her.

She rounds the tip of her arousal and claims her zenith, groaning out as her vaginal muscles contract.

The loudness of the crowd hits her as she squeezes Max's hard cock inside her body.

He comes with a roar and a series of hard smacks, and his cock begins to shrink inside as the wetness is pulled from her with his weakening thrusts.

"That was so hot, omigod," Mallory coos as she regains her upright posture.

"It was, it was incredible." Max pulls her, and she swivels to face him.

They kiss, and the party-goers watching clap and shout their approval.

Max breaks their kiss. "And you can buy her picks on the site; she's putting them up for sale."

The cheers that follow warm Mallory up. People wanting to buy her sexy pics have her on cloud nine. She beams a smile at the crowd. "And afterward, they'll go on the Only the Steamy website, but they'll cost more, so make sure you get them from Jasper's site this next week."

She catches Derek, and he looks worried. She does a double-take back to connect with him, and his expression doesn't lighten.

Max cups her chin and directs her face toward his. "Already an entrepreneur. I'm so proud of you, Mallory." His expression matches his words, and his praises pump her up for it.

"I guess so," she agrees, returning his pleasant smile.

Max hugs her and then bends to pick up her dress as they walk off the photo set together.

As Mallory dresses, she scans the crowd and can't find Derek anywhere.

Chapter 12

Derek admires the elegant arched curve of Faye's back as he releases his ponytail hold of her hair. She moans and writhes, twisting her body to grind against his pelvis. His cock is completely immersed inside her and as he pauses his thrusting for a moment, he smiles. She really is such a beautiful woman, and her kind, gentle heart has endeared her to him even more than he had expected. Her husband is watching from across the room. He's seated at a table enjoying a plate of food, but his eyes are glued on his wife getting fucked by Derek. He looks happy and seems to be enjoying it. Derek understands the man. He always wants pleasure for Mallory, too, whether it's from him or another guy or woman. Derek nods his way as a means of mutual mindset and respect. He nods back.

Derek begins his backside riding of Faye again. She drops her head and releases a heavy sigh as Derek harnesses his power and begins to ram himself into her at an ever-increasing speed. He grips her hips firmly and curls his body slightly so he can sneak a hand under and accost her clit. Her hand is already there, so Derek gently inserts his fingers to displace hers. She melts down to the ottoman, her face hitting it. Derek rides her clit aggressively, using all the moves that worked so well on her last time, starting with circles, then strong rubbing, followed by harder clit spanks.

Faye's back arches more, and she releases a loud gasp and moan. Her body twitches, and Derek braces for her contractions. He's ready to yank himself out if he can't endure them; he doesn't want to come yet. Her pussy clenches on his and as her butt nudges backward on him, he takes a step back to get his cock out of her. He will come if he stays inside her; he's way too aroused. Her body twitches as she peaks, then begins to slow, ending with sensual soft cooing.

Derek releases her clit as she twitches with her aftershocks.

"Oh, my, yes, Derek. That was wonderful," she says, then sighs again. "More, please," she begs, then releases a little giggle.

"You got it," Derek says, re-entering her body. He grips her hips, readying to pound her relentlessly until she comes again. He'll come, that's for sure, but he always stays hard anyhow so they can keep going whatever his dick does, but he's prepared to come now anyhow because she came already. He coasts his cock in and out of her easily, using her juices as their lube, and he ramps up quickly smacking himself against her bottom.

Her moans rise again as he hammers her from his backside mount and his cock bursts inside her, releasing his spunk to her walls. The beautiful thing about menopause was that Derek could do this, and Faye always said it was the best part of midlife for her, not to have to worry about the chance of pregnancy. So as a result, Derek got the blissful privilege of coming inside Faye every time they had sex, which had become every few days over the past month.

She crumples to the ottoman and flips over, a satisfied smile spreading across her face. "That was so good, thank you," she says.

"I'm still hard, do you want to keep going?" he asks.

"I'm thinking of food right now, but after?" she asks with a raise of her eyebrow.

"Yes, for sure." He glances up when he sees movement to his right. Mallory is sitting with Max at a table next to the window. She looks like a princess holding a glass of champagne, her face animated. She has a glow about her, one that Derek has often seen her have after they've been together intimately.

Max produces a rose from behind his back and hands it to her. Her face lights up at his magic trick.

Derek cringes, and then he feels ashamed, looking away.

"You okay, love?" asks Faye as she stands up. She pulls him into a hug. "You look like you could use a big hug."

Derek smiles at her, able to ignore his bad feelings for the moment. "I always want a hug from you."

They embrace, but it backfires when his gaze falls upon Malory and Max again. She's on her knees sucking Max's cock. Derek snickers and figures he must have popped a pill to be hard already again. He shakes his head, disappointed in himself. Who is he right now?

Faye releases him and steps back, and he quickly wipes his face, avoiding any evidence of bad thoughts. She grabs his hand and tugs him toward the food.

Max's head drops back as Mallory's head bobs quickly on his cock. The light fabric of her skirt flops up with her movements. She's slipped the top of her dress down so her tits are bare and bobbing as she works his cock with her mouth. His hands massage her head as she keeps going. Several onlookers are crowding around them, and soon Derek's view is blocked. He rolls his eyes. Apparently, the earlier photo shoot had them as the most popular couple at the party. Everyone wanted in on what they were doing. No matter. Derek didn't need to see anyhow, it was souring the party for him. He needs to shake this shit. He's not the jealous kind, and he doesn't like how these emotions are making him into someone he isn't normally, but Mallory's interactions with Max have him becoming someone he doesn't like.

He follows Faye to the food table, and they load up their plates. He keeps looking back at the crowd around his girlfriend and Max, but it's only thicker than the last time, and he has zero chance of seeing what they are up to now.

Faye is oblivious to his brooding, thank goodness. He doesn't want her to think he's not having a good time with her. She's first right now, and he needs to live that out.

"Oh, that glazed ham looks amazing. I'm having some of that," Derek says, grabbing the tongs. "Want some?"

She nods and he lays several slices on her plate, then on his. They load up with other goodies and then join her husband at a table.

"Derek, nice treatment of Faye earlier, I love to see her so full of pleasure," he smiles.

"Oh, it's always my pleasure. I can't get enough of her, as you know." Derek squeezes Faye's hand while making eye contact.

"Oh, I love hearing you say that," she says in a little happy voice.

"I'm glad you two are getting on as you are," Steven says. "She deserves every orgasm you give her."

"That she does," Derek agrees.

He watches as the crowd that was around Mallory and Max begins to break up. Once they've all moved, he gets a glimpse of what must have gone down behind the wall of people. Mallory is nude, and Max has no pants on. They both look exhilarated and worn out. Max helps her back into her dress, and Derek's mood sours further. He turns his attention to his food.

"You okay, son? You having some doubts about this with Mallory?" Steven asks.

Derek cringes as he watches Faye's face fall into shock. Damnit, did he have to say that, and in the presence of Faye?

"Oh, honey," Faye says as her face falls into worry and concern. "You know she loves you, right?"

Derek nods rapidly and forces a smile. "I know she does." He needs to put on a show and quick.

"You'll work through it," Steven says with a confident look. "As I've said before, you two remind me and Faye and me years ago. You'll get there."

He muddles through his mood as they discuss basketball, the weather, and the goings-on of the party. Derek tries not to hawk eye Mallory and Max like an intrusive peeper, but he wants nothing more than to watch them intently, but he's not about to ignore Faye and Steven.

They finish their food and part ways. Faye wants to soak in the hot tub, and Derek doesn't feel like getting wet. He waves as the older couple heads outside. He finds a seat on a soft sitting chair and scans the room for Mallory. He doesn't see her anywhere, nor Max. He sits with his brooding and tries to get into watching the orgy going on in front of him on the ottoman. It's really hot but he feels like a party pooper. All he wants to do is go home and spend time with Mallory. Maybe he'll just call for a ride home. But if he does that, Mallory will likely freak. He could lie and say he's sick. He sighs as he checks his phone. He's stuck and there's nothing he can do about it.

After a few minutes of people watching, Mallory rushes up to him, all breathless and beautiful. Her eyes are lit up and her cheeks are flushed, and Derek has never seen her look more lovely, which is making him feel the most terrible he's felt all night.

"Derek!" she shrieks. "There you are, I've been looking everywhere for you. It's been the best night of my life!" She's so excited and exuberant.

"Oh?" he asks, trying really hard to sound interested, but he's failing.

"Yes, I can't wait to tell you all about it." She maneuvers, lifting her right hip, then starts to lower herself down on him.

He pulls her onto his lap and tries his best to smile at her.

"I can't wait to tell you how Max made it possible for me to earn some money for us with my pics," she says excitedly.

"I know," he says plainly.

She twitches on his lap. When he's silent, she meets his gaze, a frown on her face. "Are you okay?" she asks with concern. "What's going on?"

"Nothing's going on," he insists.

"That look. Something's going on. Did something bad happen with Faye? With Sam?"

Derek shakes his head. "No, it's nothing, Mallory." He fights his strong urge to suggest they go home. It's still pretty early, so if he says this, she'll know. He doesn't want to ruin her night.

"Please, don't shut me out. This isn't us." She looks hurt.

Derek sighs, then smiles as big as he can. "I'm good, honestly, Mal. Tell me about the money maker."

She begins to spill it all, even though he was there, he was watching, so he knows most of it. Her flow of energized mood infuses into him as she talks, and he feels slightly better. Being around Mallory has always made him feel good.

"I'm excited for this, too, Mal. It could be so great. I'm actually surprised you haven't started an account before." He likes the idea of them getting more money, and Mallory getting to satisfy more of her kinks at the same time.

"I know, it's like been a dream of mine for a while. I guess I don't really know why I haven't tried it. But I'm really happy tonight has launched me there." She gets a saucy gleam in her eye. "Would you ever join me? We could have you be headless to protect your identity."

His mood swells to a happy place that she wants him to be included in her content. "Well, I'd love to, actually. That sounds really hot."

"Good." She smooths her dress down as she leans forward on her knees. She peers around the room, slowly swiveling her head. "And Max said he'd do it, too." She shivers. "Oh, Derek! This could be so good! And if I can earn money for us, we won't be so tight, and can maybe relax a little."

He agrees, but does Max have to be involved too? He can't shake it; the dark cloud descends upon him again.

She pops off his lap quickly. "Oh, Max is back. I'll catch up with you soon. Save some boner for me?" she asks with a flirty tone as she turns to face him.

He tries to dampen his dark mood and agrees. "Yes, Ma, always. Have fun."

She scurries off, her dress bouncing as she makes her way in a dash to Max.

Max looks elated as Mallory collides into his arms and they fall into an embrace, with her giggling and cooing.

Max nods at Derek, and Derek nods back. Now is not the time. Derek needs a distraction and looks around for Sam. Maybe sucking some cock would help get his brain reset. Sam was always up for that. He spots Sam by the bar and begins to stride over to him. His mood lifts as Sam acknowledges him with a head bob. The night wouldn't be complete without Derek giving Sam head after all, it had become a party staple.

"Hey Derek, how's it going? Having fun?" Sam gives Derek a happy grin.

"Yeah," he says, smiling back.

"That's it? Normally, you fill my head with every little detail." Sam reaches for a glass of champagne and hands it to Derek. "You need more bubbles."

Derek's heart sinks. Even Sam notices.

"I'd love to give you a champagne-flavored blow job is what I'm thinking." Derek takes the glass from Sam and takes a hefty sip.

Sam's head falls back as he laughs with glee. "Ah, there's my boy. Yeah, that sounds fabulous."

"Let's get you comfortable, though, or do you prefer to stand?" Derek asks before another swallow of champagne. He gives Sam a seductive look. "I'm aiming to make you explode." He downs his champagne and sets down the empty flute, then grabs for another one.

Sam's eyes dance with delight. "I'm enjoying your exuberance. How about over in the corner, near the fireplace? I'd love to see your mouth stretched around my cock in the flickering of the fire."

"Fireside cock, perfect." Derek can never get enough of this sexy man with his air of dominance mixed with elegance, his piercing eyes, and his muscular, slim physique. Derek also loves that he's hopped from an older woman to an older man, from Faye to Sam is a delicious way to spend his party time, and might just get his mind off searching out Mallory with Sam's dick commanding his attention.

Sam settles into the chair and places his champagne on the side table. "Champagne, a fire, and a blow job. My favorite."

Derek kneels before him. "I thought your favorite would have been inside my ass."

"Do I really have to pick?" Sam says with a teasing tone.

Derek grins back. "Nope." Derek makes the mistake of turning his head slightly because he catches sight of Mallory and Max again. They're slow dancing. He frowns, and he lingers watching them for a few seconds too long.

Sam folds his hands together and places them on his lap. "Derek, not that I ever want to defer you from sucking my cock down your throat, you seem off, my dear boy."

Derek quickly turns his attention to Sam. "What do you mean?"

Sam tilts his head as his expression turns fatherly. "What's going on, Derek?"

"What do you mean? I'm ready to suck the life out of you. Make you come like a machine." Derek eagerly settles closer to Sam between his legs and begins to reach for Sam's groin.

Sam blocks his hands. "I get this will distract you, but you aren't getting your lips around this cock until we talk."

Derek slumps and allows Sam to see his full bad mood by lifting his mask.

"I love you sucking my cock, but when you are feeling good and like yourself. Not like this. My cock can wait." He pats the arm of the chair next to him. "Let's talk, my boy."

"Well, that's not exactly sexy talk," Derek says in a sour tone.

"Yep, just as I thought. You have something you need to talk through, and I'm here for you, okay." Sam meets his gaze.

Derek reluctantly sits. "I could be enjoying your cock right now."

Sam titters a laugh. "And you may still, but let's hear it. What's going on?"

Derek clams up. He's not sure he even wants to admit this crap out loud. Not that he fears Sam will judge him, I mean, he could, but he doesn't want to claim these petty feelings, and if he says them out loud, they exist more.

"You can't keep it bottled up. Have you talked about it with Mallory?" His voice is tender, caring, and supportive.

Derek remains silent. He keeps his head straight so he can't accidentally see Mallory and Max. They are likely still looking happy, and he can't stomach it. His emotions are ready to spill, and he doesn't want to spew them out of control on Sam.

He stands up abruptly, turns away from him. "I'll be right back."

"Oh, no you don't," Sam says sternly. "You put that butt right back in that seat."

Sam's dominant tone always arouses Derek, and his cock begins to fill, which seems like an impossible thing given his horrible mood.

Derek freezes in place as he fights the urge to disobey Sam and zoom off across the room. All he wants to do is go find a vacated bedroom and curl up on the bed. The champagne has gone to his head and his impulses are winning.

"Derek, sit," Sam commands again. "Now."

Derek's shoulders slump, and he turns to face Sam. He allows all his dreadful feelings to show on his face.

"Aw, dear boy. Sit and talk to me. I've not seen you like this before." Sam's face is full of compassion, and Derek sinks into his care like he's a lifeboat.

He sits and fights back tears as Sam pats his lap. "Come here. You don't need to tell me, but let me help you feel better."

Derek acquiesces and settles on Sam. The hug is the comfort he needs. He melts into him, the effects of too much champagne making him feel as if he might sob. He remains still in Sam's embrace as the fire flickers, warming his skin. Sam smells like aftershave and donuts.

Derek grins at the thought. Sam strokes his hair, and Derek's nerves are wrapped up enough to settle down a bit.

Chapter 13

Derek slides off Sam and gives him a sheepish look. "Sorry," he says as he moves in front of the chair beside Sam and plops into it.

"Don't be. You're feeling what you are, and acknowledging it is the only way through it," Sam says.

Derek's heart sinks. Of course, Sam is right. He's always right. Derek watches the flames flicker, refusing to meet Sam's eyes. He says nothing but feels Sam's eyes upon him. He's in the hot seat.

"It's about Mallory, isn't it?" Sam finally asks.

Derek nods and stares at his clasped hands in his lap.

"And are you being honest with her?" Sam asks with tenderness.

"She knows something is wrong," Derek says, his voice betraying him, quivering inside.

"That's on you, my boy. You know communication is the key to relationships. Open, honest communication." Sam rubs his hand. "You two have always been honest with each other. Now is not the time to stop."

"But I don't want to ruin her fun. And I'm not like that." He pouts as he shoves his hands into his pits.

"Hey, you're allowed to feel things."

Derek shoves his hands into his hair as he leans his head back. "I can't give her what he can, and it's killing me." Tears bleep out. He can't stop them. He covers his eyes with his hands as he tries to hold back his sob. He regains control, Sam's calming presence helping, and sighs. "It's no use. I'm a horrible partner."

"No one can meet all of another's needs, Derek. That's what this club is all about. We are relational beings, meant to live in communities, which means we connect with others and get our needs met in that community. To expect it all to come from one person doesn't even make sense and goes against what this club is essentially all about at its core."

When Sam pauses, Derek becomes aware of the party sounds again. There are people talking, others moaning, and skin-smacking sounds filling the air. The sounds pull him back into the moment and out of his head, and he finally looks Sam in the eyes.

"Whatever you say, Derek, know that it doesn't change how I feel about you. I'm here for you. We're more than friends, and even more than just sexual partners at this point, and I'm happy that we are. Just stating facts. I want you to know that you can tell me anything." He grins deeply. "I've got many more revolutions around this planet under my belt than you do. So, try me, maybe I can help." He pats Derek's arm.

Derek smiles devilishly. "That's where I want to be, under your belt," he says suggestively, while raising an eyebrow.

Sam laughs heartily. "After my own heart, my boy, but as tempting of an offer as that blow job is, you're not getting my cock until we talk this out."

Derek's seduction flatlines. He shrugs with a little grin. "Had to try," he says with a lighthearted snicker.

"I love that about you. I love your libido." Sam touches his hand and caresses it. "But I also love your heart. You have a big heart, Derek. Now, how can I help it feel better?"

Derek stares at the ground for a minute, ignoring the loud goings-on at the ottoman. "Max is doing so much for her, things I can't even come close to doing. And it's not just the money."

Sam shifts in his chair. "Ah, this is about Max, then. I suspected."

Derek nods, feeling even more miserable. "I'm not a jealous man, honestly, I'm really not. I never have been, and in fact, I despise such men, but I'm feeling jealous. I want to be everything for Mallory, and I'm now seeing, I can't be. It's just not possible and it hurts."

"Do you sense you are losing her?" Sam asks cautiously.

"No, that's not it at all. I don't feel that happening." Derek glances at Sam. "She hasn't even indicated such a thing."

Sam pats his hand again. "Okay. So, you're feeling inadequate and unable to fill some needs and wants, that Mallory is meeting with Max. Is that it?"

"I'm an awful partner, and I can't tell her because then she'll know the truth that I am a horrible partner."

"Let me ask you this, can Mallory do for you what I do? What Faye does for you?"

Derek shakes his head. "No, I guess not."

"And do you think Mallory knows this?"

Derek nods his head and says weakly, "Yes." He feels sheepish. Of course, Sam is right. Sam is always right.

"You need to be honest with her. Trust her. You need to trust each other. Even just telling her what you are feeling is going to help. I can assure you of this." He shifts in his seat to more squarely face Derek. "Look, my boy, this club is fairly new for you guys, and now is a super important time as you're both cultivating new relationships with other people outside your relationship with each other while still being devoted to your own." He pauses, and someone climaxes very loudly on the ottoman, making a loud ruckus. They both laugh as their eyes connect in knowing appreciation of the wild sounds. Sam continues, "Sounds like a nice one." He chuckles. "Derek, let me tell you something I've learned. The first steps into not trusting each other are the first steps toward the death of your relationship. And trusting each other keeps everything on par when you're honest with each other about everything. Don't hold back. It's the only way through your emotions, especially the ones you didn't expect, like what you're experiencing now."

This hits Derek hard. He says, "I don't want to admit to her I'm jealous, though. I'm not that guy."

"Except that you are," Sam says, and it smacks Derek in the face. Sam's gaze calls for him to own it.

He hates that kind of jealous guy, and he hates even more that he's now resembling him. He wants Mallory to feel loved, cared for, amazing, and pleasured, and not just by him. "I just want to give her the world, you know?" His voice wavers as he feels on the verge of tears again.

"And you can, through allowing her to find what she needs that you can't give her and vice versa. No one can be everything to another. It's not even possible. It's why we have friendships, and also why I don't believe in monogamy. I believe in people and in relationships, and dedication, where it's true, not false. I believe in having that committed nesting relationship, the one you have as your grounding core, your place of return after you have both had needs and experiences you enjoyed with others, taking you places you wouldn't or couldn't have gone together." He pauses. "Is it risky? Yes. But if a relationship fails because she meets someone else, I'd argue that your relationship really wasn't meant to be. You don't want a false relationship that is only out of obligation, where you both don't really want to be there, do you?"

"Nesting relationship, meaning like Maria for you?"

Sam nods. "And I'm guessing Mallory for you."

Derek's aha moment flickers.

"Obligation alone is not a sustainable way to live out life with your partner. It doesn't work. You must both work at it, support each other. And allow each other as many graces as you both can manage, and therein lies true happiness in long-term relationships."

He's ashamed to dwell in his jealousy. "I just don't want to end up like my parents, I know that. I saw them resenting each other because they didn't talk to each other, didn't support each other in every way, and ultimately ended up not even caring for each other anymore. Their marriage just died."

Sam says, "I think you have your course of action laid out before you, my boy."

Derek's nerves settle. "Yeah, you're right. I need to tell her. We need to talk. I can't be Max to her, I'm not Max. She can't be you or Faye for me, because she's who she is." He sighs and shrugs. "I guess I was falling back into that mode I was taught as a kid, where my religious teaching, and my family, shoved down my throat that I should be the only one to meet every single one of Mallory's needs. You're right, though, that's stupid and not realistic." He relaxes his shoulders. "Community and the freedom to enjoy that community together is how I want to live my life with Mallory." He slumps his shoulders. "I'm such a chump. Max is giving her all these benefits, some of which will even help me, and I'm being an ungrateful ass." He shakes his head. "I didn't realize how selfish I was being in my jealousy, but that's exactly what jealousy is, it's not allowing your partner the ease of getting their needs met outside of you, and instead trying to lay claim on it all. Like trying to control it." He rubs his hands on his thighs as he meets Sam's eyes again. "Thank you. I needed your guidance to reach this point. I'm not that jealous guy, I just got trapped in it. All that old teaching had its grip on me again."

"It's hard to unlearn it. It's so ingrained in our culture, and when we're taught it when we're young, it becomes the only truth, until we release that control it has over us and we see it for the manipulation into falsehood that it is. We were meant to live in community situations, not as a solitary couple in monogamy. I can tell you that even monogamous couples still have friends, right? They still have work relationships and neighbors, people they socialize with. It's just that we swingers extend that one step further, into the bedroom. And thereby we are more well-rounded in getting our needs met in full, rather than getting some needs met, but leaving out sexuality and deeper, intimate relationships. We don't lay claim where claim doesn't belong. But we also have agreed upon rules and boundaries that we adhere to with one another." He smiles. "It's also a state of respecting each other's right to free will, and then also being the best partner to them that you can be. We all deserve that."

Derek smiles and agrees, feeling better. "You're damn smart," he says as his teasing bone starts to swell. "For an old fart."

Sam laughs devilishly as he pretends to slap Derek by swiping his hand in the air. "Exactly what you like me for, my boy. I'm no fool."

Derek laughs along, sliding into that comforting yet arousing notion of getting close and intimate with a person older than himself. Sam's words are exactly what he needed to hear to realign himself. He was most certainly falling into that old way of thinking, and he's extremely happy to have the insight to recognize it in himself. "You're exactly right. But mostly I just want cock now and then."

"Again, after my own heart, as I'm the same. Only my cock comes to you on my terms."

"Oh, and I can tell you, I love that too." Derek's submissiveness to Sam is one delicious way he loves to get his needs met. He laughs at himself. Mallory can adorn a strap-on and dominate him in a pegging session, but she can't be Sam. And he'd never expect her to be either, so he shouldn't be thinking he can be what Max can be to her. It's literally not even logical.

"And with that look and that kind of smile," Sam says clearly enjoying what he's saying, "now you can suck my cock."

"With great pleasure," he says, sliding to his knees and crawling over to kneel in front of him again. "I'm going to make you come hard."

"If you don't, you're going over this knee," Sam says jokingly as he swats the air.

Derek pauses and heckles. "Maybe I need to do a bad job just to see what that's like."

"Don't tempt me," Sam says in a tease. "'Cause I'll do it."

Derek's arousal thickens as Sam undoes his zipper and presents his hard cock. He descends on him and takes his full swollen head into his mouth voraciously sucking him off. Derek's night has been saved by Sam, and he wants to thank him with a good release of his load. He bobs his head and fondles Sam's balls, his arousal rising with each sound of enjoyment Sam makes. Before long Sam's fingers grip Derek's scalp and squeeze as Sam directs Derek's pace and force by using Derek's mouth like a fuck hole. Derek flops like a rag doll as he allows Sam to use his mouth and throat to bring himself to his peak. Derek sputters from the deep-throating, then gags. His eyes water as he presses his fingers into Sam's thighs. He urgently grabs his own cock and begins to stroke himself.

Sam grunts as he thrusts upward forcefully into Derek's mouth, holding his head tight between his hands, face fucking him as he flops and bucks. Derek struggles to stroke himself, and a flood of cum bursts in Derek's mouth. He manages to swallow the big load. Derek ramps up his pumping of his hand on his turgid cock and within a short time, cum erupts from his own erection as Sam simmers down.

Derek falls off Sam's shrinking cock and sits as his own cock remains hard.

"Whew, that was incredible," Sam says with great satisfaction in his voice. "I haven't commanded a good rough face fucking in quite some time. You were perfect in how relaxed you became. Thanks for allowing me that."

"It was so hot." He holds up his own hand covered in a copious amount of cum, a huge grin on his face.

"I can see that," Sam says. "May I taste you? I'd love to taste your cum off that ride."

Derek grins and lifts his hand to Sam. Sam licks and sucks all Derek's cum off his hand, then says while glancing down, "Man, I miss those days when I'd stay hard like that."

Mallory approaches. "Wow, that was really hot! I watched. Wanted to wait to approach only when you were done." She has a happy glow about her as she grins. She's alone, no sign of Max.

"Having a good time?" Sam asks.

"Oh, yes, a wonderful time."

Derek stands up and pulls up his pants over his hard-on.

"Oh," Mallory pouts. "I was just going to ask for a turn with that." She looks disappointed and slumps her shoulders.

"Mal, I really need to talk to you."

Her expression is one of shock, then it falls into a knowing. "I thought something was up. Let's go." She hooks her arm through Derek's and waves at Sam.

Mallory leads Derek toward the sliding glass door. She peers out into the darkness. "No one is in the hot tub. How about we relax in there while we talk?"

Derek nods. A soak in the hot tub sounds perfect. It will help him relax as he spills all his uglies to her. His heart is pounding, and he's trying to manage his nerves. He knows Mallory won't judge him, but showing her he's not what she thought is going to suck.

She pulls him out to the outdoors, and they both gasp from the cold.

"Shit! Why do we live here?" Mallory shrieks as she yanks Derek toward the steaming hot tub.

"I know, right? It's so bad," Derek agrees. Being with Mallory already makes him feel better, but he's still shy about saying what he needs to say. What if she reacts badly and hates him for it? The last thing he wants to do is offend her.

She drops his hand and squeals as she slips out of her ball gown. "I can't believe I'm just laying a ball gown on a frigid deck like this."

"It'll be fine, I'm sure," he assures as he attempts to remove his own clothes as fast as he can.

She slips into the hot water first, and sighing, immerses herself up to her upper chest. "Ah, that's much better."

She watches him as he removes the remainder of his clothes and then descends into the water. He bobs over to her, his heart pounding, his throat dry.

"Are you having fun at the party?" she asks, her eyes all lit with joy. "I'm having a total blast! This night has been epically amazing."

"Where's Max?" Derek asks and laments that it came out as lame as it did.

"Oh, he decided to head home. He was tired, and it had been a lot of sex. Plus, he has a big day tomorrow, so he needs a good rest."

Derek is only mildly curious about what that meant, but refrains from asking. He doesn't really care that much. "Oh, got it."

"So, are you?" she asks cautiously.

"Yes," he says plainly.

She holds his gaze. "What's up?"

He can't fool her for long. He takes a deep breath. "I'm embarrassed at how I'm feeling, so I don't really want to say it out loud."

Her expression goes grim. "It's about Max, isn't it? I see how you look at him sometimes." She seems more matter-of-fact than angry.

He shrugs. "Kinda."

"Kinda?" she asks with doubt.

"Okay, yes. It's about Max." He squirms in the water and glances around, wishing someone would walk by so they couldn't talk privately anymore.

"Is it because I spend time with him?" she asks with a slight cringe on her face.

"No, that's not it." Okay. He needs to correct her right the fuck now so she doesn't get the wrong impression. "It's not that. I've obviously spent time with Faye. It's more..." his voice trails off. He looks everywhere but at her. "I'm feeling things I don't want to admit, because I'm not that guy."

"He's given me a lot lately. I know." She reaches for his face and cups his cheek, then turns his face toward her. "It's the money, isn't it?"

He slumps. "But it's not just that. He's given you opportunities, too."

"Aww, Derek." She sounds sympathetic, and he chastises himself for worrying that she'd have reacted any other way than this.

He feels raw as he unveils the true emotions he's feeling. "I can't do what he's doing, and I want to give you the world."

She pulls him into a hug. She caresses the back of his head. "You know you're the only one I'm spending my whole life with, right? The only one I'm spending holidays with. The only one who's my one true man. Others may come and go," she says, pausing then leaning back to look him in the eye, "or stay, but that doesn't change you and me."

"And only you for me," he parrots back, his heart melting. "I don't deserve you."

"I think what this means is we need more time together, just you and me."

He nods, feeling like a loser. "You don't see me as a needy, jealous loser?"

She scoffs. "Why would I think that about my man?" She cocks her head to the side. "It's high time we had some of our own sexual fun tonight is what I think."

She glides through the water to plant herself on his lap.

"Why are you so easy to talk to?" He grunts gruffly. "And I was worried you were going to hate me."

"Hate you? For wanting more of me? Don't be ridiculous! If you didn't want more of me, I'd think our relationship was dying."

"I don't even get a lecture from you."

She snorts. "I'm not your parents."

He laughs. "That's for damn sure. And thank God."

She leans in, pressing her boobs to him as she makes ready to kiss him. Before she plants her lips, she whispers, "How about you rail me so hard and fast that we splash this hot tub free of water? Make me scream, Derek."

They fall into a passionate kiss as his cock fills between them. She squirms, and his hands claim both butt cheeks, then he moves his hands slowly all the way up her back and holds her head. They kiss hungrily as the steam flows up along their bodies and into the dark night.

He jiggles his thighs to make her bounce in his lap and her titties bob up and down. He adores how her erect nipples graze his flesh.

"I will have my way with you," he mutters with lust raging inside him.

"I want your way," she muses with a seductive grin. "Every way you want."

"Doggy," he says with a devilish grin. "I want to finger my cumslut hard and fast from behind until you cum." He purses his lips. "I own my whore tonight."

She seethes with joy glittering in her eyes. "There's my man."

They grope each other as they kiss, and the frigid air keeps them from getting too hot as they continue to make out for several minutes.

Derek bucks his hips and throws her off his lap. "Bend over."

She licks her lips. "Make me cum and then I'll make you cum."

She rises out of the water and grabs for a towel. She places it on the deck board at the edge of the tub and places her elbows on it, tipping her lovely pert supple ass to his waking cock.

"Get ready," he warns. "I'm not stopping at one."

He plays his fingers along her slit, tickling her lips and pressing his fingers firmly where he knows are her sweet spots. Then he focuses on rubbing her clit. She writhes and moans, the steam rising off her flesh above the water.

He presses two fingers into her pussy hole and starts to pump them in and out of her. He ramps it up as her sounds of pleasure flourish. This is getting so good. He fingers her super fast and hard, making sure to hit her clit, just like the elder Doms of the club had taught him. He'd learned a few new techniques on how to make her climax in mere minutes under their direction. He pistons his fingers so quick and so right that she curls into a climax, her screams piercing the quiet before her silence takes hold. He only slows a tiny bit as she whimpers. Her body twitches telling him her clit is overly sensitive, but instead of backing off, he finger fucks her aggressively, making her body gyrate rapidly.

She screams, then whimpers, and then her body shudders. She mewls and drops her head to the towel. "Fuck," she says panting heavily.

He smears his cock all around her slit and slides in quick. He knows he doesn't have much time before she gets cold, being so much of her is out of the water. He rides her from behind, gripping her hips. He grunts as he packs his cock inside her cunt over and over again. He allows himself to come quickly.

He pulls his cock out and they both descend quickly in the hot water.

"I've never been so happy about you coming fast," she jokes with a giggle.

"I know, same," he says as he relaxes in the warmth.

"We didn't exactly follow the rules about no cum in the water, though," she snickers.

"I'm sure we aren't the first," he says with a happy grin. "I've drained my balls so many times tonight. I think I broke my record."

"Nice," she says, as if it's her triumph, too.

"How is it that you are so understanding?" He shakes his head. "I tell you I'm a jealous loser, and you respond by saying we just need more time together." She's so wonderful, and he can't quite understand how he got so lucky finding her in this big, wide world.

"Well, it just makes sense. If you were getting your needs met with me, you wouldn't be jealous."

"I don't want to be unreasonable."

"I don't think you are being unreasonable. But yeah, we can both see Max is giving me what neither of us can, but that doesn't mean I'm choosing him over you in any way. He's just tending to some of my needs, is how I see it. It doesn't make you less in any way. Just different."

"Yeah, Sam helped me get that. Sam's really smart," he says with a big grin.

"And sexy as fuck!" she announces.

"Yes, I'll second that, and first it!" He pauses as he scans her. "I love seeing you naked in the hot tub," he confesses.

"Same," she coos. "I am getting a bit tired, though, too. Are you ready to leave soon?"

He nods. "Yep, once we're warmed up and pruned out, I'm ready to head home."

"I had a wonderful time tonight, and my favorite was with you." She smiles a devilish smile. "I wish was had just filmed that so we could put it up on my new account."

"Oh, good call! We should have."

"Maybe we can come back some night, and Sam could video us. That would be really hot. And who knows what would happen after?"

"Ah, and I love that idea so much. Sam would love it too."

"And Maria," she says smartly.

Chapter 14

Mallory collects her ball gown in her left arm while squashing it with her right. She's been struggling getting the puffy skirt to nicely fit in the garment bag to the point where the zipper won't snag it.

"Ugh, this is impossible!" she shrieks. "This bag is just too small."

She steps back from the couch and glares down at the massive dress.

"Here, let me help, babe," Derek says as he hurries to rescue her from her frustration. "It might just be a two-person job."

She smiles at him. "Yeah, I'm thinking so." Her excitement is not at all diminished by this minor technicality, though. She feels ready to burst with sexual energy.

They both muscle the dress down to a flatter state, and while Derek holds the poofy skirt down, she slides the zipper up quickly. "Would have been easier to just wear the damn thing there!" she says with a guffaw.

"Yeah, that's probably true." He grins sheepishly. "Too late now."

She cackles. "Yeah, I'm not opening that up until we arrive after all that effort."

Her phone buzzes with a text, and she snatches it off the coffee table.

Max texts: I'll be there. I'm so excited for this, Mallory. Thank you for including me. A package should be arriving for you soon for tonight.

She glances at Derek's back as he leaves the living room. Her heart sinks. Another gift from Max, and now instead of joy, she feels dread. She knew Derek hadn't meant to tarnish her relationship with Max, but it was inevitable. She feels guilty for a gift she hasn't even received yet. Her thinking is all wrong, but that isn't stopping it from choking her.

Should she prepare Derek with a warning about the delivery, or just wing it and hope he isn't crushed? Instead of worrying about it, she shoves it from her brain. It's not her place to shield Derek from any emotions.

Mallory texts back: Oh, I'm so excited for tonight and for the package. Thank you in advance. And you are coming, right?

She hasn't told Derek that Max is for sure coming to the video and photo shoot. She really wants to shoot some scenes with both Derek and Max, and Sam, and even Maria, but she knows that it may be a pipe dream. All she knows is she's about to burst with energy, and she can't contain her excitement about the idea of creating a huge amount of sexy content for her new account. She's already gaining traction from the few things she has posted, which is a dream come true. She loves the idea of turning strangers on and being sexy in the online space. Sexuality should be celebrated, not hidden away, well, at least for people like her who desire to share, that is. Plus, the people who want to view it. It feels like being at one of their parties, but on a much larger scale.

She'd heard the stories of people getting fired from their jobs for this type of thing, then going full-blown into it as a career and making tons of money. So, she wasn't worried about losing her job. She's passionate about this. Plus, with Max backing her, she can't lose. Sam is also supporting her by offering to be the videographer, and Maria said she'd help direct the scenes. It's like all her friends are joining in the effort, yet she is the only one who stands to make money from it all. Maria had said she thought it would be fun, as did Sam, and that's all the motivation they needed. They are almost becoming family to each other, and it's incredible to be a part of such a thing.

Derek hands her a piece of banana bread. "Fresh from the oven."

She accepts it greedily, loving the melting butter oozing across it. "Oh, I love your banana bread. Yummy." She takes a bite. The warm, sweet bread and the melted butter are exquisite. "So good," she mutters over a mouthful.

Mallory catches sight of a delivery person dropping a package on their front step. She rushes over to open the front door. Derek follows.

"What is it? Did you order something?" he asks casually.

"No. It's from Max." She glances at Derek with a slight cringe.

He appears to be unaffected by it, so either he doesn't care, or he's masking his emotions. She hopes he isn't masking again, but it's his default, so she remains guarded.

She snags the box and carries it inside, then sets it on the couch.

Derek goes for the scissors, but she's able to rip them open with her hands.

She pries back the flaps of the cardboard box, and it's filled with so much lingerie that it could stock a small shop. "Oh, my God. Seriously?" She begins picking them up with wide eyes. "This must have cost a fortune. Holy shit! Look at this, Derek!" She grabs handfuls of fabric, lace, and string and holds them up in the air. "This man is unbelievable!"

Derek's eyes widen. "Shit. That's all lingerie?" he asks in disbelief. "I've never in my life seen something like this."

She's floored, absolutely floored that Max would do this, especially after all he bought her in the past few months. She watches Derek's face, fearing he will take this as another bid from Max to buy her love.

"You know this doesn't mean anything for you and me," she says, assuring him.

"I know," he says happily. He hugs her. "The thing is...I get to enjoy these on you forever, and every day, and they're ours."

She relaxes, melting into his embrace. "I love you," she coos.

"I love you."

DEREK PARKS IN THE driveway of Sam and Maria's massive home.

He chuckles. "It looks so different in the day."

She nods, amused. "It really does. I guess we've never come here this early before."

He turns off the vehicle and hops out. He grabs the box filled with lingerie from the back.

Mallory slides out and snatches her duffle bag.

They smile at each other across the seats as they both stand in the open doors.

"This is going to be so much fun, and I'm happy we're both excited for it," she says as warmth fills her heart.

"Yes, I am, too. This is going to be epic." He steps away from the vehicle as a big gust of wind blows. "Now let's get inside. It's awful out here."

She squeals as the frigid wind whips along her frame. "Yes, let's go!"

They scurry toward the front door as the wind beats their bodies.

Sam swings the door wide open, and they rush in. "Another day of brutal weather." He shakes his head as he shuts the door. "Isn't it spring yet?"

Mallory shudders and gasps. "I know, right? It should be."

Sam takes the big box from Derek, then sets it on the bench. "Oh, I'm intrigued by this."

Mallory giggles.

They both remove their coats, and Sam takes them to hang in the closet.

Soft music plays, and it's soothing to Mallory's shivers, along with the warmth of the house, her body stills. "Whew. That's so bad."

"I'm really excited about this. How are you two feeling?" Sam's demeanor is always arousing to Mallory, his warm, caring leadership, like an overseer who dotes.

"Yeah, I'm really excited," Mallory muses, her smile gently growing. "I can't wait."

Sam smiles a slow, seductive grin. "I can easily say the same."

Derek tilts his head to the right. "I'm more than ready." His smile is genuine, and Mallory doesn't even sense a twinge of ill feelings.

This might work after all.

Sam leads them down the hall with the box in his hands. "Anyone going to clue me in on what's in this monstrous box?"

Mallory's heart beats faster. She can't wait to be modeling it in front of everyone. "It's a big box of lingerie that Max sent me. It's unbelievable. He must have spent hours shopping."

Sam stops cold and glances at Derek. "Really? Is that so?" He sounds unsure.

"Yeah, I see it as a gift to us," Derek says quickly. "I'm the one who is going to get to see her every day in person in them, so it's also a gift to me."

Sam nods, mirroring Derek's grin. "That's my boy."

"Well, he's not wrong," Mallory says with glee.

"This feels like a small store, or a booth at the very least," Sam jokes.

Mallory swipes it as Maria approaches. She has on a sexy little red dress with a deep V showing her lush cleavage. "Wait until you see this, Maria!"

"What is it?" she asks.

"It's a giant box of lingerie. From Max."

Maria jerks her head back in surprise. "That's a lot of lingerie." She also falls into a look of concern.

Everyone is worried about something harmless, and Mallory knows it. Her heart is Derek's. And even Max knows this, so she isn't going to let them darken her mood.

"Let's go lay it all out on a bed," Mallory says excited. "I haven't even looked through it all yet."

"We might need more than a bed!" she exclaims.

"I'm thinking we should have started this morning rather than waiting until the afternoon to begin," Sam says with amusement.

Mallory follows Maria down the hallway, practically running after her to catch up, which is a bit cumbersome while carrying the box.

"That man is one of a kind," Maria says as she sweeps her hand across the king-sized bed. "Let's see how many we can fit here."

"I seriously couldn't believe it when I opened this box. He's the most generous man on the planet!"

"He really likes you, Mallory. Dare I say more?" Maria asks with a raise eyebrow.

"Yeah, might be," she says, busying herself with pulling out pieces of lingerie. "Wow, look at this one!" She holds up a strapped piece for a torso. "I've always wanted to wear one of these. The idea of being controlled by the pulling of these straps during sex, and the capabilities for creating more resistance, is intoxicating."

"Yeah, those are incredible for that. It's a very subby desire, I've done it both as the Domme and as the sub with Sam. It's very sexy. Personally, I love it." She takes it from Mallory to inspect it. "I have a similar one that Sam bought me. Oh, the memories! Now I'm getting aroused," she says with a laugh.

"Well, I can't wait to try it." She puts it on the dresser. "This is the must-do-today pile."

"Noted." Maria straightens out the lingerie on the bed as Mallory takes out each piece.

Mallory's joy launches. "Look at this one! I'm like in serious heaven here." She dangles a sheer purple nightie with purple and pink flowers along the top hem. "It's like sexy Christmas!"

Maria laughs. "More than that, even." She fixes a red, fluffy hem on a sheer red number. "This is like sexy Christmas on steroids."

The women continue to pull out piece after piece, commenting and oohing and aahing over each one, tossing it to the bed, the dresser, or the new maybe pile on the loveseat by the window.

"We still have half of the box to go through. Maybe we should just use what we've sorted and save the rest." Mallory gazes upon the piles of lingerie still in the box. "I just cannot get over this. How much money do you think this cost?"

"Thousands. Definitely thousands of dollars." Maria shakes her head. "If you were single..."

Mallory shakes her head, not wanting to go there, but she says, "Yeah, I wouldn't be." She regrets saying it the second it leaves her mouth. She glances at the door to make sure no one overheard. She widens her eyes at Maria. "I only want Derek. I'm committed to him," she says quickly.

"I know, honey. I know." She smiles at Mallory. "Let's start. I'm dying to see you in some of these." She laughs. "Well, all of these."

Mallory gives her an interested look. "I love your dress, by the way. You look hot as fuck." She really can't take her eyes off Maria for very long; it's like her gaze bounces back every time to watch the older woman move.

"Thank you, love," she coos, clearly enjoying the compliment. "You know, I'd love to see a few of these on you. You know, before we go out to the men. Just to find the hottest one."

Mallory's heart flutters. She'd love nothing more than to model a few of them for Maria. "A private showing. I like it."

"Okay, go sit on the loveseat, and I'll make a pile. Then we'll switch spots and you can try them on and strut your sexy self around the room." She grins deeply, with a hint of salaciousness that triggers Mallory's arousal. "Then we can see what happens."

"Okay, I'm in. This'll be fun." Indulging in some alone time with Maria is exactly what she finds sexy and super-hot. She pushes the lingerie to one side of the loveseat, sits, and closes her eyes.

"Good girl," Maria says with calm authority.

Mallory's getting horny as she anticipates this little lingerie show, and she adores that Maria is picking her favorites. With the whole group, she never envisioned getting some alone time with Maria. She loves the men, but things are different when it's just the two of them.

Time is taking too long, and Mallory begins to shake her feet. She crosses them to try and curb the fidgety way she feels, but it doesn't help.

"Patience, I'm almost done," Maria instructs.

Mallory giggles. "I'm not very patient."

"You will be," she says. "Anticipation is a great form of foreplay."

Mallory's clit lurches at that, confirming that Maria has plans for their time alone, juicy plans. She simply nods. She's more than happy to listen to Maria's guidance. Her mind drifts to the men, and she wonders what they are doing. Sam and Derek may be getting busy themselves, but if Max has arrived, likely not. Or at least not likely out in the open because Max isn't into watching two men, but two women, he'd be in heaven. Part of her wants to invite him in to watch her and Maria, but mostly she's excited about their first alone time.

Maria hums as she works; her soft voice is like a mellow purr.

"Keep your eyes closed," Maria states.

Mallory senses her coming close, but she doesn't tense. Instead, she melts into the lush thoughts of potential sexual activity with her. Mostly they'd played in the middle of orgies at parties so having her full attention is a treat indeed. Her mind drifts to imagining Maria and Sam fucking on the bed and her heart begins to pound, her breath begins to hitch.

A soft fabric graces Mallory's cheek. Maria drags it slowly across her skin.

"I like the expression on your face. What are you thinking about right now?" Maria asks as she draws the fabric across the exposed flesh on Mallory's chest.

Mallory smiles. "I'm imagining you and Sam fucking on the bed and I'm watching from this loveseat."

She chuckles softly. "Oh, I do like that idea. We could certainly fulfill that quite easily." Maria caresses her cheek softly with her fingers. "Maybe Derek could be beside you."

She nods aggressively. "Oh, yes. I'd love that."

"Open your eyes, love," Maria says in a soothing voice. "Look at the end of the bed. I've compiled my favorites. We'll see how far we get into them before we can't resist."

Mallory opens her eyes to see a pile of lingerie. All the rest of the pieces have been shoved off, so the pile is properly isolated. She rises and moves past Maria, fighting every urge to grab the woman and instigate a kiss.

Maria hands her the one she had been dragging across her skin. "Start with this one."

Mallory takes the black lace and holds it up. It is a onesie of very soft lace with a deep V for the cleavage. "This might be the softest lace I've ever felt. It's not at all scratchy."

Maria nods. "Yes, I have a few of their pieces as well. Whoever invented the scratchy lace for lingerie should be shot."

Mallory chuckles. "I know, right? Once I wore a lace thong to a football game, and the lace hurt so bad that within ten minutes of arriving, I wanted to murder. So I rushed to the bathroom and removed it. I tossed it in the garbage!" She laughs, remembering how irate she was.

"This one will feel luxurious against your skin. Let me see it on you, please." Maria has polished the act of being patient, and Mallory rages, feeling anything but. Her smooth skin shines in the soft lighting, and her eyes spark with lust. She holds an air of dominance that coddles Mallory, and she finds it interesting how Maria's form of dominance is almost gentle, but no less commanding than Sam's. It makes sense, though, because the feeling she gets mirrors what kissing Maria feels like.

Mallory begins to undress for Maria's eager eyes. The woman relaxes back against the loveseat and spreads her legs, resting her right hand on her thigh with her thumb resting near her mound. She'd love it if Maria stroked her clit as she watched her dress and undress. Mallory can't keep her eyes off Maria's hand as she removes her clothes in a slow, seductive reveal. She shimmies her hips as she undresses, then reveals her top half, quickly removing her bra.

"Oh, yes," Maria says, clearly appreciating the view. "You're so beautiful, honey. A vision of beauty and a goddess of sex. I could look at you all day." Maria's hand creeps closer to her pussy.

Mallory smiles and spins for Maria so she can see her bare bottom.

"I love your ass too, wow. You're just spectacular." Maria's fingers meander up her skirt, and as she wiggles, her skirt hikes further up her thighs.

Mallory watches intently as Maria reaches inside her panties and begins to move her hand rhythmically. She curls her body so she can step into the lace bodysuit. Her breasts hang down, her nipples taut to points, with her areolas puckered.

"You really have the best nipples I've seen. I'm not lying." Maria slowly moves her fingers across her pussy beneath the fabric of her panties.

"Thank you," Mallory coos, loving the praise. She desperately wishes Maria would move the panties so she could see Maria's glistening pink pussy.

She pulls the lace up and over her breasts, placing the straps on her shoulders. She struts around the room in front of Maria, sashaying her hips and making quick pivots to change direction, much like a model on a runway. She poses by leaning forward to create a deep line of cleavage, then she straightens up, glancing at her own erect nipples beneath the sheer lace.

Maria catcalls softly to show her appreciation. "Fucking gorgeous, honey. You're making me so hot."

Mallory turns her back to Maria and pulls the straps down off her shoulders. She bends over and bares her ass, then lets go of the fabric so it falls down her legs. It pools at her ankles, and she steps out.

"Fuck," Maria whispers, her voice strained. "Keep going. Do that white one next."

Mallory plucks it off the bed and wiggles it in the air as she gives Maria a seductive look. "With great pleasure." She dons the lingerie and twirls for Maria.

"Edging myself," Maria says breathlessly. "Now the red one."

Mallory loves how turned on Maria looks. Her own breathing has ramped up and her clit is ready for Maria's touch. She's aching for something more, but she also loves submitting to Maria's leadership.

"Whew, fuck you are so sexy." She pulls her hand away, and the panties snap back into place, fully covering her.

"Damn," Mallory says under her breath.

"That's it, work it up your legs, baby, yeah, just like that. Beautiful."

Mallory pulls the piece over her hips and then secures it over her breasts.

"I can't stand it anymore," she slurs, then rises to stand. "I need you."

She strides toward Mallory. Her heart pitter-patters, then quickly charges into thunder as Maria lays her hands on her covered breasts.

Maria cups and strokes her body, and she sways and curls herself in a dance to Maria's soft groping.

Maria's hands continue to roam her body, then as she holds Mallory's ass, she pulls her close so their bodies are fully touching, breasts smashed together.

They fall into a tight embrace, and their mouths seek each other. They kiss deeply, their tongues gently, but hungrily exploring each other's mouths.

"I can't wait to make you come in this outfit," Maria says as she firmly squeezes Mallory's ass cheeks.

She nuzzles her face into Mallory's tits, then drags her tongue across the tented fabric over her hard nips. She takes a covered nipple in her mouth and sucks it. Then she grasps the fabric and pulls it down so Mallory's nipple springs free. Maria attacks her nipple and sucks as she squeezes and caresses her body. Maria does the same with her other breast, then plants open-mouthed kisses all along her chest, up her neck, and across her chin.

Mallory moans softly and drops her head back as Maria tastes her flesh.

Maria steps back and removes her clothes, keeping eye contact with Mallory as she does. "Keep yours on. I want to watch it move across your flesh when I make you come."

Mallory bites her lower lip and nods. "Yes, ma'am."

Maria presses her naked body to Mallory and they kiss again, both their hands entwined in each other's hair, gripping each other's scalps. They kiss deeply, both moaning as they alternate kissing with suckling each other's necks.

Maria scoops up Mallory and carries her to the bed. She lowers Mallory onto the big mound of lingerie.

She squirms in the luxury of all the fabrics, all soft, all different colors. It's like a sea of sexual promises.

The women smile at each other.

Maria presses the fabric up Mallory's thighs to bare her mound, then presses her thighs apart. She tickles her fingers along her slit, saving her clit for later.

"Please," Mallory begs, her eyes begging just as hard as her plea.

"Not yet," Maria scolds. "I want more evidence of your submission before I move on."

Mallory writhes. All she wants is for Maria to play with her clit. She suppresses her words until she can't anymore. "Please," she says again.

"Make no mistake, I'm making you come." Maria slowly inserts her two fingers into Mallory's wet hole, then drags her fingers to spread her wetness all along her labia. She dabs her fingers all over as Mallory allows the woman to guide her arousal slowly higher.

When Maria finally touches her clit, Mallory jolts in response.

Maria laughs softly. "Ah, you're very sensitive and wanton now. Just where I want you."

She rubs Mallory's clit harder, then presses two fingers inside her. She rides her hole and clit rapidly, then withdraws.

Mallory opens her eyes and whimpers as she glances down her body. Her surprise falls into a smile as Maria settles between her thighs. Maria continues to pump her fingers in and clamps her mouth around Mallory's clit.

Mallory bucks from the suction, and her sounds of pleasure easily exude from her open mouth. She twists and wiggles as Maria eats her out aggressively.

Maria comes off her clit. "I want you to come when you're at that point after you can't stand it anymore, but you must count to ten at that point before you do."

Mallory nods. "Yes," she whispers. "I will."

"Good girl," Maria says.

She takes Mallory's clit head into her mouth again and sucks hard, her full force causing Mallory to twist. She grasps the sheets and pulls them taut as Maria also fingers her G-spot.

Mallory screams as she slams into her peak. She can barely hold off climaxing as Maria works her over. She counts out loud to ten because it seems to help her not lose grip on not coming. "Eight, nine, ten." Her voice is strained, and as she falls silent, she releases control.

Her clit begins to clench, sending wavs of sensation out her core to the rest of her body. She thrashes with undulations traveling her torso, then her back arches in a visceral move that she can't control as the full breadth of her climax claims her. She moans and whimpers, cries out, then falls silent as the full orgasm shakes her body.

Maria doesn't let up, and she launches into a second peak. She tries to push Maria off because the sensation is too much, but Maria has a tight grip on her thigh, so she's pinned in place. The sexual bliss is both agony and ecstasy as she comes again.

Maria falls off her pussy than laps at her slit, slurping and making mouth smacks.

Maria rises. Mallory opens her eyes. Maria's eyes are ablaze with passion as she situates herself placing her pussy to match up with hers.

Mallory feels woozy from coming so hard, but her excitement at the idea of Maria being so turned on launches her into action. She quickly responds with aligning herself along Maria in the scissoring position, each with their legs bent so their pussies meet.

Maria begins to rub her pussy against Mallory's and the women fall into a rhythm as they gyrate their hips tribbing.

Maria's head falls back as her body curls, so Mallory rubs her harder. Maria shudders as her climax overtakes her.

Watching Maria climax is so hot and sexy that Mallory reaches her peak too.

At their near-simultaneous climax, both women's sounds are a beautiful song.

Both women lay back. Mallory feels cum drunk and it's so luxurious, she absolutely loves the feeling.

Mallory notices movement in the room, and she glances toward it sighing with a giggle when she sees Sam holding up his phone, videoing them. "Oh, wow! How long have you been there?"

Derek and Max are behind him with giant grins.

"Wow, ladies, that was absolutely hot as fuck and I got it all on video."

Mallory falls into easy laughter as she meets Maria's glance. "Did you know?" Mallory asks.

"I saw him before I scooped you up and motioned him in."

Sam stops filming. "And we have our first video of the night. Totally epic. That was so natural and perfect." He shakes his head with a smile on his face. "That was just beautiful. I couldn't have directed a better scene. It was so authentic."

"Well, I loved it, and I'm ecstatic you captured it." She didn't feel violated at all; she felt exalted. It was a celebration of mutual sexual pleasure. "And it's only the first one. Let the celebrations of fucking begin."

She grins at all three men, then at Maria, her heart beaming as much as her smile.

Chapter 15

M allory takes the next piece of lingerie from Maria. She smiles at her choice. It's a strapped bodice outfit with a sunray pattern that will gather near her belly button, then spread up her chest like the spokes of a wheel. It will leave her breasts bare and her pussy too. She smiles at Maria, who smiles back.

"Nice one," she coos, smoothing the straps with her fingers.

Maria caresses Mallory's bare flesh with a knowing twinkle in her eye. "You'll look irresistible in that. You're going to kill it."

Mallory notices movement across the room. It's Max. He moves near the ottoman where Derek and Sam are talking. She really wants a scene with all three men, but she doesn't think Derek will go for it. She isn't entirely sure Max would either. The thing is, an age gap MMFM sounds extra fun and spicy in her mind. She licks her lips as she imagines it. She'll have to settle for separate scenes with them, she supposes. Of course, Derek and Sam with her is a for sure thing. Max and Sam would clash, though, both being dominants, and that doesn't even touch how foreign being super up close with two men having sex is for Max. He always says it doesn't bother him, but he never seeks to watch it or participate in such scenes in the lifestyle club. It's more like he's just tolerant of being around it, which seems more accurate than anything else, honestly. Maybe he'd do it, though.

Mallory frowns. She honestly hasn't noticed Max having sex at the parties with anyone else but her since they started their relationship. She gets the impression that his devotion to only her is something very new for him. This is a swingers' club, but in reality, he's no longer swinging. Worry grips her. He needs to fuck others too. She is, and she intends to keep doing so.

She watches Max talk to the others as Maria begins to fuss over the scene's aesthetic by moving pillows, lighting a candle, and arranging lighting on all sides of the planned area for filming. Mallory stares at the strappy outfit in her hands. She has hopes for a future with Max in it, but with Derek's increasing jealousy, this seems less likely. If Derek notices Max isn't having sex with anyone else, his hackles will be raised even more.

"This will be perfect here for positioning," Maria states as she places a blue felt wedge pillow on the couch. "Sam adores this cushion, as do I."

"It's the perfect shape," Mallory agrees as she dismisses her worries with a smile. Her nerves are starting to flare up. But it's not that she's anxious, it's also more of an excitement to be embarking on this new venture. The thought of lots of people watching her have sex is extremely arousing. "Doggy, the reverse, beneath my back to make my tits pop. So many possibilities with that, my mind is reeling."

Maria picks up a pillow and fluffs it. "Never underestimate the good grinding action of a simple pillow. It was honestly my first sex toy." She grimaces, then laughs. "It's got to be firm, though. No squishy-squishy."

Mallory releases a short laugh. "Oh, wow. I never thought of that. A pillow was mine too, then, other than my hand."

"In my case, it was a response to being shamed for touching myself. My mother," she says, rolling her eyes. "Growing up with sexual negativity shoved down my throat was a sucky way to mature into a young woman. Took me years to overcome it." She sheds the disdain from her face and smirks. Her grin grows big. "But look at me now."

Mallory scoffs. "Oh, you've completely overcome it, I'd say. Running a sex club out of your home with your swinging Dom more than qualifies."

"And basically, I've erased it. Though the memories haunt me." She grimaces.

"I didn't have that kind of crap to deal with growing up," Mallory muses as she starts to step into the straps.

The men saunter over.

Hello, ladies. We have a plan. Max is going to go first, then Derek and I, while Maria films. That work?" Sam asks with a lusty leer. "My cock is already ready. My dear Mallory, you look scrumptious, baby doll." His gaze drifts up and down Mallory's body as she fits all the straps in place.

Once she's fully into the straps, she shifts her body back and forth slightly, enjoying his horny expression. "Yes, and I can't wait." Her insides flutter as Max approaches. "Hi, Max. How are you?" She extends her arms for a hug.

He looks suave in his suit. "I'm wonderful, sweetheart. I love this on you." He fingers the straps and tugs them away from her body. "Useful," he says with a daring look. "I can't wait to try this out."

"Well, you picked it, and you did an amazing job shopping for it all. I seriously cannot believe you sent me so many."

"I had fun. I kept imagining you in them, and I couldn't stop hitting 'buy now.'" He laughs, his eyes are bright and happy. "Let's just say there are a lot of stores very happy with me at the moment."

"Yeah, I can understand why! I think it will take me a few years to wear them all." She glances at the box and can't keep the delight off her face.

He pulls her tighter into an embrace and bends his head down for a kiss. "I think we can manage to speed that up." He kisses her lips in a peck. "If we really try."

His cock is a full rod against her, and she raises her eyebrow as she allows her lust to show on her face. "Well, you are ready, now aren't you?"

"I was ready a long time ago," he says with a deep chuckle. "When I watched you and Maria. That was very, very hot, by the way. I thoroughly enjoyed it."

She laughs with glee. "As did I, clearly." Derek and Sam are looking at Sam's phone while discussing video app features.

"I think we may be shopping for a better video camera soon," Sam says, nodding.

Max pulls her head close enough again for another kiss. While staring into her eyes, he presses his open, hungry mouth to hers. They fall into a deep kiss easily, their mouth smacking filling the air. Max's hands begin to roam her body, and she grasps his biceps, squeezing them, groping him right back.

"Mmmm," she moans as she gives him a saucy look.

He grips the straps across her shoulder blades with both hands and tugs her body back and forth, swaying them both.

"Mmmmm, so good to taste you." Max kisses along her cheek, then trails kisses down her jawline and her neck.

She melts into his arms, mewling, allowing his mouth and touch to arouse her. She opens her eyes and glances around as Max kisses her chest with clear intention of making his way to her nipples.

She gasps in surprise.

Sam is already taking a video.

She's loving how he just starts filming to capture the authentic moments. She really values real situation porn, with amateur always being her fave go-to. Derek is the same way. They both chose it as their top choice over corny, scripted videos.

With Max in his formal suit and her dressed in scantily thin straps, Daddy Dom is her take on this scene. It's how she and Max naturally are anyhow, so why not play off reality? She adores such play, the man in a suit, and a naked woman. The suggestion of dominance and submission is often her go-to fantasy, so she knows many other women are the same. A commanding hungry man who showers her with gifts, compliments, sex and orgasms, yummy food, that's her dream. Someone who lifts her up, supports her, and loves to make her come on repeat, then actually desires to take care of her. Where Derek does all that too, Mallory has to admit, Max has him beat. Perhaps it's just his age and experience, but she finds him incredibly attractive. This is something she cannot deny, and it sends her brain into a confusing spiral, especially when she catches glimpses of Derek. She needs to focus on the now and stop her trek down those thoughts.

She glances at Derek for a lingering pause. He's watching them intently, but without a sour expression.

She releases a sigh of relief, then refocuses her gaze on Max. "A giant box of lingerie is certainly an enticing gift, Daddy," she coos.

"You're worth it and way more, my princess." He devours her right nipple, and she drops her head back with a decadent moan.

Derek and Maria both look ready to dive into the fun, which she loves, but she's hoping to have a Max-only scene. She's all on board with the Daddy Dom vibes. It would have been a good idea for them to talk about all this before starting to film, but she's all good going with the flow, too. She hopes it will give the watchers a sense of reality, even if they don't plan it out to the T anyway. The knowledge that people will be watching this someday makes her even hotter as Max travels the front of her torso with his open mouth.

He's suckling her flesh, making her titties into pointed peaks.

His mouth moves, arousing her further. She leans back and allows herself to land on the couch.

Max dives in to kiss her belly while still cradling her lower half against him.

She's not going to overthink any of this, though she's watched a few porn star interviews where they found it hard to watch themselves afterward. This will all be an experiment until she finds her groove. The women were sometimes shocked about the reality of how they looked, and it took away from their pleasure as they obsessed about that. She doesn't want that. She wants to enjoy it. She desires to feel it all come about naturally, and let the reality of the scene be her top focus so she can simply react. She could always edit parts out anyway, so enjoyment has to be her top priority. That will surely give them the video nuggets of viral gold, too.

She moans as Max grasps the straps to position her. She allows him to place her where he wants. His gruff tugging of her body with the straps, tweaks her submissive bone hard. "I'm your fuck doll, Daddy. Make me be the way you want me." She moans. "Fuck me, Daddy. Fuck me good."

Max growls as he snatches the little wedge pillow and works it beneath her upper back. With her tits the top point, Max falls between her legs. He nestles her thighs open with his face, his scruff lightly scratching her sensitive inner thigh.

Max isn't a hard or sadistic Dom, so his going down on her in his suit while taking control of her body gets her heart pumping. He's the perfect mix to satiate her kinks, and denying it won't do anything but intensify it for her.

"Pimp this pussy to your will, Daddy. Make this little bitch pay her dues." He already has command of her, but her saying it, permitting him, highlights her willingness to give that power to him. She smirks. She can't wait to edit this video. She's thinking with a director's brain even though she's been trying not to. Editing is another skill she will need to learn if she wants to be a content creator. However, Derek seems to enjoy the task of editing as part of the team. And she'd happily give it to him. Her patience for technical stuff is a bit thin.

Max's mouth commands her attention. He's suctioned firmly to her clit, which snaps her back to falling into the lush ecstasy of his touches. Max grips her thighs and sucks her bits with his strong mouth. Bless him for forcing her to live this experience more in the moment.

She rolls her body in response to him eating her out, toying with the straps as she writhes in pleasure. She twists her head back and forth, thankful she's sinking easily into the throes of passion. All she's got on her mind is Max and the fabulous pleasure he's giving her.

She chuckles inside as she glances at him. She's amused that he hasn't even loosened his tie as she charges closer to her climax.

He releases his suction and murmurs into her pussy, "Come for me when you want, baby. I need you to come for me." He fastens his mouth on her quickly, and her body torques in response.

She moans as his slurping sounds escalate. When she opens her eyes for a split second as her eyelids flutter, she sees Sam has taken hold of the phone tripod and is getting a closeup shot of Max's mouth on her pussy. He's literally inches from their union.

She launches into her peak, slamming into her blissful orgasmic high with a new rage. Thoughts of men and women getting off to this scene send her flying, and she comes so hard her body bounces, her torso curls, and she cries out as more of her nerves fire. She falls silent as the contractions strengthen, delectably overwhelming her into blind ecstasy.

She pushes on Max's head as the sensitivity skyrockets, and she is hurdled into another peak, and then another. She shrieks in desperation, even though she really adores the powerful sensations. She loves the orgasmic plateaus with multiple peaks. Max is getting so good at routinely helping her get there. A multi-peaked orgasm, and Sam was expertly getting it on video. How perfect. She's so excited and pleased. This is going to be so amazing!

With her clit throbbing, Max hastily grabs her straps and flips her over on her belly like she's a rag doll. She's a wet noodle, cum drunk from riding her multi-peaked highs. She gasps as Max aggressively manhandles her to reposition her on the wedge pillow, making her ass pop up higher. He's rarely this rough, but his horny urgency is a huge turn-on.

"Yes, Daddy, fuck me from behind. Make me your obedient hole like never before."

He unzips his pants and grunts. "Oh, you're my hole, babe. My hole to fuck." He quickly lines up his cock brushing it along her throbbing, wet lips. He penetrates her quickly and begins to ride her with more aggression than usual. "Take my cock. Take it deep. Take your Daddy's thick cock," he commands while increasing his slamming into her.

She lets him use her, deeply loving the fact that he is. She doesn't even reach for her clit but savors his unrestrained using of her.

His round protruding belly smacks her bottom on repeat as he chases his own climax like a rabid beast, grunting and growling. After about two minutes of bold thrusting, he pulls himself out, and his sounds of release spill.

His orations are satiating, and she grins with her face flush against the couch cushion. His cum shoots onto her with his exerted groan. He collapses on top of her, resting himself along her back; his panting is rapid and labored.

She smiles loving that he got his, and that her flesh will smell like his cum.

His mouth is near her ear as he whispers, "I could take you to a cabin in the mountains and pleasure you every day like this." His voice is raspy, soft, and subdued. "I'd take care of you, all your needs, wants, and desires. Anything you want and everything you want, for the rest of your days. And I'd help you make all the videos you want. I'd fully support your career, however you want to do it."

Mallory's eyes widen at his proclamation. She's shocked he's said this in front of everyone and on video. But she wonders, did he say it to put on a show for the audience? Or did he say it because he means it?

"Cut," Sam announces. "Very good show! You two nailed it! This will be so hot. I can't wait to watch it back."

Max rises off Mallory, then extends his hand to help her stand up.

Derek looks pleased. She wonders if he heard Max's words, but he looks so calm and not perturbed at all. He must not have heard, or if he did, he must have thought it was part of the show.

"Have fun?" Max asks casually, as if he didn't just offer to have her run away with him.

She scans him. He seems very happy, but he just came, so, of course, he's happy.

"That was a really hot scene," Maria exclaims, fanning herself. "Whew! I might need to go find a toy."

Derek raises his hands and cocks his head. "Here I am. It's my pleasure to be your toy."

Mallory hasn't seen Derek and Maria together yet, and she wants to watch.

"Really? You'd be in?" Maria asks with interest in her tone.

"Very." Derek looks quite randy. "Let's go."

Maria looks back at Mallory as Derek snatches her hand in his. "What about the shoot?"

"Go, enjoy, Maria. I'll get a snack. Derek's good to go for multiple rounds, so don't worry about that!" she says with a snicker.

"I'll be the bartender, meet me at the bar," Sam instructs.

Max puts his deflated cock back in his pants and pulls Mallory close. He kisses her forehead. "Thank you. And thank you for including me. I really enjoyed that."

"Oh, I did too, Max. I most certainly did," she says, smiling up at him as he cuddles her close in a bear hug.

"Really sexy having these straps to grab onto. I liked that a lot."

She releases a deep sigh. "Ah, that was so good. I agree. I came hard, with multiple."

"Yep, I could tell," he says as he presses his forehead to hers. "It wasn't just for the audience, baby. I mean it."

She freezes and stares up at him, a million questions burst inside her head like a handful of balloons cut loose. She looks into his eyes and sees the love there.

"Think about it," he says, then releases her,

More confused than ever, she follows him to the bar, where Sam is ready to fix them some drinks.

Chapter 16

Mallory turns the car onto Buttermint Way, the road Max had instructed her to take to get to his new cabin. Her brain spins, running over all the crazy things that had happened. She still couldn't believe she'd been fired. They used some lame excuse for a screwup, and they gave her the boot. She'd walked out of the office in utter shock, escorted to empty her locker, then led to the door. She hadn't even been given the common courtesy of telling her coworkers goodbye. She also suspected that all her coworkers were likely told she had just quit without notice. There's no way management would tell the truth and make themselves look bad. No matter. The word would get out. She'd shared her story with Sara last night over drinks, and Sara is a blabbermouth. She'll tell everyone of the injustice.

She knows exactly why they fired her. It's because she'd started doing adult content on the side, and she'd made a huge splash. Her new endeavor has been basically an overnight success story. The writing was all over their faces when they let her go. They'd clearly gotten wind of her success, or someone ratted her out. The management couldn't just let her be herself, in her own time. When had her leisure time become any of their business? It was ludicrous. Doing the videos and nude pictures in no way impacted how she did her job. In fact, she'd been a top employee for years. However, that didn't matter once they discovered what she had done in her private life. And the key words here, "in her private life," should have kept her safe in her job. All the support they'd boasted about for years was a total fallacy. If they found out something they didn't like, they fired the person. It made her think of when they fired Marty. It hadn't made sense last year why they'd let such a hard worker go. But now it all made sense to her. They'd likely found out that Marty is gay and then they axed him. Free country my ass!

She shakes her head, trying to release some of the frustration. She doesn't want to think about any of it. The only thing that is keeping her sane is that she now earns more money creating content than she did in her previous job. That's jarring. Money suddenly doesn't matter as much, which also impacts her relationships. Her heart sinks as she recalls the little white lies she's told. But they are a necessary evil until she figures out what she's going to do.

Derek had been so understanding, too. Of course, he was. He's that guy, even though he'd lapsed into jealousy, it was just a blip, and she can let it go. He seems over it, completely. Especially when he was okay with her going to the cabin with Max, he said he understood all the stresses she'd been dealing with in the last week, and he encouraged her to take some time away. She doesn't like not sharing everything with him, but if he knew what Max had whispered in her ear, would his jealousy have flared up again? With all the stress, she hadn't wanted to find out. So, what if it just looks like a little vacation? She honestly isn't sure if that's what this is or not, herself. She needs some time to think.

Both Derek and Max support her desire to create content. Both men want to help her do it, record it, edit it, and be an integral part of it. Previously, she needed Max's money to back her, but now she has her own, and she's making more daily, without even lifting a finger; her content is selling like hotcakes. She's flabbergasted. She can buy gas without trying to make it one more day on fumes, she can buy a new pair of jeans without having to cut back on the food she eats, and she can even think about saving some money after bills.

She's floored. She never in a million years expected she could more than support herself; she can support a partner, too.

Having sudden mountains of cash has made her a profitable business owner, just doing what she wants to do. It's unreal!

She glances in her rearview mirror, and it's still a vacant road. Max has chosen a cabin way off the beaten path. She passes by gate after gate. This is how the rich live, gated driveways with secret mansions hidden by massive trees. Every now and then, she catches a glimpse through the trees of the houses. Even with the tiniest hint, she can tell these houses are more castles than mere dwellings.

She drives for another five minutes and sees on the app that she's almost there. As she spots it, she pulls her car over and stops at the closed gate. She spots a video camera and rolls down her window to wave at it.

"Hi, I'm here," she says cheerfully.

The gate opens, and she drives in. As she rounds the corner, the full structure comes into view. She hits the brakes as she stares at it in absolute awe. The cabin is not a cabin at all, but a stunning three-floor mansion. Either Max has come into more money, or she has no idea how wealthy he really is, because this place looks as if it belongs to a movie about the super-rich.

She slowly begins to drive down the long private road as the full realization sinks in. Max has been downplaying his worth. This isn't just plain wealthy, this is millionaire wealthy. Billionaire? Who knows?

She shakes her head, trying to wrap her head around everything she's done with Max and has it all make sense. He always had money, that was never a question, but there's money, then there's money. And if he is this wealthy, it seems he has been keeping it hidden. But then again, it's not as if he owes her an explanation about his bank accounts. He has always been overly generous.

She parks her car in the space on the far right, which basically could be called a small parking lot. The grounds are natural mountain forest vegetation with big pine trees and other leafy giants. The mountain peaks in the distance remind her why they are often called majestic.

"Whew!" she exclaims as she gazes around. She's basically stepped into a painting.

Max appears out of the front door. He's smiling and rushing toward her. "You found it." His arms are raised. "I'm so happy to see you."

"Hi, Max," she says softly as he takes her into his arms.

He kisses the top of her head and caresses her hair. "I've missed you."

As Mallory presses her full body to Max, his erection pokes her belly. "I can tell." She giggles as she gazes into his eyes. "And I've missed you."

"I have so much to show you. I've been busy preparing for your arrival."

She cocks her head wondering what the heck that means. He's only known she's been coming for a few days. "Oh, yeah?"

"Yes," he says, leaning back. His grin grows. "I can't wait to show you. Come in."

"When you said a 'cabin,' this isn't exactly what I pictured."

His eyes twinkle as he chuckles. "Yeah, it's a bit big. I know. But I wanted to invest in real estate, so why not something like this?"

Mallory shakes her head. "Max, how many *homes* do you own?"

He snickers. "Well, it depends on how you classify them."

"Them?"

He laughs casually as he places his hand on her back. "Five."

"Five? Holy shit, Max! That's insane!" She and Derek own one small house, and they have barely been able to afford it, that is, until now, with her new job. She smiles as she shakes her head, her eyes wide. "You've been holding out on me."

"It's nothing. It's really not a big deal." He smiles widely at her. "Let me help grab your stuff."

He looks so happy, and it warms her heart.

She pops the trunk, and he reaches in.

He stares into the trunk. "I'm so happy you came, but I expected you to have more with you."

She cringes. An uncomfortable smirk takes hold of her face. She tries to erase it quickly, but it's too late.

"You told Derek, right?" He freezes as he eyes her up, his expression losing its recent zest.

"Max..." She trails off, the pit of her stomach clenching.

"No matter, honey. It will all work out." He smiles at her as he sets the suitcases down. "Come, let's go in. I can't wait to show you what I've been working on for you."

She collects more bags from the back seat. She needs to calm the worry train and just live in the moment, because she can't fathom how the future will unfold.

"How are sales going?" Max asks as he leads her through the front door.

"Really, really good. I'm blown away, to be honest. I couldn't have dared to expect this."

"I'm so proud of you. Starting your own business isn't easy."

She scoffs. "I don't think most businesses do this well this quickly." She gazes around the mansion foyer. It's very plush and perfect. "I imagine you must have a cleaning crew with a place like this."

He nods. "Yes, when I'm here, they come once a day, but when I'm away, it's like once a week."

She takes in the elaborate paintings on the walls, which, since she can see the brushstrokes and occasional thick areas of paint, are clearly originals. Most of them are nature scenes, and all of them have mountains. "This place is stunning."

"Thank you. It's relatively new, as I mentioned over the phone. But I'm really happy with it. I love the views out the back. Wait until you see." He leads her deeper inside and then turns down a hallway, leaving her suitcase at the start of it. "Come this way for my surprise."

"Does it involve me screaming your name?" she asks coyly with a sly grin. "Because those are the best surprises."

He laughs. "Yes, it will lead to that, eventually." He grabs her hand and smiles down at her. "You make me so happy, Mallory. I think you're going to like what I have to show you."

They walk holding hands down the hallway. Mallory gazes upon more artwork on the walls, which are mostly beautiful women in gardens.

"All this artwork is like...wow!" She stares at the one with a woman on the beach, her body in a bikini, and her skin seeming to glow. "Just beautiful."

"I hired an interior designer. I can't take credit." He smirks as he stops at a closed door. "Welcome to your new studio." He presses the door open wide.

Mallory peers inside, her interest piqued. She spies sex furniture, sex toys, a big king-sized bed, lighting, and those umbrellas photographers have, plus a video camera on a tripod. On the far end of the room in the corner, she spots a sex swing hanging from the ceiling, then a stockade next to that, a massage table, and what looks like a chair at the dentist. There's a spanking bench in the other corner and paddles and whips on the wall. The shelf next to it has so many different colored dildos that it rivals a big box of crayons.

"Holy fucking shit, Max! This is incredible!" She drops her jaw and is unable to close her mouth as she stares at all the sexual paraphernalia. "I'm literally speechless."

"You can shoot any scenes here you want. I'll hire a videographer and a video editor. Any porn stars can come and shoot with you. I won't restrict you at all. I just want to support you. Help you realize your dream. Help you make the best content you can." He holds her face in his hands and peers into her eyes. "I'll do anything you want. We can still swing as much as you desire, too."

Her heart fills with a mix of hope, excitement, and dread, all at once. He's making her decision even harder. "But..."

He shakes his head. "There's no but."

It's unspoken, but she knows exactly what he wants. She's not going to say it.

He gropes her back and crawls his fingers down to her ass. He gives her buttocks a hefty squeeze, lifting her body off the floor. "Now, about that screaming my name business."

She smiles as her seductive siren uncoils from its slumber. "Shooting will be fun, but so will using all of these things with you." She wishes Derek were there too; he'd love this room. "You know what a great place this mansion would be for one of the parties? It would be ideal."

He nods as he leans his head down to hers. "Yeah, that's what went through my mind as I toured it. We can do that; be the host for a party if you'd like. I'll give you anything your heart desires, Mallory. I want you to know that. Anything." He presses his lips to hers.

But you have to leave Derek...

However, Max didn't say that. The problem is that the unsaid words sit in her throat, choking her. She walls off her worry and refocuses her thoughts back to the moment. If she's to move on, she must do this, and those impossible decisions don't belong in this moment.

She caresses his arms as she presses her pelvis to his, feeling his hard-on with her belly. "You're so generous with me, you blow my mind."

"I'd like to blow your clit head. Let's have you lie down. Dentist chair? Bed? Couch?"

"I want you to use me, Max." She purrs as she drags her finger along his jawline. This is a fantasy she's harbored, especially with how generous Max always is with her. "Use me. I beg you." Max using her will fully command her brain, free her from this worry that has settled upon her since losing her job and deciding to come to Max's place.

"Honey, I'd love to pleasure you." He looks confused, his eyes full of concern.

"Use me, Daddy. Take me. Let that sexual masculine energy reign." She runs her hand down his chest, not stopping as she coasts down his covered erection. "Shove that thing in me, Daddy. Fuck me like the cheapest whore on the planet. Then leave me alone in a crumpled heap."

He furrows his brows as a smirk settles across his face. "Ah, I see your game. I can play along."

"No, no playing. Just use me like a tissue for your cum. Fuck me, do what you want without regard for my pleasure." Her clit twitches as her desire for the kink blossoms. "This is only hot with you and me. Fuck this hole, this meaty tunnel right here, until you shoot your jizz up my cunt." She plays with her slit through the fabric, aggressively mashing her labia lips and poking at her opening.

His eyes rage with male dominance.

She quakes as she melts into his intentional gaze.

An evil smile creeps across his face, making him look ravenous.

"Dig deep and live that rage, Daddy. Fuck your pussy like I'm a lump of plastic." Her clit lurches and her pussy lips flare with the desire to be rage fucked. It needs to be said. "Ravage me. Rage fuck me. I'm your fuck doll. Do what you want." She makes her body go slack and drops her gaze to the floor.

Max runs a hand through the gray parts of his hair above his ears, which have grown larger over the past few weeks. It only turns her on more. He grunts as he wraps his hand into her hair and pulls her tight to him. "I'll use you, like a fuck doll should be used."

Mallory realizes she's charting new ground, but they'd talked about similar things, and she has her safe word. She wouldn't advise this leap to others, no matter how small, but with Max, they've said enough. She falls mute and demure, hoping he will take advantage and live out a fantasy he perhaps never has.

He claims her mouth in a kiss. His tongue intrudes into her rough and fast, sliding along her tongue. She keeps herself relaxed as he tongue fucks her mouth. He breaks the kiss and tugs her along with the stronghold he has on her locks.

"Your hole is going to make me come. Going to fuck you raw. Doggy. Beast-like. Pounding into your ass like I'm spanking you with my body." He roughly pulls her to the spanking bench. He reaches for the hem of her dress and lifts it off her body in one tug. He searches for something on the shelf of the bench. He unsheathes a knife.

Mallory gasps, but remains still. Her heart responds with quickening beats, and her breathing becomes more labored. A little mewl escapes, but she resists the urge to move.

Max grasps her bra and slides the knife beneath the strap. He lifts it up, cutting the elastic. Then he moves over to cut the other one, and then yanks down the bra to expose her breasts.

He grins and raises an eyebrow, his beast mode slipping for a second as amusement fills his eyes. He corrects it right away, then cuts the remainder of the bra from her body. Then he grabs the thong at her hip and cuts then repeats it on the other side. He plucks the fabric from her labia and pushes it so that it falls to the floor.

"Bend over, present yourself to me," he demands without even a hint of asking. "Your hole is mine. You're not coming, and if you do come, I'm spanking you over this bench until your ass is red." He grins, deep evil lurking across his face. "Do it, bitch. Give me your ass, now."

Mallory quakes, sinking into the humiliation like it's a hot bath. "Yes, Daddy."

"I'm not your Daddy, I'm your Master. Now bend over and tip your ass up. Head down." He spins her roughly and presses on her middle back with a hard shove. "Be a good cocksleeve and shut the fuck up. Give me that butt."

Hearing his talk this way rages her lust, and she obeys without hesitation, her arousal erupting. She's not so sure she won't be able to stop her climax. She keeps her lips closed as Max reclaims her hair in a wraparound twist. He presses her head lower than her hips and promptly lays a sharp slap to her right ass cheek.

She squeals, the harsh slap hurting more than she expected. She squirms slightly as she hears him unzip his pants.

He slaps her again, and she flinches.

Fuck.

The cold leather of the bench's cushion is smooth on her cheek. She licks her lip, tasting the cherry of the lip balm, and shivers as Max humps her butt.

"Just like this, but with my fat cock up your cunt sleeve." His voice is gruff and scary. "You exist for my dick."

She instantly wishes they were filming, wondering if they could somehow rig it so that at the press of a button, they could capture authentic encounters like this that they fall into spontaneously. It would make such fabulous content. She smirks, realizing her brain won't shut off from business mode these days, even in a scene like this.

He pulls his fist tighter in her hair, and his taut grip hurts her scalp. She holds in the desire to say "ow" because she fears it will make him stop. Instead, she remains still like a lump of rubber as he rams himself into her backside.

He presses the head of his cockhead at her pussy lips. "Going to fuck you hard. Fuck you red and raw like a proper toy." He presses himself into her, shoving his cock in hard with several thrusts bottoming out in her cavity.

She gasps and grunts as he brutally takes what he wants. He hits her so hard her feet leave the floor with his powerful thrusts.

Then he pulls out of her and backs away. He rummages around for something, making an excessive amount of rustling noises. Then he returns and grabs her wrists. He leans down on her back, his hard-on a hard bat between their bodies. He whispers in her ear, "This is the only way I'll ever trap you. You understand me? You are free." He secures the straps around her wrists and clasps them together. He presses her bound wrists to her back and penetrates her again.

He grunts as he pounds himself into her, taking time to slap her butt now and then as he fucks her hard.

She whimpers as he tightens his hold on her hair again, then, grunting loudly, he slams into her with a barrage that rocks her body into violent jerks.

Her arousal is peaking, and she's about to lose control and come. But since she's getting no clitoral stimulation, she thinks she can hold off and last without a climax, but only because he's so close.

He growls and yanks her head back by her hair while pelting her bottom with his pelvis. His cock slides in and out of her making sloshy wet sounds, and that combined with the skin smacks makes her inch a bit closer to her peak.

"Fuck," she whispers, hoping it's quiet enough for him to not notice with how busy he is fucking her.

He groans like he's in pain, and then she feels increased wetness. He keeps pumping himself into her as his sounds calm down.

"Oh, my God," he mutters as he slows his pumping. "I came so hard. I can't even explain how hard."

Her arousal settles down. She made it without climaxing, but part of her wishes she hadn't, just to see what he would have done.

He slides his softening cock out of her and then grips both her hips. He pulls her down and presses her to the floor. Then he walks out of the room.

Mallory is panting, her own lust its own ragey animal. She needs to be fuck and now. She looks around the room for something she could fuck, or grind on. There are pillows on the bed, but they look too soft and squishy to be any good for grinding on. There are wood structures that might work, like the bed frame, the spanking bench, or the sex chairs.

She eyes up the shelf of dildos and rises to stand. With her hands still bound, this will be interesting. She glances along the shelf noting the werewolf looking dildo, the sea monster fat grill dildo with bumpy scales, the purple dragon cock, and the one that looks like a piece of gnarled driftwood. That one has a suction cup on the bottom, so she chooses it. She goes on her tippy toes and takes the cockhead of the dildo in her mouth and plucks it off the shelf. This is a trick. She carries it with her teeth clamped around it to one of the sex chairs.

She bends down and tries to push the suction cup onto the plastic seat to secure it. A laugh bursts from her. This is not easy. She bobs her head on it like she's giving it a blow job to try and get it to take hold. She can't get it to stick, and it haphazardly falls to the floor, so she chuckles at herself. She swivels and stoops down with her backside facing the dildo. The challenge doesn't frustrate her, she's got this. With her bound hands, she picks it up, then stands. Squatting down, while trying to look backward proves tough. But she presses the dildo and finally gets it to stick.

She smiles at her triumph and wiggles her wet slit along the tip. She slides down gently, hoping this suction cup is a good one. She begins to ride it, wishing like hell she could accost her clit. Then she'd come so fast.

She keeps riding it, easily rising off it and re-impaling her cunt over and over again.

She spies movement out of the corner of her eye and turns her head.

Max is in the doorway filming her, a humor-filled smirk on his face.

She guffaws and crumples her shoulders as a laugh escapes her, but she keeps riding. She's so close to her climax tipping, which spying him filming her as she has struggled has helped along quite efficiently.

"Ride that till you come," he instructs. He laughs at her.

Her humiliation kink explodes, sending her soaring over the edge of her climax. Claiming control eludes her. She shrieks, her body shuddering as strong contractions belt out of her vaginal walls. She gasps and hollers as her body instinctively crunches up. The contractions are some of the strongest she's had, and she shudders, the delicious overwhelm, a thing of ecstatic beauty. The need for silence consumes her as the pulses squeeze the dildo inside her.

She falls forward, barely catching herself before she falls. "Holy fuck," she slurs. "That was fucking huge."

Max grins and walks toward her, still holding up his phone.

Gasps and pants claim power over her voice as he gets up and close to her face. She crumples to the floor, panting, and he continues to keep filming. Smiling, she looks right into the phone. "That was fucking hot as fuck."

Then Max taps the recording off.

"Wow!" he exclaims, his face beaming. "That was out of the park! I'm still soaring."

"Same," she says through her pants. "That was incredible." She relaxes on the floor, her whole body going limp.

Max releases her wrists from the restraints, then helps her to stand. "Let's go snuggle on the bed."

She follows him, her whole body throbbing and still overcome by the monumental climax. "We need to do all that again."

"Yes, we do. I certainly enjoyed it, too."

They crawl onto the bed, and Max moves to spoon her from behind.

"You were reluctant at first."

"I was. It's not my usual go-to. You know me. You first, babe. You know I always like to make you climax before me. But I really enjoyed unleashing my aggression, and I love how you embraced it too, and submitted to it. How did it even turn you on?"

"Oh, it totally did. And I'm so glad you tried it."

"I'm mostly a teddy bear, but I do get those occasional streaks where I feel aggression overcoming me. I don't know. Maybe it's a surge of testosterone or something." He cradles her body to his, wiggling so their skin rubs together.

"Well, I think it's hot and I love it. I want to do it again. Let you use me. We can have a lot of fun in here together."

He kisses her shoulder. "So you approve of the studio?"

"Oh, hell yes, I do." She almost adds, *enough to live here.*

Chapter 17

Mallory blinks. She smells Max's scent and that's because he's hovering above her face. She gasps and then giggles. "What's this about?"

"Tea bag me, and then I'll tongue butter your lips as I eat you out." Max snickers as he gyrates his hips above her face, his cock at full attention.

"I never thought I'd wake to balls in my face, ever, in my life," she says with humor laced in her words.

"There's a lot of nevers flipping their switches for you these days," he retorts, his tone amused.

"That's an understatement," she coos. Yeah, like never would she have thought she'd be dating a horny older man and be committed to Derek at the same time while creating sexy content and porn for a huge online audience. "My life has changed just a bit," she muses sarcastically.

"You and me both." He sighs. "Now, about my balls."

She laughs. "It's a good thing I like sex, or I'd bite your balls like donut holes and shove you off me like a used wrapper," she says in a teasing voice.

"Oh, I'm safe then," he says with a heckle. "You don't eat donuts."

She stares up into his eyes with salacious intent. "You're only safe if you're okay with me attacking your balls," she says in a sassy, seductive voice. "Who says I don't eat donuts?"

"I've never seen you eat a donut," he says, then chuckles.

"I've never seen you eat prunes; that doesn't mean I should assume you wouldn't." She licks his balls, then nibbles on his freshly shaved flesh with her lips.

"Ah, fuck," he mutters. "You got me on that." He bounces above her face, his ball sac dangling above her mouth. He moans as she drags her tongue around his balls. "Open up, baby, time to dip."

She cackles as she grips his thighs and opens her lips.

He dips himself into her mouth, and she presses her fingers into his thighs, her fingernails leaving indents.

He groans out deeply as she begins to suck him. "Oh, fuck, that's incredible." He grips the headboard as she works him over. "F-f-fuck!" he stutters as his breathing launches into heavier panting.

She grips his turgid cock with one hand and strokes him as she sucks his balls.

His body tenses above her as his sounds of pleasure escalate. "Oh, baby," he says in a slur. "Want a taste of my cock?" he asks in a hopeful tone.

"Please," she says with desire. She adores that he's woken her this way, and it's likely something she'll never forget. She adores how Max is doing things he probably never thought he'd be doing, too. They are both breaking new ground in their lives on a daily basis.

He positions himself with the tip of his cock at the parting of her lips.

She opens wide and allows him to push himself into her mouth.

He rides deeper into her mouth with each thrust, gently fucking her face.

She grips his thighs as he coasts in and out, his groans of pleasure arousing her further. She allows him to use her until he's so deep she gags, then she grabs his cock and takes over the blow job.

He almost crumples on top of her as his body jerks, his cum bursting onto her tongue.

She struggles to swallow his cum, but manages with a sputtering gasp.

"Your turn," he states with determination. "I'm going to make your body shake." He climbs off her and crawls backward down the bed, keeping his gaze on her.

Max had been on an aggressive diet. He'd told her he was determined to lose some of his gut, and it was working. What she liked most was that fucking him had become a little smoother without it, not that she really cared about his pouchy belly, but this was an improvement she liked. She'd never minded his extra fluff; she adored snuggling into him. She also figured it had something to do with being on camera, since he had expressed an interest in doing some videos with her, faceless videos, that is. She loved the idea and knew that she'd adore sharing them with her fans as much as she's enjoyed sharing the one's of her and Derek fucking. Max had appeared in a couple of videos so far, and no one ever fat-shamed him, so she figured it was all his own idea of getting healthier. The pics of her and him at the party had blown up her account, then all her other photos and videos were skyrocketing her to the top 0.2 percent on the platform. It was wild, and she'd never expected such a following so quickly. And these people were devoted to her, and all she'd done was be herself. It was jarring to experience such rapid success.

Max settles between her thighs with a giant grin. "I'm not stopping until you're shaking like a leaf and spent, cum drunk."

"Yes, please," she begs with a big grin.

He plows into her pussy and sucks her without mercy, his mouth working full force. She careens her neck, her torso arching as she quickly skyrockets into a lush climax. Her body jerks as she travels through the orgasm. He doesn't let up his suction and she peaks again, and then again, her body twitching, her moans filling the air.

He keeps up his stimulation until she is limp, whimpering, blubbering, and begging him to stop.

"Please," she says weakly, barely getting it out.

She's ready to fall asleep when her phone buzzes on the bedside table. Max is grinning at her with a wet face, where he is leaning back against his pillow. She grabs her phone and glances at the screen. It's Derek.

She taps into the call. "Derek," she says breathlessly. "Hi, good morning."

"Hi, you sound out of breath." Derek sounds happy.

"Yeah, I ought to be. Max just made me come like twenty times."

"Oh, very nice," Derek says, blissful without a trace of jealousy.

"When will you arrive?" she asks, her excitement evident.

"I'm leaving in about ten minutes. But I wanted to ask if you needed anything from home before I leave."

"Oh," she says, pausing as she considers. "Yeah, will you bring that black bodice that laces up the front? Do you know the one I wore last week? It's still hanging on a hanger in the closet, I believe. I hung it there to dry. It needed washing after we got it so messy." She snickers and glances at Max, who simply grins back.

"You got it. And anything else?"

Derek is a good man. She isn't sure what she's done to be so lucky as to have these two amazing, supportive men in her life. Having Derek has always been incredible, but adding Max? And she is the luckiest woman alive!

"No, just you, and your cock so that we can get some good film."

"Oh, we'll be there! Hard, eager, and ready for action! I've missed you, and my cock has missed you." He clears his throat. "Have you seen your stats today? Mallory, you're blowing the roof with all this. You've hit ten thousand subscribers."

"What? Are you fucking serious? I have? Oh my gosh! Max, check my account on your phone. Derek says I've hit ten thousand!"

Max pulls his phone off the bedside table. She watches his face as he checks. His expression turns proud.

"You have indeed. See here," he says, showing her his phone. "You're doing it, babe. You are now more than able to support yourself."

Mallory's jaw drops; she's speechless. To be independent and earn this much money all on her own, without being reliant on anyone, is incredible! She never thought she'd be in this position, and certainly not so soon. "I seriously cannot believe this." After all her struggles, both financially and with her previous career, this was the most significant gift in life she could have ever hoped for. And to not be dependent on a man is such a top achievement that every strand of her feminine energy blooms with feminist vigor. All the roadblocks patriarchy had put in her life, all the sexism, all the insults, all the threats to her safety and well-being seemed to fade away. She was empowered and using her own body and her sexuality not only to survive but thrive.

Sure, she had the support of her two men and the support of Max's finances, but now she had true freedom. Her gumption swelled. Her power had fully evolved, and she no longer had to rely on anyone. Instead, she could even maybe help others. Tears well in her eyes as the full realization hit her. She is sovereign. She is a self-made woman, and she is a powerhouse.

A sob escapes her lips.

"You're doing it, Mal, you're succeeding!" Derek sounds so excited, and it warms her heart.

"And you're a part of that success, Derek." She sobs slightly, trying to stop as Max beams a smile at her while rubbing her leg. She finds it hard to speak, so she lets the need to speak go.

"I'm hopping in the car. I'll be there soon. I love you, Mallory."

"I love you, too, Derek. See you soon."

The news is so jarring, she remains still while it's still sinking in. "I'm a full-blown legit entrepreneur." She slowly raises her gaze up to meet Max's. "I'm mentally adding all this up." She falls silent as she thinks about it. Her face lights up. "Max! With that many subscribers and all the other sales I have made, I'll likely break three hundred thousand this month. Holy shit, Max!" She knows it will fluctuate, but she'll take the early success with grace and hope.

"I'm so proud of you, Mallory. I cannot tell you how proud of you this makes me. You are doing it, babe. You're incredible! You're really doing it! I knew you would. How could people not love you?"

"I knew things were going well, but I didn't expect this." She shakes her head as shock fills her on a renewing basis. This is beyond all her wildest dreams. The news is like the sun upon her, and it feels so good. She can't wait for the future, but how could it possibly top right now? It couldn't. She is on top of the world!

Max pulls her into a hug, his gaze warm and sparkly. "Mallory. You're the most beautiful, talented, and smart woman in the world, and I'm the luckiest man alive to be with you." He cups her face in his hands and looks directly into her eyes. "Do you even realize how amazing and sexy and wonderful and talented you are? You, my dear, are not just a phenomenon; you are a goddess of sexuality, of femininity, of female power. You were meant to do this and to be worshipped by hundreds of thousands of people for your beauty, your goodness, and your sexuality. Nothing can stop you. And I'm going to help you do it all. I'm not going anywhere. I'll do whatever I can to help you do whatever you want in this world. And it will be my pleasure." Tears well in his eyes. "You have no idea how much you've made a difference in my life. You've brought the magic back, even given me some I hadn't even fathomed possible."

She can't stop the tears, and another sob escapes.

"Babe, you're a natural at this. It's why you are such an immediate hit. People see your sparkle, your zest for life, your openness to share the most intimate parts of yourself with others. They see how genuine you are. You aren't faking this. It's who you are. And baby, you're a star."

She manages to calm herself enough to speak. "Max, I wouldn't be here without you, though. It's not all me."

"Oh, no. It's all you. They want you. They don't want me." He laughs aghast. "I'm a crusty, old, fat, rich, white guy. A dime a dozen. No, babe, you're the star."

"But you just said it yourself. In this world, if it weren't for you, my supportive, incredible, generous, amazing man, I wouldn't be where I am. And that's a fact." She sighs. "The realities of being a woman in this world lie with the restrictions or freedoms her man gives her. If you or Derek were not open, I wouldn't be able to do this. Even aside from your money, Max. A woman with a supportive man behind her, that's the real power. Not that women can't do it on their own, but to have that, it's like insurance to be free for who she is." She thinks of several of her friends whose husbands restrict them, and they're nowhere near their potential in life. "Trust me on this, you've made all the difference in my success, too."

"Well, I'm not taking credit for how incredible you are, babe. That's all you." He smiles. "I'm just here for the ride, for as long as you'll have me. I'll be honored and blessed to be by your side." He caresses her face. "Unconditionally. I'll never stop loving you, no matter what. Do you know that?" He pauses and looks intently at her. "I hope you realize that. You couldn't do anything to stop my love. I'll love you for the rest of my life, and for eternity. Nothing could kill it. No matter what you do." He pauses, then says with pain developing in his eyes, "Even if you leave me someday. I won't stop loving you. It's not possible."

His declaration is huge. It's making her feel invincible and even luckier than she did a few minutes ago, which she hadn't even thought was possible.

"I'm serious. Dead serious. And I'm not looking for a response, I'm just looking to love on you. Now. And. Forever."

His generosity and his capacity for love amaze her. It's hard to wrap her head, and her heart, fully around it as she gazes into his loving eyes. No words will work. She climbs into his lap, and he holds her tightly. He's somehow made her feel even more empowered than before, and yet she feels the best she's ever felt simply by being cradled in his arms. "I'll never douse your light. You should shine as you were meant to. For you. Plus, the world needs it."

She's on a high she's never attained in her life, and it feels damn fucking good.

Chapter 18

He pulls his car into the driveway, and as the full structure comes into view, his jaw drops.

"Holy fucking shit," he mutters. "This is a cabin?"

The house isn't a house as much as it looks like a mini hotel. He and Mallory have a small home that would fit inside this one probably seven or eight times, or more. How can he compete with this?

His heart sinks as he parks near Mallory's car. He grabs his bag and the items she requested and lumbers toward the entrance. Moving forward is more of an effort than it should be, but when she bursts out of the front door, his spirits are lifted. She looks so happy. He always feels better when he's around her.

"Hi," he says, opening his arms. "It's so good to see you. Whew! You look incredible, Mal." Apparently, cabin life suits her.

He gazes upon her, taking in her bright red dress with a deep dive at her cleavage. She has her nails done in a matching shade of red. Her hair is swept up in a sophisticated hairdo, but he knows her, and she likely simply shoved her locks into a binder in a flash. Yet, it somehow comes off as an elegant up hairdo on her. "You look so sexy without even trying."

"Hi," she says coyly, a smile spreading across her face. "Thank you."

"I'm so happy to see you. You have no idea how much I've missed you."

"And I'm so happy to see you! Come in, we have so much to talk about. I think it was really good to have you come up today to get you all settled in, before the big day of filming and all." She shimmies her shoulders. "I'm excited and nervous, but definitely more excited. I can't wait."

"Yeah, I agree. Plus, it'll give us some time to catch up before the hoopla starts." His eyes widen as he enters the mansion. He gasps. He marvels in awe that it's even nicer inside. "Holy crap, this place is incredible. It's like a movie set." He scans the hall and peers further in. "It's unreal." Do people in real life live like this?

The opulence is extreme and makes their house look like an absolute dump. This crushes him further. He tries to smile at her as she beams a huge grin. His offering to her in life is shrinking smaller and smaller by the day.

"And Derek! Just wait until you see the studio Max has created! It's like a dream come true! It's so incredible! All the toys, the furniture, it's like my best fantasies coming to life, and then some." She grabs his arm and tugs him toward the hallway. "Wait until you see it. You won't believe it!" She giggles. "We'll have so much fun!"

She rushes along, pulling him while glancing back now and then. Her eyes are lit and her expression bright.

"Is Max here?" he asks as he takes in bedroom after bedroom. "Geez. How many bedrooms does this place have?"

"He's working. And I think it has like twelve or something insane like that." She's so nonchalant about it.

They make it to the end of the hallway to the open door. He peers in. There is a blow-up couch with the hand and wrist straps against one wall, and several sex chairs with holes in the seats are next to it. He scans the shelves of multicolored and shaped dildos and all the various sex toys. On the wall are some BDSM restraints, floggers, and paddles. There is a free-standing stockade, which hurls his brain back to the memories of Mallory at the party. The bed resembles a set from an upscale adult film, complete with plush pillows and a fluffy comforter. A sex swing and a big St. Andrews cross occupies another corner. The spanking bench is covered in toys laid out on towels.

"You did the dishes, I see," he says with a smirk, motioning toward the drying toys.

"I did." She beams a huge grin. "It's amazing, right? Can you believe it?"

"It's fucking incredible. I can't stop looking at it all. He's thought of, well, everything." He spies an exercise ball on the edge of a workout mat, plus a workout bench, and a bunch of foam squares and triangles by the wall of mirrors. "I think he bought the whole catalog of sex toys and furniture." He shakes his head as he gazes at the hardware. "And lights and a camera. This is seriously like a professional studio."

"Oh, I wouldn't doubt it if he bought the whole catalog. That sounds like him." She nods, seemingly unfazed by the extreme level of expense Max has gone to in creating the studio.

Great. She's now used to the opulence. He tries not to let his worry show on his face.

Max appears in the room with a happy grin.

Derek can't hate the man. He's been so generous to Mallory, and he himself has also benefited from that. But despite his liking, Max, taking care of his woman, shrank back at the sight of him.

"Derek, so good of you to come." He wraps his arm around Mallory's shoulders and squeezes her. "Like the room?"

Derek snorts. "What's not to like? This is a total dream." He scans the area again, seeing a small bar with bar stools in the far-off corner, complete with a mini fridge and a see-through wine cooler. It looks fully stocked, of course. A couch, an easy chair, and a bean bag are arranged adjacent to each other, creating a cozy sitting spot. "It's incredible." He can imagine numerous potential film setups in this room, let alone the rest of the house and the grounds. "There are endless stories to be played out here. You have quite the cabin."

Max beams.

Mallory claps in delight. "I know! Right? And I've been planning out some scenes. Max and I have been brainstorming." She scoffs. "Well, we got a little too turned on while planning this morning and had to fuck, but we got a few ideas down."

Derek nods, thinking he'd love some time alone with her in the room himself, but with Max there, it seems like an impossible feat. "I can imagine." Despite his feelings of doom, his cock twitches. He's been missing having sex with her terribly. Seeing Faye helped him feel better, but he also wants Mallory. She's the love of his life. "Maybe you need a schedule sheet so I can book some time for you," he says jokingly, only he's not really joking.

"Oh, I like that, and yes. But that would be kind of a hot idea, too, like a brothel scene or something." She muses. "I love this state. So much more flexibility and allowance here." She waves her hand in the air. "Less prudes. Less control. Fewer restrictions. They let people live more how they want with less hassle here."

Derek knew that was going to be a thing. He's beginning to wonder if he and Mallory should move to this state. He'd find a job pretty easily, no doubt, and with all the money she's making now, he'd be able to be a little picky about what he decided on for work. The truth is that her success is going to be a padding for him, too, and afford him flexibility. He has to be grateful to Max for that. He looks up at Max as he looks so proud, having his arm around her.

Derek is jealous, and he needs to deal with it. It's not on her to alleviate his jealousy, though. He's not that guy. He refuses to be. He just wants some alone time with her. Hopefully Max will have to go back to work for the rest of the day and he'd get his chance to fuck his woman. He's not accepting that it won't happen. No way.

"Well, how about you show him to his room and he can get settled?" Max asks kindly of Mallory. "I need to get back to work. Make yourself comfortable, Derek. Anything you want, just eat it, drink it, use it. My house is your house."

Max takes off, and that leaves the two of them staring at each other. His trick will be to not ruin their time together with his petty fears and jealousy. He's been reading a book about swinging and compersion, and it's been helping him cope, but having it flung in his face like this is sending his resolve flying off into space.

He takes a deep breath. "Mallory..."

She raises her hand. "Derek, let's just enjoy each other. The rest will come in time," she says with begging eyes.

She's right. He nods slowly, and his fate is sealed. He'll go along with it for now.

"I'll show you your room, then you can freshen up, and we can do whatever we want. Sound good?"

He agrees and follows her down the hall, realizing for the first time that it's being called "his room." He bites his tongue and keeps up with her gait. He doesn't want to lay claim to her, but at the same time, he does. He'd stupidly assumed they'd be sharing a room to sleep.

His patience dissipates as they get there. "Are you sleeping with me here or with Max?"

She pauses, then spins to face him. "With Max. But I'll come sleep with you, too, don't worry." She looks so calm. "Maybe I'll take turns. How about that?"

At this point, he's considering one big king bed for the three of them.

She moves to embrace him, and he takes her into his arms. She feels at home and it stirs his emotions. He might cry. His heart aches for his love, for being by her side, for all the times he never wondered if she'd be with him, because he knew she would be. He also knows he can't take her for granted, when couples do that, they stop trying, and the relationship dies. It's one thing that being polyamorous does; if someone isn't valuing the other, the relationship falters in such a way that it dies, and rightfully so. Either step up and show your partner how much they are loved, wanted, and appreciated, or expect that they won't choose you. It keeps the relationship honest, fresh, and communication must be top-notch. He finds it's more like when they first started dating and he has to try hard, but that might also be what makes them last. He won't be getting lazy on her. She could just as easily get jealous of him and Faye. The door must swing both ways freely for both of them for it to work.

"I've missed you so much," he murmurs into her neck.

"As I've missed you." Her soft voice both arouses and excites him.

He leans back and gazes into her eyes. He believes her. "I need you, Mal. And when we aren't together, I realize how much I really do, even more so." A swell of emotion threatens to overwhelm him, but as he gazes into her eyes, he starts to relax.

She smiles back, and his heart melts.

He can't tell if she agrees, but it doesn't matter. She's here in his arms, right where he wants her, and it feels amazing.

He leans in for a kiss, and she folds right in. They fall into a deeper embrace, their hands caressing each other, but quickly they turn to more aggressive, hungry grabs. He's taking his time, though, no matter how much he wants to launch into wild primal sex, he's reigning that in. He's going to savor her. She's his and he's hers, but it's not an ownership situation in that way. It's an enjoyment and a sharing, fully consensual, and a hearty, enthusiastic yes, or it's a no.

Their passion erupts as he kisses down her neck.

She quivers and moans, her lust practically visible. "I've missed you so much, too." She grips his back as he kisses the curve of her neck, traveling down her chest in a series of open-mouthed kisses.

"I need you, all of you. Need to be in you." His cock is filled to the max and feels as if it will burst it's so packed. He wants nothing more than to ram it home and release a nice big juicy creampie inside her, but he's using all this restraint because he intends to show her his love. His climax will come, there's no doubt about that, but his love, he wants that to linger in the air between them and live as a special memory in her mind.

He bares her breast and devours her nipple, slathering his tongue all around her puckered flesh. The nugget is firm and reactive as he suckles.

She moans and threads her fingers through his hair.

He takes his time tracing the map of her nipple with the tip of his tongue, then he consumes her in a full mouthful, suckling hard.

Her fingers press his scalp as he pleasures her nipple. Then he moves to the other one. Oh, how he's missed the scent of her. Fuck he's missed her sounds, too. He needs to get one of those Bluetooth toys for long-distance play when she's gone like this. His heart sinks a little as this solidifies as a real thing. She'll be away at times with her new career, which is to be expected. He clears his mind. He doesn't own her; that's just a kink. He wants her empowered freedom. She deserves it.

He presses his fingers into her breast as he mouths her peak. After a few minutes of tasting and arousing her through nipple play, he kisses down her belly. This is going to be a worshipping fuck. She's coming multiple times before he goes inside her. He's not taking anything less.

He kneels before her and cups her butt cheeks. Then he leans in and kisses her soft, smooth mound, wiggling his tongue along her lush divide. Her lower lips are plumped with arousal already, and her sounds are telling him she's ready for more. But he's slowing it way down.

He carefully takes her flesh into his mouth, one section at a time, to arouse her in a slow tease. He's looking forward to edging her right to her brink, then guiding her into the scrumptious plunge.

The room is quiet except for her moans and the lapping sounds of him gently eating her out.

"Please," she begs. "Please, Derek."

He smiles, then forms his mouth flush with hers. Pressing his fingers into her ass cheeks, he presses his face fully between her legs. He tackles her labia, then wiggles his tongue inside her, but pulls it back out. He slurps upward until he is with her clit. He unearths it with the tip of his tongue, coaxing it out of its hood.

"Mmmm, fuck," she murmurs, then coos like a dove.

It wouldn't be fun without all of her moans and whimpers. Blissfully so, she's gotten even more vocal since they joined the club, which he adores. The club has changed them, and for the most part, in better ways. But there are things he still can't settle, like her staying here so long with Max. He isn't sure how he's supposed to be okay with that.

He also knows he's never been prevented from coming here. They've both made it clear he's welcome, so he needs to get out of his head and stop being a dipshit.

He groans as he re-consumes her clit with firm suction.

She goes weak in the knees, and he spies the bed behind her. He nudges her backward, and she takes the hint, slowly backing up toward it. She lays back and he tracks her bodily movements hovering above her pussy as she settles back into the puffy comforter.

He spreads her thighs and darts downward, aggressively eating her out within seconds of her lying back.

She squirms and shrieks, her sounds telling him she's close already. He backs away to coax her back down from the high, then restarts. She's right there on the edge; the pause didn't do much to drop her arousal.

He releases his hold on her and says, "Come for me, Mal. I want your cum on my tongue. And keep coming. I'm not stopping." He gives her an aggressive snarl. "Grind into me. Take your pleasure."

She nods with a tiny grin, her eyes lit with happiness and lust.

He gets back to work and busies his mouth. She grips his hair and presses the back of his head further into her. She moves her hips in tune with him.

Her body jolts as her sounds escalate. Her torso rocks in gyrations as she climaxes. He stays true to his word and keeps it up. She quickly soars again, her body curling, her shoulders rising off the bed. She's gasping through the highs, but he still isn't giving her a break. He keeps working her over, and she blasts into another peak easily.

She's gasping and sputtering, her body twitching from aftershocks.

One more, she needs at least one more.

He ramps up his efforts, and his stimulations hurl her into what seems to be a double-peaked orgasm. His favorite. He loves that all their play has helped her learn how to do it. It's remarkable how she had to learn it, but playing it alone also helped. All the toys Max has gifted her have also been a gateway to her learning more about her body. And he's enjoyed the ride there as well.

"Please, Derek. Put your cock in me. I need it. I want you to fuck me. Don't hold back. I want all of you."

He lets go of her and climbs up her body. His love for her swells. He gives her a passionate, hungry, kiss then lines up his cock. Feeling overcome with desire, he penetrates her quickly and begins his riding of her body. She accepts him easily, and their bodies undulate together in the beautiful sounds of their pleasure. Skin smacks, moans, sighs, and growls fill the air. He's randy as fuck and he's going to come fast, but he's okay with that. His jealousy of Max is warring with his logic, he wants her to remember the pleasure he's giving her more than he wants her to remember anything else about the day. He hates that these thoughts are invading their time together. He refocuses on her, as he should be.

She grasps his biceps, fingering and squeezing as her enjoyment crescendos and dips, and when she starts to rise again, he loses it and his cum bursts inside her.

He rises and keeps slamming at the angle he knows will get her there. With his cock obediently staying hard, he fucks her until her body shudders and her moans tell him she's climaxing once more.

Victory.

He keeps going though, since his dick is still hard, and after several more pumps, he comes a second time.

He slows his thrusting as their breathing settles, then he lays beside her opening his arms, and she snuggles in.

"That was beautiful. I love making you come. I can't get enough. Ever. I'm addicted to you." He's super emotional after making love to her, and he almost lets a sob fly, but he holds it in. Holding her this close again after they've both spent time has got him so on edge. Tears spring to his eyes, and hard as he tries, he loses it, and a cry escapes his lips.

"Oh, Derek," she says with so much compassion and love that his sobs balloon.

"I wasn't going to..." he says but stops to gasp, his embarrassment at losing control consuming him, "...to say anything but I've missed you so much, Mal. This is...more than I hoped for."

She caresses his chest as she kisses the other side. She lays kisses all along as she squeezes her arm across his belly. "It's okay. We're together. Always. Remember that even if we're miles apart. I love you, Derek."

He cries for a moment, but then calms. That word...together. What they always said they'd be was "together." But they haven't been "together," they've been miles apart. They need to make that change. But what does that look like? Does she want to stay? Him living here with her and Max? That sounds weird and hard. And does he even want that? His family would freak, not that he fucking cares about them after all they've done. Many of them have been so cruel to him that he chooses to stay away from them most of the time anyhow. They might never even know the situation.

He tries to quiet his mind as he lays with her, flesh to flesh. This is what he needs, and all the rest will come later. He just needs to drink her in and be with her.

"I love you, too, Mallory," he whispers in a shaky voice. "I'm sorry I lost it."

"Derek, don't be. I love you, and I'll never tell you how to feel." She gazes up at him. "I want to see all your emotions, all of you. You know I love your sweetness and all the way through to your rough and aggressive sides. I love all your moods and all your modes. Who wants the same thing every time they have sex? Not me!"

"True. And I'm the same way, I love your variety. It's one reason we get along so well. We have the same views and opinions on it all."

"Yeah, that's so true." She caresses his belly.

After a few minutes, their breathing returned to normal, and things seemed to calm down.

"I don't want to ever move. I feel so floaty."

"Mmmm, me too."

"Love being close to you."

"As do I."

Chapter 19

"I can't believe the day is here!" she shrieks as she jumps. "I'm just so excited I can't sit still." She dances in place.

Another crew member arrives, and she watches Max lead them to the studio so they can set up. He's enjoying being the director of the event, and Mallory is grateful that he is, so she can try to relax with Derek at the table. They are getting a front-row seat to the parade of people arriving for the shoot. It's more people than she had expected. In her head, she was thinking of one person to operate the camera and possibly an extra. Still, Max had hired makeup artists, several people to film from different angles, and even a consultant to guide them in setting up the best scenes. None of the stars have arrived yet. The first one is due any minute. And Mallory is on pins and needles waiting for Maria and Sam to arrive, too.

"I feel like a little kid getting my best birthday party ever!" She stretches. "I'm getting lucky today like it's on steroids!"

Derek smiles at her with a deep chuckle. "Yup you are. And you deserve it." He looks so relaxed now, much better than he had looked yesterday when he arrived. He really had looked awful and ragged. Her absence took a greater toll on him than she'd expected. Her mind is a swirl with all the emotions from her enjoying time at the cabin with Max, to her tender lovemaking session with Derek, to the filming day. She is being pulled in two directions with her men, and her heart wants them both. But today, it's all about the filming so all that complexity will have to wait. She's not tackling any of that on a day like today.

She squeezes Derek's hand. "Are you nervous?"

He chuckles lightly. "Only a little. I'm more excited. How about you?"

"Yeah, same. A bit of both. This is a monumental day." She taps on her phone and scrolls. "I have so many fans waiting for this." She glances at him. "I've already sold one hundred and five, Derek."

"What? Are you freaking serious right now?"

She nods. "Totally. They are preordering it like crazy. I never would have expected this in a million years. And I'm guessing that orders are going to go up a lot over the next month. I have people literally begging me already. I've been toying with adding another level with a higher price tag for early access. What do you think?"

"I told her I think it's a fantastic idea," Max says as he comes up behind her and places his hands on her shoulders.

Derek startles at his sudden appearance. "Yeah, for sure. You should."

"She's got such a brilliant entrepreneurial mind. I'm so proud of her." Max looks proud, and Mallory beams a smile up at him.

"Yeah, she really does." Derek looks surprised, but Mallory lets it go. It's not like he looks angry.

"She can do anything, and she's already proven that." Max pats her head. "Pretty soon you'll be funding your own films."

She shakes her hands excitedly and shrieks. "You really think so?"

"Yes, I really do. Your numbers are looking good, babe."

"They are looking good." She claps. "I never thought I could be such a success. It feels incredible." She shrugs. "Who'd have thought I could do this?"

"I did. And I've got my team on the next set of ads already."

"Oh, that's amazing! Do you think I should make the new level now? I mean, it literally will take me a minute. Then I could announce it on social media that I created an early access." She pauses. "How much time do you think the editors need?"

She glances at Derek, and he's oddly silent with a weird look on his face. This concerns her. She needs to find time to ask him what's going on, but the day is ramping up at an alarming rate as the two male stars plow through the front door. She doesn't mean to leave him out of all this, but their chat will clearly have to wait.

It's Jasper and Wesley. She jumps up and squeals. She claps her hands and then rushes toward the door. "You're here!"

"We're here," Jasper repeats, a huge grin on his face. His blond hair is extra spiky today, and he wears mirrored sunglasses that cover his blue eyes. He's wearing a muscle tank top, which shows off his incredible abs. His habits are showing in his bulging muscles; he's a total gym rat.

She was ecstatic when he said "yes" to the collab. Her luck just keeps clicking. She's been a fan of his for so long, well, a fan of both of them. She was thrilled when she scored them for the filming because they are two of the hottest performers. Well, the salary Max offered them ensured it would be a sure thing, but she wasn't complaining one bit about that. "I'm so excited to work with you both."

She scans Wesley. His dark flesh is a stark and beautiful contrast to his white suit with a pale pink button-up shirt beneath. He's not one to dress to blend in with a crowd.

"Hey, babe, looking smoking hot. Can't wait to hit that." He points to her lower half.

She grins as shivers zing through her. She's never felt more alive in her life. "I'm excited to be hit." She swoons and almost wilts as she sways. "I'm super horny today and so ready."

"Ah, that's exactly what I like to hear," Wesley says in a cool, suave tone. "We watched you all evening yesterday to get ready." He chugs his closed fist up and down in front of his crotch.

She shrinks back as her face blossoms into a huge grin. "Wait. Really? You really did?"

"Yeah, hell yeah. You're the hottest, hon. I subscribed." Jasper slides his tongue through the V of his two forefingers on his right hand. "I'm ready to make you scream."

Jasper gives a pelvic thrust toward her.

This is hot. She might just lie down right there and let them start with how aroused they're getting her. "You know how to start the foreplay right," she coos.

"Damn straight, I do. The foreplay begins way before the bedroom. Any lover worth anything knows that. Wooing never stops. Only those with no game stop," he says with a snort and a tip of his head, "lame dick losers." He grins brilliantly, his white teeth shining. "And goddesses like you deserve all of us moronic slaves to our dicks first worshipping you before we fuck. Am I right or am I right, Wes, my man?"

He might come off as arrogant to some, but she sees the truth in it. He's got an understanding most men lack, proven from that sentence alone.

"Damn fucking right." He nods, then peers behind him. "That Derek? Hey, bro! Can't wait for your mouth to be wrapped around my cock."

Derek hoots from the table. "As I said in our DM's, I'm more than ready, Wes."

"Good. I'm already hard. But I gotta piss first. Where's the pot?" He grunts, then shakes his head. "I hate pissing with a full hard-on."

"Down this way," Mallory leads him down the hallway while snickering. She's glad she doesn't have that kind of problem to deal with. She glances back at his crotch and startles, then stands still. The mound beneath shows how big and long his cock really is. He's one of the adult film legends with an eleven-inch cock, all natural, too, it's been reported. A genetic anomaly cock king standing right before her. She literally cannot wait to play with it.

He simply nods at her with a grin. "That's right, it's all true."

She giggles, then peers into the bathroom. She motions with her arm for him to enter as he strides in.

He whips around and snatches her neck in his large hand. His eyes gleam with hunger. He presses his body to her, and she slams against the door. His cock is a fat monster of a rod pressed to her abdomen.

"If I wasn't full of piss, I'd fuck you right now." He gives her a meltingly charming smile. "But for now, a kiss will do."

He presses his mouth to hers, and they fall into a deep embrace.

She gropes him, her horniness launching into hysterics. She'd happily let him fuck her if he wants, she wants it, too. She moans as they kiss longer. Her desire for him skyrockets even higher as they make out. His cock is so prominent, she's going to have to work really hard at restraining herself to wait until the shoot.

"Just wait, baby, I'm coming for you. You're mine. I don't care who you are, but at that moment, you'll be all mine. Gonna dick you down hard. You're going to be so full of hormones you'll feel drunk. A limp quaking cunt dripping before my raging cock." He leans back from her and snaps his fingers. "Cloud nine is where I put my ladies, but you are going to cloud fifteen."

Her clit lurches at his declarations. He's cheesy as fuck but a total turn-on at the same time. And she believes every word he says because his reputation precedes him. His words and his come-on efficiently melt her into a wet noodle. "I seriously can't wait, Wes!"

She backs away as he starts to shut the door but then opens it wide.

He snickers. "Watching me piss isn't hot." He smiles as he shooes her away with his hand. "I know you want to see it, but you'll have to wait, babe." With a cocky smile, he doesn't bother to shut the door before he walks to the toilet. She hears him grunt. "Fuck, cooperate you fucker." Then a loud stream of pee hits the toilet water, the sounds reaching her in the hallway.

She smirks, giggles, then starts back down the hall. He's right, peeing isn't hot. When she reaches the kitchen, Derek and Jasper are deep in flirtation mode. Derek may be busier than her in this shoot! She stifles a laugh. She wants him to shine, too. He's living out his fantasies as much as she is, and more power to him. He's come so far away from the shame his parents instilled in him that she's constantly blown away by what he does now, but so happy for him. He knows more love now than he did for most of his life, and for that, she knows she's played a ginormous role.

She settles into the seat next to Derek and places her hand on his.

"Yeah, you too are together, right? Like a nesting couple?" Jasper leans back in the chair. "I want to know the lay of all this. I respect that."

She nods. "Yes, we are. We've been together for two years. This whole adventure started with us swinging together." She pauses as she watches Derek's face. "And we're polyamorous. I'm with Max, too, the owner of this place."

"Nice. Solid. Got it." He grins. "Lucky men. And what a fucking house, man, whew!" He hops up when Wesley appears. "My turn to piss." He skedaddles down the hall awkwardly, then turns back, giving the rest of them a goofy clown face.

"This is going to be so much fun," Mallory coos. "All the fun personalities. Everyone is sexy as fuck." She shimmies her shoulders. "And I'm the only pussy who gets to have you all."

"That was by design, wasn't it, darlin'?" Wes asks as he sits.

"Fuck yes, it was."

Max appears in the room and raises his hands. "The crew is ready. Are we still waiting for anyone?"

Mallory lifts her head toward him. "Yes, Sam and Maria haven't arrived yet."

"Maria?" Wes asks with interest. "Sam?"

"She's not filming this time. She's here for me, like my personal assistant. But she said she'd consider it in future collabs, possibly."

"Nice. Can't wait to meet her. What's she about?" Wes asks.

"Sexy as fuck. Midlife hotwife vibes. Queer. Loves sex." Mallory rubs her hands together. "I've already been with her, I can vouch for her. She's a Domme to me, but also a switch, so submissive usually otherwise. But I've seen her dominate men."

"Like me," Derek says proudly. "When I'm in the mood for it."

"And Sam?"

"DILF. Dom. Queer. Amazing." Mallory pats Derek's hand. "Derek's Dom, and mine, when we get together, but Derek gets with him more. He'll be participating."

"Sweet. Always love meeting another Dom."

Wes peers at Derek. "You're a switch or a sub, my man?"

"Switch. I'm dominant mostly with Mallory, though."

Wes and Jasper both nod.

Mallory wondered how it would all unfold with so many dominant men, but she also knew they were professionals, and they could find a way to mesh on a scene, at least for a while. And if things get heated, she has a plan to split the day into separate filming sessions. However, she's really not worried. These guys are dominant, but not arrogantly macho and stupid. They can co-exist for the purposes of a collab. Plus, Derek will be there, and another switch in the mix almost always smooths things over. Plus, she could beg Maria to join in, and that would cool any hot heads in a flash.

They all chat around the table while enjoying lemonade for twenty more minutes. This is perfect for everyone to get to know each other better.

Mallory is bursting at the seams as she checks her phone. "Yay! They'll be here soon!"

Before long, the door is flung open and Maria and Sam enter with their usual brilliant flair.

"This place is magnificent!" Maria declares with her arms spread wide and high. She's her usual theatrical self.

"Wow," Sam agrees. "Max has outdone himself with this place. This is way bigger than his place in the north."

"Place in the north?" Mallory glances at Max. "You have another place you haven't mentioned?"

"Well, yeah, I do have that one, but that was in the number I told you." Max looks proud of himself. "Mallory and me were talking about hosting a club party here soon. Everyone could make a weekend of it. Would you two come?"

"Absolutely. Right, Maria?"

"Sure thing." She goes to Mallory and quickly hugs her. "I've missed you terribly, love."

They kiss on the lips. Maria grips her head and goes deeper.

The men hoot and holler cheering them on.

When Maria breaks them apart, Mallory exclaims, "Wow, as if I weren't already horny enough."

Maria beams.

"Are you sure you aren't going to join in, Maria?" Wes asks. "Sexy as mother fucking sexy. My woody just pushed into a legit brick."

Mallory giggles. "He's not lying about the 'brick.'"

There's significant laughter.

Mallory states, "Well, let's get you two settled, so we can start filming. Do you need a snack? A drink?"

"Yeah, maybe something small. And water, or some of that lemonade. I'm so parched." Maria pulls Mallory back into a hug. "You have no idea how good it is to see you. You are positively glowing, honey."

Mallory squeezes her shoulders together. "Honestly, I feel amazing."

"And I was just on your account. You've hit superstar status, Mallory. I knew you could. Congratulations!" Maria pats Mallory's back as she gazes at her.

Mallory leads them down the hall and helps them settle into their room. She leaves them, then gets them set up with refreshments. After another half hour of them all chatting and getting to know each other, it feels right to Mallory. It's time.

She rises and lifts her arms up. "Well, I'm feeling the vibes. Is everyone ready? Because my pussy is calling all your names and she wants to be fed cock, now!"

"I'm in, and more than ready," Jasper says, grabbing his crotch, giving it a jiggle. "Been ready for a long time." He grins.

The other performers and camera crew indicate how ready they are, and Mallory gives a wave of her arm. "Well, then. Let's get going!"

She intends to stop off for a quick makeup check as she scoots down the hallway. She was grateful to the makeup artist at the house earlier, as they did a fantastic job. Better than she could have done on her own. The air is heavy with anticipation, and she can practically taste the brooding masculine energy. Her own femininity is glistening with desire, and the shoot promises to be epic, given how everyone is getting along. She had wanted a get to know each other session before the sex, so her wishes got met. The connections made will make a difference in how they connect during filming. Not that she couldn't just get down to fucking right away, she was built that way, but she liked the personal connections added. She's so ready to be dominated, and she has picked the perfect men to do it.

Chapter 20

Mallory dabs the powdered brush along her nose and forehead to de-shine her skin.

Maria slides into the bathroom and snuggles up behind her. She presses her body to her backside and wraps her arms around Mallory's tummy.

"You look absolutely gorgeous, honey, stunning." She sways slightly. "You ready for this? There's a lot of very experienced cock out there."

She nods and melts into Maria's embrace, allowing her body to be easily swayed. "I'm so ready. And I'm super excited. Everyone knows their roles, and I told them to follow the director, too, but also, I told them spontaneity is our best and most effective tool." She leans her head back on Maria. "I want it to be genuine and authentic, too. So, I'm hoping everyone will go with the flow." She swivels to face Maria, and they embrace, forehead to forehead.

"You look really happy. Everything going okay?" She doesn't look concerned, but inquisitive.

"Yes, I'm doing amazing."

"And Derek?" Her voice dips.

"I think I need to do something there. He seemed a little lost yesterday. But after we reconnected and had sex, he seems good." She shrugs. "He probably just needed reaffirmation that we're still good."

"Good. He seems good to me, it's just that he seemed off when he came to our house last week. He and Sam talked quite extensively, alone, but I wasn't within earshot. So just checking in to support you in any way you need. You know I love you two."

"Thank you for that." She leans in and kisses her on the lips. "And I love you, too."

"Love you to the moon and back. Now let's get you orgasming so much you forget your name." She steps back. "I want to see you coming so hard you're blubbering nonsense. And know that I'll be at your side to get whatever you need. Water, a snack, makeup, and lube. You name it and I'm your servant. I'll get it."

"You're the absolute best!" In truth, she needs Maria there. It's not a want.

She grabs Maria's hand, and they exit the bathroom. The walk down the hall takes too long, and Mallory has the urge to run, but she remains calm. She doesn't need to be panting yet, and not for that reason.

They enter the studio, and everyone is already in place. It's like walking into an orgy that is set up to be focused just on her, which, is exactly what it is.

Butterflies erupt inside her. This is her dream coming true. Full control over filming what she wants, experiencing what she wants, and then getting to sell it to an already interested audience. She's living her best life. Nothing could possibly tarnish the day.

Derek smiles at her with an encouraging expression.

Max salutes her from his post next to the cameraman with the largest video camera.

Wesley is leaning against the bed, looking delicious in a black tailored suit with a white button-up shirt open at the top. He's changed but still looks sexy as heck.

Jasper is wearing casual dress clothes, including khaki pants and a pink, flowered shirt, which complement his blond hair and blue eyes. He looks like he's on vacation on a beach somewhere.

Sam is also dressed up, wearing black slacks and a maroon button-up shirt with a navy tie.

Her eyes swing back to Derek, who has also changed into a suit. A new suit she's not seen yet. He looks fantastic. They all do.

She glances down at her own lingerie dress, which is a white, see-through lace, off-the-shoulder design with spaghetti straps, and features a flared skirt that reaches her mid-thighs. She opted for the lace stockings, garter, and belt, and a soft thong. She feels elegant and beautiful, and very feminine. Max helped her pick it out and paid the three hundred-plus bill to get it delivered to the cabin yesterday. She gave strict instructions that none of the men were allowed to rip it. Ripping of fabric scenes would have to wait for another filming day; she loves this outfit too much to bear it being torn to shreds.

"Okay, are we ready? Everyone knows the plan?" she asks as she scans their faces.

All nod in agreement, and she steps further into the room. They all congregate in the living room section of the large studio, where there are five glasses of champagne on a coffee table. When Max had hired a stager to set up the room and the scene, she had been surprised by the little things, and big things, the woman had suggested, like a corner of the room to be a living room area with poured drinks set out, another to be a bar with high top tables with snacks on them, a bedroom area that looks like it's from a designer magazine, a sex dungeon area to drool over, and little things like a stack of games on a shelf near the couch, a pile of books on the coffee table, a fake TV remote. The other little things, like drink coasters and a tissue box, also make it seem like a real living space.

She'd seen some videos with just a white wall and a white couch, and while the starkness of the room had helped her focus only on the couple fucking even more, it also made the scene seem more fake, and cheap. The sexy fun at home slant seems most effective these days. She's hoping for realistic videos that are more like amateur but better coordinated for maximal sexiness and appeal. She wants it to seem like the viewers are getting a special peek into real, private, sexy times. She hates fake videos with seemingly over-staged scenarios that seem not true to real life, which are made even worse with bad acting and inauthentic moans. Those are the ones she drops out of in her alone play time. She knows what she likes, and that's her goal: to shoot a film that she herself could get off to and enjoy.

She knows her audience, and her audience includes herself. She gets into place.

Max raises his hand and then shouts, "Action." He drops his arm.

She takes the champagne glass offered to her by Derek. The cameramen start to move around. She has to consciously not let them catch her attention, so she doesn't turn to look at them. The movement is hard to ignore, but she focuses on Derek, and that helps.

"Cheers to a job well done," Derek says as he tips his glass toward her to clink.

"Thank you, Derek. I couldn't have done it without you." She squints her eyes as she smiles. "Literally. You and that cock of yours." She reaches down and squeezes his meat through his trousers.

"Mm, love that, Mallory. A gold nugget of a reward for me."

She swivels to clink glasses with all the other men, who have swiftly gathered around her—she imagines what each of their cocks look like inside their pants. This arouses her significantly. She had suggested Max join in to make it MMMMMF, but he declined. He said next time. This time he wants to oversee and direct, being it's the first one at his place. It's her show, but he's been such a huge part of planning it with her, it feels like his baby, too. And she loves that he's taking a piece of owning it. It will make it even more exciting to watch in the end when they're alone together.

"Cheers," Jasper says, a twinkle brewing in his eyes. "To a successful launch of your career."

"Here, here," Wesley says as he also clinks her glass. "Can't wait to see what you do."

Sam smiles at her, then tips his glass. "To you, my lovely young woman. Oh, the places you've already gone since I met you, and the places you'll go. You're incredible. And now the world is getting to taste that too."

"Not like we'll get to taste!" Jasper pipes in with a heckle.

She had given the men a loose structure but told them to speak as they normally would. It seems to be working. She didn't want this to be scripted so much, but fluid within a very loose framework of actions and reasons.

The men all laugh as she dips her chin down, a huge smile growing on her face. "You're all so amazing."

"You come first," Derek states.

"I want to thank you all for coming to my celebration. I'm so excited to be at a point where celebrating is warranted. And that's all thanks to my fans." She stares right into the camera. "They've made me the creator I've become, and to them, I'll be forever grateful. They helped me build this empire. So, thank you, my wonderful fans." She scoffs then giggles, dragging her gaze away from the camera to the men. "I can't even believe I have an empire. But it feels wonderful to be so wanted."

"Hey, babe, you're a winning combo. You're sexy, sweet, kind, considerate, and kinky as fuck, and willing to try new things. The kind of woman most partners dream about." Derek beams. "I should know."

"True, you should know." She moves closer to him, then takes a drink. "Champagne kisses. This is a fulfillment of my promise. I'm giving you champagne kisses today and going forward."

Derek takes a drink of his, too, and then they fall into an open-mouthed kiss.

Someone takes their drinks as their kissing deepens. He gropes her back and then slips his hands down to her bottom, cupping each cheek in a palm beneath her skirt.

Her one caveat is that she and Derek were to have sex first in the video, and she won't stray from that. Other than that, she's open to what goes down and how it does. Derek said he'd submit to all the other men after the initial sex with her, and then the orgy would be in full swing. Her audience knows she and Derek are together, and they also know Max and she are together, but she's not touching on her relationship with Max in this video because he's not in it, of course.

It will invariably propagate lots of questions from her audience that Max is not on film, but she doesn't mind fielding their questions. She rather savors that they actually want to know about her life and her relationships.

Derek kisses down her neck and cups her right breast, squeezing it through the lace. He caresses her nipple and pinches it as it pops up erect.

She groans to express her delight in his attention and for the audience.

He pulls her breast free of the lace and fondles it.

"Mm, nice," Wesley says in a smooth voice.

"Mm-hmm," Jasper agrees. "Perfect tits."

The cameraman moves, and she closes her eyes to focus on the sensation Derek is bringing about in her. He kisses down her breast and then suckles her firm tip. He bares her other breast and plays with it, too.

"I want your cock in me, Derek."

"Not until you come. You know the rules, babe," he says sternly.

She smiles and bites her lip. "Did I ever mention I love your rule?"

"Yes," he says with a knowing grin.

He massages his hands all over her breasts, then kisses down her body. He kisses her covered mound, then rises. He pulls her forward and flips up her skirt so the cameraman can get a nice shot of her thong string up her ass crack. He pulls it then lets it spring back in place between her butt cheeks. A few chuckles ripple through the room as he does it again.

He flips her around and humps her butt a few times, then pulls her back to a standing position. He gives her bottom a slap.

She startles. She hadn't expected that.

Derek grabs her hand and pulls her across the room. The camera operators zoom to keep up.

"You need a little punishment. I've not seen you for days." His expression is stern.

She loves how he's using reality for a kinky scene. "I know. What are you going to do about that?"

"Give you a spanking." He gives her a strongly wicked stare.

"Oh, this will be good." Jasper scrambles to follow along.

Wes and Sam join the parade.

"Spank you in front of them," Derek says with authority.

She was not expecting this at all, but she's game. He knows her views and wants, so she can just fall into the fantasy of it and not worry about a dang thing.

Derek pushes her over the spanking bench and her opening flares in response. Her clit lurches to life when he opens the drawer to the right that houses the spanking paddles. This is progressing much faster than she had expected. She knows this is exactly what her audience wants, though, so she's good with it. They want sex, and more sex, and more sex, and her being dominated. Story films will happen, but this first one, she's good with oodles of sex and kinks. Her story already exists online for her fans, however, and this video is just an adjunct to it all. Maybe new fans would need more prep, but her aim with this is to hit her audience square where they indicated they wanted it. Sex. Sex. And more sex. And that includes a bit of strong domination, too.

Derek flaps up her skirt to bare her bottom, then tugs down her thong to trap her thighs. He spreads her ass cheeks for the camera.

"Have a peek," he says with an arrogant snicker, very uncharacteristic for him. "Take this view and do what you want. I do."

He releases her cheeks, then slaps her ass with his bare hand three times.

She whimpers, even though it doesn't really hurt. She wonders if what he just said has any validity. She doesn't care, but now she's curious if he masturbates to that idea.

He takes in a big breath, which she assumes is part of the wind up of his down swing, and then smashes the paddle into her ass. Hard.

"Oh," she exclaims. That one hurt. It was a much harder hit than she expected.

He hits her two more times, and it stings. Then he grips her hips, digging his fingers into her flesh. He humps her butt fully clothed, and his pounding whaps against her tender flesh.

She whimpers as he slams into her without hesitation. His domination is turning her the fuck on, especially with all the watchers.

The other men snicker and hoot.

Wesley claps. "Beat that butt."

Spanking, domination, and humiliation are on her okay to do kink list. Derek doing this arouses her so much, she's already close to coming. She had assumed one of the other men would have done this type of domination. But to her delightful surprise, she also thinks her audience will get a big kick out of seeing Derek behave this way.

"You're taking my fat cock up your quaking cunt, my sweet little bitch." He slides his fingers between her lips and moves them around, tickling, pressing, kneading her flesh.

She moans because it feels so fucking good. When he presses her clit, she shouts.

Again, the men respond with appreciative hollers and whistles. They like this. They are likely waiting for Derek to hurry the fuck up, though, so they can ride her, too. She likes being ridden; it hits the being-used kink in her. She loves being pleasured, though, more. It's all so juicy.

He finger fucks her from behind, hard and fast, the way Sam taught him. It always makes her climax quickly. He ramps it up higher, and she catches the wave.

"I'm going to come," she exclaims in desperation. Her panting and her sounds ramp up, and she screams. She presses her fingers into the cushion of the bench as her body tries to curl into its unyielding presence. Her back arches as a result, and her body rocks through a big climax.

Derek wastes no time and unzips his pants. He plows into her pussy and fucks her in a loud ruckus.

The poundings against her sensitive ass hurt, but it adds to her eroticism, and she reaches below her pelvis for her clit. A hand smacks hers away and takes over. She thinks it's Wesley. He rubs her clit aggressively as Derek grunts, then creampies her.

Sam pipes up. "I need a good ride. Let me get in there. It's been too long for me, too. Get ready for me, Mallory."

"It's never been for me," protests Jasper good-naturedly.

She smirks but remains silent. She's way too overwhelmed to speak anyhow.

Sam slides into her. Wesley keeps working her clit and she launches into another peak, her contractions squeeze Sam inside her. He grunts, indicating he's using significant effort not to come too soon himself. He uses her body, then pulls out, smacking his hard cock on her ass.

"Whew! I almost couldn't stop," Sam says, heckling himself. "Saving this hard meat for you, my boy. Let's go back to the couch. I want to relax as you suck my cock, Derek." He tilts his head. "Naked. Strip, my boy. Strip. For the camera."

Derek begins a slow strip, getting into the erotic dance kink of his as he removes his clothes seductively for the camera. He'd have been good on a stage.

She watches him, her sexy man, relishing how he's getting into this as Jasper taps her closed lips with his cock. "My turn to ride this bitch."

"She needs a bit more of a bright red ass, though," Jasper says wickedly.

He snatches the paddle and begins to smash her ass with it. "Get you to obey and get in line, you sassy, power-hungry wench."

She shudders and cries out with each hit. Her ass already feels bright red. Thankfully he decides it's time to fuck her and he enters her body in a rush. He thrusts into her as Wesley still mans her clit.

She floats in ecstasy, and shudders again as a smaller orgasm rises her up off the bench, her clit throbbing as she sputters through gasps. She gives Wesley a look, hoping he catches her drift that they need a new position to keep things fresh. Plus, she's tired of being spanked. She chose these two men, Jasper and Wesley, for their known dominance, but also for their reputations of prioritizing their partner's pleasure over their own needs for complete blind compliance. She wants men who are open to her voice, her wants, and her desires. She'll settle for nothing less.

She loves being dominated, but on her terms. The way it's supposed to be. It wouldn't take much for her to flip into an area she didn't want, so her collab partners will always be explicitly chosen by her, and no one else.

He takes her cue. "Jasper, let's try out that sex chair over there. And I'd love to spit roast her over that exercise ball, too."

"Good idea." He pulls out and yanks her off the bench. He throws her over his shoulder, her tits flying as she soars above him.

"Whoa!" she exclaims. She hits his back hard, her hands slapping against him at touchdown. She looks up and spies Derek over in the sitting room area. His head is bobbing above Sam's lap at a fast rate. One of the cameramen is up close getting it on film.

Jasper runs with her across the room, caveman style, and then whips her body back over his shoulder, easily twirling her before placing her over the exercise ball. "I choose this."

Wesley hoots. "That working out pays off, bro." He laughs further, but she has no clue why. She'll have to wait to watch the video to know.

"Rag doll," Jasper says. "Ass or mouth?" he asks Wesley.

"Mouth, I'm hankering for a gag."

"With your giant, that's a given."

Mallory isn't sure how she'll handle this, but she knows it'll be brief, another stipulation.

She loves this whole plan. She gets to have sex with four men, upon her terms, while climaxing heavily herself, and then she gets to make money on it. And she doesn't even pay for anything because Max has already covered it all, and told her not to pay him back. How has she gotten this lucky?

The men waste no time in manipulating her body. Her ass is higher than the rest of her on the ball as she holds her front half up with her arms. She feels wobbly and weak after climaxing. Wesley commandeers her head between his large, dark palms.

"Open," he commands.

She meets his gaze and obeys by dropping her jaw. He snatches up his hardness and presses it into her mouth. He grips her scalp and wastes no time getting going.

Jasper nestles against her backside and feeds his meat into her pussy. His slide in is super easy, and he begins to rock her body with pelvic thrusts.

She was curious to see how it would feel on this ball, and it's brilliant. Her body bounces as they each move in and out of her holes. The give of the bouncy, blown-up ball flows with them as they spit roast her.

She gags almost immediately as Wes pumps to the back of her throat, then down it. Her body lurches forward, curving around the ball, but since he has her head pinned, he stays inside her mouth. She can barely stand it, with her eyes watering. This needs to end.

She smacks his thighs, and after another gag, he pulls out. She gasps and sputters. Enough of that shit. She gives her head a slight shake. That's a "no" fellas.

She's not mad, though, so she grins at him with humility and gives another tiny shake of her head. Time to move on. She doesn't even care if it's noticeable on the video. This is her show, she gets to decide. Besides, she likes her audience to know she lets the men use her, but ultimately, it's her call.

Jasper rides her pussy from behind as her body bounces on the ball. She decides she likes the ball very much. She can't wait to use it with Derek and Max.

As she's getting fucked by Jasper, she watches as Wesley strolls over the to the toy shelf. He scans the shelf and comes back with a clit toy. He slips it under her, and her body curls instantly from the jolt of stimulation. Next, he moves to the restraints section and selects a spreader and wrist cuffs. She watches every move he makes as Jasper pounds into her.

"Group event," Wesley announces. "Finish that blow job and get your asses over here. Three minutes. No less."

Wesley secures the wristbands as she braces her front half as still as possible with her palms on the exercise mat beneath her. It's tough to be still as Jasper rocks her body forward relentlessly. Wesley waves the spreader bar in front of her face to taunt her.

She simply grins saucily at him. The lewd motherfucker. Of course, he'd choose that. He was the one in videos always leading group play in doggystyle, like a train of cocks lined up at the ready.

"Gonna take ours from you," Wesley taunts.

"You gonna come?" Jasper asks through panting breaths.

She nods. She's getting there. "Yeah," she whispers.

The cameraman gets really close to her face, then backs away.

As Derek and Sam arrive, it tips her over the edge. Them watching her get so righteously railed is such a turn-on. She cries out as the contractions launch, then rockets through her pelvis. She gasps, babbles, and stammers as the strong orgasm chugs through her body. Her nonsensical orations spill. Maria will be happy.

Finally, she can speak, "Fuck." She draws in another breath, then releases it. "That was strong."

They grab her and so many hands position her in place as Wes secures her in the spreader. They drape her over a sex chair, which is somewhat uncomfortable, then Sam locks her wrist cuffs.

Her body is on fire before they even touch her. The dopamine in her brain has her floating in a state of hormonal ecstasy. This is top notch fuckery and she loves it. A camera comes up close to her face once more. She realizes she's not looked at Max in quite some time. She's been so lost in the oblivion of the sexual haze of their scene that she even forgot about him for a bit. She spies him, and he looks happy, and this soothes her.

She loves the power of turning men on. It's a superpower that many men shame yet want at the same time. A weird dichotomy. She's harnessed her superpower, and will use the fuck out of it, while both enjoying the ride and getting rich, hopefully. She brings men to their knees daily, feeds on their lust, and drags them into her world of sexual liberation and freedom. Who's the dominant one here, anyway?

She stifles her laugh as Wesley settles himself on her backside and presses at her hole.

She draws in a deep gasp as he enters, then bottoms out deep inside her. He's huge, as he reaches her cervix, he makes her whimper, and her eyes bulge. He had entered slowly, thank goodness, but his cock is so deep, it's the longest cock she's ever had, and that includes dildos.

"Shit," she coos as she tries to relax and take it.

He chuckles. "Take that monster cock, baby. All up, pinning your cervix to your stomach."

No shit he is. She whimpers as he begins his riding of her hole. Thankfully, he doesn't slam all the way back into her. Her body adjusts to its size after a few pumps, but only because she's so dang aroused.

Derek sneaks beneath the sex chair and somehow wiggles his body into a weird position where he can lick her clit. She imagines Wesley's balls will hit him in the face with each thrust. That's hot. She can't wait to see it on the video.

Sam holds the tip of his cock to her mouth, and Jasper slides underneath to suckle her tits. All the bases of her are covered. She's getting serviced like a queen.

The motion of them all at once is overwhelming, though. Sam takes her mouth with his cock and mouth fucks her. Her senses are on high-voltage octane as they all manipulate her body. Their grunts and growls egg her on, and she falls right into a bursting climax, loving imagining Wes's balls hitting Derek's head. She rolls about in the sensations like she's drunk. This is so fucking ideal, she couldn't have imagined anything better.

She climaxes again, and Wesley pulls out.

"Fuck, that's too tight," he mutters. "Can't stop if I stay in."

She loves his honest declaration, which is something not often seen in films.

"Come on, boy, you haven't taken my monster yet. Get on this meat before I lose my jizz."

She watches as Derek drops to his knees and takes Wes in his mouth. He gags instantly but keeps trying. His sounds are obscene, and likely some will find them disturbing, but it turns her on to watch Derek get dominated. She knows he's loving every second of it.

Jasper and Sam spit roast her, and she falls swiftly into another big O.

Jasper pulls out and goes to wait in line for Derek's attention next.

It's Sam and her alone now. She also relishes the time she gets to spend alone with Sam. This is turning out perfectly. She hopes the video will reflect the ecstasy she is feeling. She's not masked a single emotion, but let it all happen naturally.

Sam scoops her up and carries her entangled body to the blow-up couch with the hooks. He lays her on the ground, his cock bobbing above her as he works to remove the spreader. He pats the couch, and she climbs on top. He secures her wrists to the latches and settles between her thighs.

"Going to make you come so hard you scream. I'm not stopping at one either."

She can't recall being eaten out by Sam. Usually he's fucking her doggy or she's giving him a blow job. Maria raves about his oral skills, so she's legit excited. What a great time for him to debut this for her!

She quickly glances at Derek and there's a camera on them as he sucks Jasper's cock and strokes Wesley's snake...it's a snake, it's too huge to be called anything else.

Sam commands her attention as he presses his fingers along her swollen flesh around her opening. Her eyes half close as the hormones lull her, which is likely intensified by being flat, so she's relaxed and fully supported by the blow-up furniture.

He dives into her with a force that satisfies already upon touchdown. His suction is immediate, full, and strong. She longs to play with his hair and press his scalp with her fingers as he aggressively eats her out, but she's tethered. She moans and whimpers as he sucks her bean, his arms wrapped tightly around her thighs. The slurping sounds he makes add to her arousal, and she rolls into a ready-to-explode high. She both loves and hates being restrained, but it's a turn-on nonetheless.

The other three men appear, and Sam slows his eating out of her. Derek kneels at her face and hovers above like he's about to kiss her. Jasper and Wesley each take a side of her and take her nipples into their mouths. Sam reattaches himself to her pussy and hoovers up her aroused clit in a rush, making her gasp.

Derek kisses her as the others give her pleasure. As he kisses down her neck, her orations peak and her climb to her apex is accelerated like a shot. She screams as Sam hankers down on her harder and she bursts into another ginormous orgasm. He keeps going and her orgasmic high plateaus with two more significant peaks, never fully falling down from any of them, her body is deliciously spent.

They back away from her limp body as she pants heavily. Her eyes are half closed. She lies there, floating in the lasting reverie of the wonderful climaxes. She feels so incredibly sleepy and exhausted, but she doesn't want to sleep. Not now. But something is pulling her under, and she can't stay awake. The last thing she sees is Max's smiling face above her.

Chapter 21

When she wakes, she's lying in the bed in the studio. She feels refreshed and amazing. Shit. She fell asleep. They fucked her to sleep. Damnit. She hadn't wanted that. She's the party pooper. Max rushes to her side as she stirs.

"I fell asleep? I'm such a loser." She smiles up at Max. "What about the film?"

"It was perfect, don't worry." His face is loving, and his eyes are amused. "You were pretty worked over. Have any idea how many times you came? Break a record?"

"I think I did. I didn't really count, though. They were big. Many were really big. I'm thinking that mushroom coffee I had before the shoot made a difference, too."

"We'll order more, then." He sits on the bed and caresses her cheek. "You're a sex goddess, you know that? A true goddess. You came so many times, and you gave them so much pleasure, too. It was incredible. The film will be stellar because of it."

"Do you think they got good stuff?"

He nods. "Very good. They've shot many scenes over the years, and they are confident they got some magnificent footage."

She rises up. "Where is everyone? Where's Derek?"

"Wesley and Jasper are on the patio. They kept going but are now in the hot tub. Sam and Maria have not come out of their room yet."

She laughs. "I'm not surprised! I'm sure Maria was going ballistic watching all that and not participating."

"I know I was." He caresses her nude torso. "I'm not going to ask for sex, though. I want you to recover first. You hungry? Thirsty?"

"Yes," she says, but her concern flickers to Derek. "You didn't mention Derek."

"Well, babe, he left." He looks forlorn.

"Left? What do you mean he left?" What the absolute fuck? Why would he leave now after the filming? He just got here. "Like, you mean, he took his stuff and left?"

"No. But he didn't seem happy, babe. He left in a huff. I don't know what happened." He caresses her cheek. "I'm sure he's coming back. His suitcase is still here. Maybe he just needs some time to get some air. That was pretty intense."

She nods. "It really was." Her worry escalates to the extreme. This isn't a good sign, not after how he looked when he arrived yesterday.

She sits up, and he helps her stand.

"You, okay?"

"Yeah, I'm a bit woozy. And a little sore." She chuckles. "I sure got used."

"Indeed. So, what did you think?" he asks as he keeps his arm around her as she walks.

"Well, I loved it. I thoroughly loved it. But next time, I want you and Maria in it."

"Done."

He guides her down the hall to their room. "Shower or bath?"

She nods. "Shower."

He turns on the water and then helps her enter it. "I'll be waiting on the bed. If you need help, holler."

She smiles, grateful for his aftercare. He points to the counter. "There's a water here and a cookie."

She laughs. "Thanks, Dad," she says sarcastically.

He grins at her. "You mean Daddy? Or Master?" He snickers with a raise of his eyebrow, then disappears.

Her flirty grin remains long after he's gone as she stands beneath the steaming water and lets it fall down her flesh. Her ass still hurts a bit, too. They got a little hog wild with the paddle. She shakes her head. However, it truly was a scorching scene.

"Totally epic," she whispers.

After her shower, water, and the cookie, she and Max return to the living room.

She peers onto the patio, and Maria and Sam have joined the other two in the hot tub. Their swimsuits are all hanging on the rail.

She smiles. "I'd like to join them. You?"

"Yes," he says, pulling her into a hug. "I'll get my suit on." He chuckles. "Then take it back off."

She sits on the couch and lets her back rest against the soft, puffy back cushion. She feels more incredible than ever. The shoot went better than she'd expected, and she got so caught up in it, she was her authentic self. It was ideal. Hopefully, it will come through on the final product. A few moments of solitude are just what she needs, though. And she's going to savor it. She closes her eyes until she hears the front door open.

She pops open her eyes to see Derek rushing in, looking around wildly and holding something small in his right hand.

"Derek. Hi. Where did you go?"

"Anyone else around?" His tone is urgent, and his eyes are wild.

"Everyone is on the patio in the hot tub. Max is getting his suit." She frowns. "Why? Are you okay?"

"Good." Derek looks all googly-eyed and freaked out. He takes a big breath, clearly trying to calm down. "I need you, Mal. I need you every day. And I mean every day." He rushes to her and falls to one knee. His eyes are scared, tender, and then they fall into a full expression of love. He closes his eyes once more and takes a big breath in, then out. "Mallory, the love of my life, my partner, my friend, my lover, and my muse."

Her heart leaps to her throat as he turns over his hand and opens his fist. "Oh, my..." she exclaims.

"Mallory, will you do the honor of marrying me? Will you be my wife?"

Her heart beats rampantly as her brain spins. Panic seizes her. This is the last thing she expected. She's thought about this many times. There are no words. Everything is failing in her head. There should be an instant answer, but she has too many thoughts to reconcile, the biggest one being shock.

"I know this is a lot and unexpected." His eyes are understanding and supportive.

Max wanders into the room in his suit and robe. His jaw drops. "Oh!"

Mallory and Derek stare at Max as he stares back at them.

The answer to his question fills up her throat.

THE END...WELL, FOR now! Stay tuned for book 2, "Power Plays."

https://books.ruanwillowauthor.com/powerplays

About the Author

Ruan Willow is an award nominated open door spicy romance author, sex blogger at https://ruanwillowauthor.com/ , sexuality and erotica fiction podcaster at the Oh F*ck Yeah with Ruan Willow Podcast, and an audiobook narrator/voiceover actor. She is also published on Medium, Frolic Me, Theo Reads, and Literotica. She loves spending time with family and friends, interacting with fans, cooking, sharing/chatting with and educating people about sex, reading, travel, being outdoors, swimming, learning about sex, podcasting, and more sex. Did you catch all the sex? She's giggling right now thinking about you reading all about sex. She values openness and talking about the natural act of sex. And. Yup, she loves to laugh!

Pen Names:

She writes general erotica/erotic romance/erotic rom com/ menage as Ruan Willow, hotwife erotica as Ruin Willow, taboo erotica as RuAnn Willhoe, and R.U. Ann for open door romantasy/ erotic horror/paranormal fiction.

Ruan has been nominated for Best Erotic Writer by the ASN Lifestyle Magazine Awards 2025.

Thank you!

Thank you to all my family and friends who support me. I wouldn't be where I am without you. You are all the magic and the light in my life, the love that grows in my love. I am honestly thrilled and humbled by the supportive people in my life. Love you!

To Fans:

Thank you for purchasing and/or reviewing this book!

I peddle fantasies for the purposes of your enjoyment, entertainment, and expanding your sexuality and openness. Always remember that no fantasies are bad. You should enjoy your sexuality and your fantasy life as much and as often as you can.

Thank you for reading my book! I write for myself and for my fans. My fans are my main focus though, but of course, I want to like what I write too, and I thoroughly enjoyed writing this story.

In writing erotica/erotic romance, I'm always excited for the erotic journey! I'm personally on a path of sexual empowerment, enlightenment, and enjoyment. Thank you for reading this and I'm honored to be a part of your journey as well. I strive to spin stories where the characters get to enjoy lots of pleasure, and I hope you have also gotten pleasure from reading this book. Enjoy your own journey!

I am where I am because fans have responded to me and my content, so I owe everything to you! Thank you! Thank you! Thank you! You are a blessing in my life, and you give me more joy than you will ever know. I love interacting with all of you and I will never give that up.

My stories are open door erotica and erotic romance, so they have a generous amount of sex in them, as I believe our relationships should have as well. I hope you enjoyed this novella for what it is, literature that is in the erotica genre where sex is a part of the plot, storyline, and character development. It is very different from a closed door romance, and there are different levels of heat in the erotica genre as well. Explore them all! I personally love open door romances because I want the full story of the relationship, not a partial one.

If you'd like more of my work, please see below for my list of published works on the following pages, visit my sexuality and erotica podcast, find my audiobooks, visit my website, my Patreon, visit my profile on Medium, and my linktree with all my links at https://linktr.ee/RuanWillow

Thank you for purchasing this book, I'd love to hear your thoughts in an honest review on the site where you purchased the book from. I'd absolutely love it if you shared my book with others. It warms my heart profusely when I see someone who has taken the time to review/share my book. Love you all very much!

All my best, yours truly, with overflowing love from a full heart,

Ruan Willow, Erotica author, sexuality/erotica podcaster, and erotic book narrator

Ruan's other books
and novellas:
All books:

Https://books.ruanwillowauthor.com/[1]
Other links/URLs:
Ruan Willow on Goodreads Ruan Willow Goodreads Author page[2]

Ruan Willow on BookBub https://www.bookbub.com/profile/ruan-willow

Sign up for Ruan's newsletter: https://subscribepage.io/ruanwillow

ARC copies are usually on BookSirens and StoryOrigin App. Check those sites for FREE ARC of books and audiobooks.

---

1. https://books.ruanwillowauthor.com/

2.   https://www.goodreads.com/author/show/21312130.Ruan_Willow